"I explained in my letter. After my sister died, I needed to be with my grandmother."

"I understood that." Mal hit his signal and checked his blind spot before shifting to the right lane. A thought occurred to him. "Did you think I'd try to talk you out of leaving? I wouldn't have."

"I know that now."

"Then why did you tell me not to contact you?" Mal clenched the steering wheel and his teeth to stop the flood of words rushing out of his heart.

"I thought it would be easier that way." She gestured toward the entrance of the large, sprawling town house complex on their left.

Easier than what? "I'm glad it was easy for you." He pressed his left turn signal and waited for the few cars in the opposing lane to crawl past.

He regretted engaging in this conversation. It was pointless. Grace had made her feelings about a relationship between them clear four years ago. He wasn't going to make the mistake of falling for her again.

Dear Reader,

I'm thrilled to introduce you to the Touré Security Group and the three brothers who lead the family-owned company: Hezekiah, Malachi and Jeremiah.

In *Down to the Wire*, we reunite Malachi Touré with Dr. Grace Blackwell, the research scientist who broke his heart four years ago. They've both made sacrifices for their families. His sacrifice brought them together, but her sacrifice broke them apart. What will it take for them to heal their families—and their broken hearts?

Thank you for taking a chance on The Touré Security Group series. I hope you enjoy Malachi and Grace's love story.

Warm regards,

Patricia Sargeant

DOWN TO
THE WIRE

———

Patricia Sargeant

HARLEQUIN

ROMANTIC
SUSPENSE

HARLEQUIN®
ROMANTIC SUSPENSE™

Recycling programs for this product may not exist in your area.

ISBN-13: 978-1-335-59377-1

Down to the Wire

Harlequin Enterprises ULC
22 Adelaide St. West, 41st Floor
Toronto, Ontario M5H 4E3, Canada
www.Harlequin.com

Printed in U.S.A.

National bestselling author **Patricia Sargeant** was drawn to write romance because she believes love is the greatest motivation. Her romantic suspense novels put ordinary people in extraordinary situations to have them find the "hero inside." Her work has been reviewed in national publications such as *Publishers Weekly*, *USA TODAY*, *Kirkus Reviews*, *Suspense Magazine*, *Mystery Scene Magazine*, *Library Journal* and *RT Book Reviews*. For more information about Patricia and her work, visit patriciasargeant.com.

Books by Patricia Sargeant

Harlequin Romantic Suspense

The Touré Security Group
Down to the Wire

Visit the Author Profile page at Harlequin.com.

To My Dream Team:
* My sister, Bernadette, for giving me the dream.
* My husband, Michael, for supporting the dream.
* My brother Richard for believing in the dream.
* My brother Gideon for encouraging the dream.
And to Mom and Dad, always with love.

Acknowledgments

Sincere thanks to Dr. Jeffrey Froude for answering my multitude of questions regarding scientific research.

Chapter 1

"*O*h, *no, no, no, no, no!*" Dr. Grace Blackwell's fingers flew across her keyboard.

Malware-protection warnings popped onto her ancient laptop's screen with nerve-wracking frequency like over-caffeinated whack-a-moles. Seated at the dark wood table against the back wall of her home office, she'd deleted the email with the attachment that had started this mess.

Faster!
Faster!
Faster!

Internet, disconnected. Documents and programs, closed.

She released the breath she'd been holding before launching her anti-malware software to scan her hard drive. She wanted to make sure all the malicious little invaders had been quarantined.

"*How* did this happen?" she asked herself and all the cybersecurity fairies who were supposed to keep her systems safe.

They wouldn't answer, but she knew someone who could. Grabbing her cell phone from the desk, Grace tapped the icon programmed to dial the personal mobile of her friend, mentor and former graduate school professor Dr. Bennett MacIntyre. The call went straight to voice mail. Odd. It was as though his phone had been turned off. She frowned as his greeting gave her instructions for leaving a message. According to the clock displayed in the lower right-hand corner of her computer screen, it was twenty minutes before his eight o'clock Friday-morning class. Wasn't that early to have turned off his phone?

The greeting ended. Grace put a smile in her voice. "Good morning, Dr. B. It's Dr. B. I think your system may have been hacked. The attachment you emailed this morning tried to upload malware to my hard drive. I'm running a scan now, but you should check your computer, too. We'll talk later."

Grace ended the call, but her unease persisted. Her anti-malware software had quarantined six threats. So far. She was afraid to touch anything until the scan was completed. Stepping away from her filing table, she stretched as she paced across the midsize guest room she'd converted into her home office. Sunlight streamed in from the two windows that overlooked the front landscaping of her sprawling town house complex. It made the eggshell walls appear brighter.

She stopped beside her cherrywood desk and touched the framed photograph of her with her grandmother and her deceased older sister. The picture, which stood beside her laptop, had been taken almost eight years ago during her Thanksgiving visit with her family in Florida.

Grace moved away from her desk, stretching some more and massaging the spot where her shoulder met the side of her neck. The breach had tapped into all her paranoid responses, including the one that was bugging her to keep trying to reach Dr. B. Fine. This time, she dialed his direct office line. The call connected on the second ring.

"Dr. Bennett MacIntyre's office. Doris speaking. May I help you?"

The female voice was unexpected. It scattered Grace's thoughts. Doris Flank had been Dr. B's administrative assistant for years. Grace lowered herself onto her desk chair. "Good morning, Doris. This is Dr. Blackwell. Is Dr. B available?" There was a long pause. *Had they lost their connection?* "Hello?"

"I'm so sorry to be the one to tell you. There was an accident. Dr. MacIntyre died last night." Doris's response was thick with emotion.

"What?" Grace's voice broke, making the word two syllables. "How?"

Doris sniffed, then cleared her throat. "He tripped and fell down a flight of stairs late yesterday evening. A security guard found him. His neck was broken."

Grace's right hand flew to her mouth, pressing against her lips. Her throat was on fire with emotion. She couldn't breathe. She couldn't think. Hot tears streamed down her cheeks.

Dr. B.

"Doris." Grace didn't recognize her voice. The words were raspy and unclear. "I'm so sorry. Thanks for letting

me know." She disconnected the call without waiting for
a response. Folding her arms on her desk, she lowered
her head and sobbed her heart out.

Sometime later when the storm had settled, Grace
pushed herself to her feet and shuffled downstairs to
her townhome's kitchen for a glass of ice water. Once
she felt a little stronger, she thought she would call
Dr. B's wife and children to express her sympathy
and ask if there was anything she could do for them.
Anything at all. Her eyes stung with more tears as she
thought about their loss and pain. To wake with your
loved one in the morning and then that evening learn
he'd died. The shock and grief would drop you to your
knees.

Wait. What had Doris said?

Dr. MacIntyre died last night.

That would've been Thursday night. Then who'd sent
her the email this morning?

"Why are you here?"

Malachi Touré glanced up from his laptop early Tuesday morning. His older brother, Hezekiah, frowned at
him from the threshold of his office at their family-
owned company, Touré Security Group, in Columbus,
Ohio.

Their parents had died almost two years earlier, leaving Malachi and his two brothers a third of the company
each. They ran the company together, but Hezekiah had
assumed the leadership role. It made sense. He was
the oldest and he'd worked for the company the lon-
gest. Even before graduating from The Ohio State University more than ten years ago, his older brother had
been deeply involved in the business, including the fi-

nances, marketing and contracts. And he dressed the part. Today, he looked acceptably conservative in a tailored navy-striped suit. Malachi would've chosen a more subdued tie, but he didn't have any quarrel with Hezekiah's bold paisley one. The black combination-lock attaché case added to the corporate look. Their brother, Jeremiah, would have gotten a rash just thinking about those clothes.

"What're you guys doing?" *Speak of the devil and he appears*, Malachi thought. Jeremiah, the youngest of the three Touré offspring, balanced a mug of coffee as he squeezed past Hezekiah. His loose-limbed stride carried him to the closer of the two black cloth guest chairs in front of Malachi's desk. His slender six-foot-plus frame was clothed in black pants and a long-sleeved emerald jersey.

"I *was* working." Neither brother acknowledged his dry response. Since they'd trashed his concentration, Malachi sat back against his black cushioned executive chair and gave his siblings his full attention.

He drew a frustrated breath, catching the scent of strong hot coffee coming from the black coffeepot on top of the iron gray filing cabinet beside his white mini fridge. The smell reminded Malachi of the half-full mug beside his right hand. He took a deep drink of the rich, sharp brew. White cursive lettering on the mug's black surface read I'm Not Antisocial, I'm Just Not User-Friendly. His brothers' idea of a joke and proof they could work together—if they tried.

"You're supposed to be at the client's office, tracking down the hacker. What happened?" Hezekiah's frown remained stamped on his broad sienna features.

"What's with the tone, Number One?" Jeremiah

rested his right ankle on his left knee and linked his fingers over his flat abdomen. "Mal doesn't report to you."

"We report to each other." Hezekiah tossed their youngest brother a quick look.

Malachi answered, foiling Jeremiah's first attempt of the day to start an argument. Others always followed. "I can trace the hacker from here. The client gave me the login for remote access to their network."

"That mug is so you, man." Jeremiah chuckled. "Are you really surprised he's working from here? I would've been surprised if he wasn't."

Hezekiah propped his right shoulder against the open door and rubbed his eyes with his left fingers. "Mal, would it kill you to interact personally with our clients once in a while?" He pinned Malachi with a direct stare. "We need to raise our profile so we can expand our client base. One way to do that is to increase our visibility with current and prospective clients."

Malachi blew out a breath and reached for the same argument he'd been using for the past two weeks, every time Hezekiah brought up this subject. "We're already well situated in our niche market. We need to focus on what we've always done best: partner with small to mid-sized businesses for their security needs. That's what Mom and Dad built the company on."

Hezekiah turned his attention to Jeremiah. "What do you think?"

"I think you're both crazy." Jeremiah's shrug was nonchalant, but Malachi caught a brief look of discomfort before his brother hid behind a mask of bravado.

Hezekiah pressed him. "Should we expand or double down in our current market?"

Jeremiah shook his head. "They're both good ideas."

Hezekiah narrowed his eyes. "It's not like you to not have an opinion on something. You have an opinion on everything. You love to argue, whether you know what you're talking about or not. So why are you holding back now?"

"What do you care?" Jeremiah slumped on the chair and scowled. "You're going to do what you want anyway."

Hezekiah shook his head. "That's not true. I wouldn't ask for your input if I didn't want it."

Jeremiah planted both feet on the floor and leaned forward on his chair. "You're always telling Mal and me what to do, like you're somebody's boss. Just now, you barked at Mal because he's working from our offices instead of the client's."

"I didn't bark at him."

"You're always bossing us around. We're not kids anymore. We—"

"That's enough." Malachi's patience snapped, pressing him against his chair. "What's wrong with both of you?"

Jeremiah glared at him. "What did I—"

Malachi cut him off again. "I don't know why you won't tell us what you want for the company, but that's your choice." He turned to Hezekiah. "Don't bring your arguments into my office. Do you think I enjoy being in the middle of your spitting contests?"

"You're right." Hezekiah shifted his briefcase to his left hand to check the bronze Rolex on his right wrist. "We're too busy to get distracted by petty arguments."

Jeremiah stood. "Yeah, it was a stupid argument."

Malachi caught Jeremiah's eyes, searching them for

an explanation for his inexplicable behavior. His brother lowered his gaze, turning away to leave his office.

Hezekiah stepped aside so he could pass. With his attention on the doorway, he lowered his voice. "Do you think he's been acting even stranger than usual?"

Yes, but it's not for me to explain Jerry. He has to explain himself. "The two of you need to talk. I'm getting tired of the constant arguing."

"You're right." Hezekiah's sigh lifted his broad shoulders. He turned toward the door. "And I don't want to chase you away again. Good luck catching the hacker."

"It's skill, not luck."

Hezekiah tossed a smile over his shoulder as he left Malachi's office. It was a dim imitation of his usual expression.

Jeremiah had told him he'd been thinking about leaving the family business and offering his own brand of fitness and self-protection training through a local gym. Why wouldn't he also tell Hezekiah? Why was he keeping secrets?

With effort and another long drink of coffee, Malachi pushed concerns about his brothers from his mind. He had a hacker to catch.

This hacker is not *going to give me the slip.*
At least, not for much longer.

They'd already avoided him for the better part of Tuesday morning, leaving a trail of subtle breadcrumbs that had led him ever deeper into the network only to find…nothing. Malachi scrubbed his face with his palms, then leaned back against his chair to roll up his sleeves. The hacker was smart but not that sophisticated. They knew enough to plant red herrings but not enough to cover their tracks—at least, not from him.

His black Apple Watch vibrated. Time to stand. With a sigh, Malachi stretched before circling his desk. His mother had bought the device for him the year before she died.

"Sitting is the new smoking. You jog every morning, but that doesn't mean you can sink into your office chair for the rest of the day." She'd pointed at the watch as she chided him. *"That will remind you to walk away from your desk and look around once in a while. If you sink any farther inside yourself, I'll have to send a search party in there after you."*

Mal smiled at the memory. She was always trying to push him out of his comfort zone. He hadn't made it easy for her. *Miss you, Mom.* She'd been so bossy. She'd also been so right. The mandatory breaks from the computer made him more productive. He did a few jumping jacks to get his blood flowing and clear his mind as he stared at the view outside his office window.

Touré Security Group was in a corporate complex in a sleepy neighborhood not far from Antrim Lake, where he and his brothers did their six-mile morning runs. The asphalt parking lot was ringed by young linden trees, firepower nandina bushes, and vibrant red, gold and purple coleus.

After twenty-five jumping jacks, his watch vibrated against his left wrist again. He'd completed another hour toward his stand goal. Satisfied, he drew a deep breath, straightened his shoulders and returned to his laptop with a renewed determination to nab the hacker.

"No more chasing after you through network operating systems that turn up empty." But before he could enter a command thread, a message appeared on his screen.

Who are you?

What the... Malachi's fingers froze above his keyboard. The hacker had sent him a message. How? One of those breadcrumbs must've been a hack that led them back to his laptop. Malachi grabbed his head and squeezed his eyes shut as a series of curses exploded in his brain. He gritted his teeth and shoved his irritation aside. Sitting up, he glared at his screen.

The hacker had repeated the message.

Who. Are. You?

He sensed their anger and frustration as though they were sitting right next to him. Malachi grunted. "You wanna play? Let's play." Perhaps his fingers hit the keyboard a little harder than necessary.

Who are you?

He waited for a response. It didn't take long.

You're not with Buckeye Dynamic Devices, are you? But you're not the hacker.

Malachi frowned, narrowing his eyes at the message. He responded.

What game are you playing? You're the hacker.

Liar! Who are you and why are you here? Are you after the formula?

What? He mouthed the question before typing.

What formula?

His cursor blinked at him indecisively, poking at his impatience.
Finally, the hacker responded.

We need to meet.

Good idea.

Buckeye Dynamic. Half an hour. They won't have you arrested if you answer their questions and agree to stop infiltrating their systems.

A longer pause.

You haven't a clue. Cakes and Caffeine Coffee Shop on Old Henderson and Godown. Thirty minutes. Come alone. I'll enlighten you.

He raised his eyebrows.

Enlighten me about what?

Meet me and find out.

Oh, really?

How will I identify you?

How will *I* identify *you*?

Malachi rubbed his forehead with his fingertips. This hacker was straining his patience. Cyber experts were a suspicious group, but this was next level.

I'll be reading The Gospel & the Geek by Bernadine Cecile.

Another long pause.

Thirty minutes. Alone.

Malachi logged out of the system. He grabbed his dark gray sports coat from the back of his chair and Bernadine Cecile's book from the shelf above his desk. On his way out, he paused at Jeremiah's office. "I need you and Zeke." He didn't respond to the concerned frown that settled on his younger brother's chiseled features. Instead, he crossed over to Hezekiah's office. He addressed both men. "The hacker's asked to meet in thirty minutes."

Hezekiah looked up from his computer. His thick black eyebrows rose. "That was quick."

Malachi held up a hand. "*They* found *me*."

Hezekiah frowned, exchanging a look with Jeremiah. "Where's the meet?"

"Cakes and Caffeine Coffee Shop on Old Henderson." Malachi shrugged into his jacket. He only had thirty minutes, and it was a fifteen-minute drive from their office.

"I'll come with you." Jeremiah started to return to his office, probably for his coat.

Malachi caught his upper arm. "I'm supposed to go alone."

Jeremiah held his eyes. "Screw that. We can sit at separate tables."

Malachi felt a smile curve his lips. "I don't think the hacker will miss the family resemblance." Looking at Hezekiah and Jeremiah was like looking into a mirror, except Jeremiah still had a full head of tight, dark curls. He and Hezekiah had shaved their heads a couple of years ago. Male-pattern baldness wasn't a joke. Malachi felt Jeremiah's bicep tighten under his palm. He let his hand fall away.

Jeremiah's features stiffened. "You're not going into this without backup."

"I agree with Jerry." Hezekiah stood behind his desk. "Come on, Mal. This person hacked a defense contractor. Who knows what they're capable of, how many of them are involved? Who knows anything about them? Your plan was to track the hacker and turn the information over to the client, not to confront them."

"New plan." Malachi checked his watch. He was running short on time. "You know where I'll be and when. I'll text when I get there. It'll be fine. *I'll* be fine."

He didn't wait for their response. Malachi jogged down the three winding flights of stairs and across the polished gray concrete flooring of the black-and-silver lobby. He pushed through the front glass doors into the parking lot and got into his black four-door SUV.

Malachi exited the lot and merged with traffic, nudging the engine of his car a bit above the speed limit. He wanted to get to the coffee shop before the hacker. That way, he could survey the customers to see whether the hacker had brought backup. He could also select a seat that allowed him to monitor the full space. But for all he knew, the hacker had been sending messages from the café. He had to be aware of all possibilities. He couldn't walk in unprepared.

The scent of fresh coffee and warm, sweet pastries struck Malachi as he entered the shop. He adjusted his hardcover copy of Bernadine Cecile's book, holding it in his right hand so the cover was visible.

The café was full, a testament to its popularity. He did a thorough scan of the room as he strolled to the counter to order a coffee, his third of the day. Sunlight poured in through lightly tinted windows set into the stark chalk-white walls. A stone fireplace stood in the center of the dark hardwood flooring. A handful of retirees were culed up on fluffy armchairs beside it, reading books or newspapers while nursing hot drinks.

Scarlet-and-gray booth seating lined the café's perimeter. Cushioned gray armchairs and cozy dark wood tables were positioned around the room. Several customers occupying those booths and tables were working on laptops. Some were working alone. A few groups seemed to be collaborating. None of the patrons appeared to be waiting for anyone. No one seemed to be looking at him. Then what was causing that prickling sensation along his spine?

He paid for his coffee, then filled the porcelain mug at the self-serve station. The uncomfortable feeling got stronger. He chose a booth bench in a corner of the room close to the rear exit, which gave him a clear view of the space and a quick out. Pulling his cell phone from his jacket pocket, he sent a text to Hezekiah and Jeremiah: Arrived. Waiting.

He tucked his phone back into his pocket. Placing the book faceup on the edge of the table, he picked up his coffee.

"Mal?" The scents of roses and powder had preceded the soft, hesitant, feminine voice. Their familiarity stopped his breathing and clouded his mind.

He shifted on the gray cushioned bench to look behind him. Shock surged through him like an electric current. He wanted to stand, but his legs ignored him. He tried to speak, but his voice wouldn't work.

Grace Blackwell.

Seeing her standing in the archway that led to the café's restrooms, his body reacted as though they hadn't been apart for four long, miserable years. She could've stepped out of the dream that was never far from his mind. Maybe he was having it now. He took in her pale silver scoop-neck polyester blouse and slim black slacks. A lime-and-black knapsack hung from her right shoulder. Her dark brown hair was longer and gathered into a ponytail. That was different. Her face and figure were slimmer. There was an air of tension around her that hadn't been there four years ago.

"Grace." His body stiffened as he waited for her to disappear. She didn't. "What are you doing here?"

Her long-lidded cinnamon eyes dropped to the book on the table. She lifted it for a closer look before holding up the cover for him to see. "I'm meeting you."

His thoughts scattered to the wind. "*You're* the hacker?"

Chapter 2

Grace sank onto the bench seat on the other side of the café's table as gracefully as she could under the circumstances. Her head was spinning and her legs felt like licorice rope.

Malachi Touré.

Her heart had lodged in her throat when he entered the coffee shop Tuesday morning. She'd tried to convince herself she was mistaken, but her body had called the lie. She'd gone weak at the knees. Her grip on the threshold that separated the hallway to the restrooms from the main café had kept her from collapsing to the ground.

He'd shed some pounds—and his hair—but her memories had burned his chiseled sienna features onto her retinas. Sharp cheekbones, a stubborn chin and a strong nose could fool you into thinking he was cold and aloof. But full, talented lips told a different story. Almond-shaped ebony eyes could find all your secrets, even the ones you didn't know you had. His long, loose-limbed strides brought back memories of the way he'd felt in her arms.

She'd lost her breath when she saw the book he was holding, *The Gospel & the Geek* by Bernadine Cecile. She'd been shocked when the hacker referenced the title. It had pulled her four years into the past. She'd remembered it had been one of Mal's favorite books. She hadn't known anyone who had talked about it as much. Apparently, she still didn't.

"You look great." Where had that come from? She gritted her teeth to trap any other inanities behind them. This wasn't a reunion, no matter what her heart wanted it to be. This was a reconnaissance on cyber theft, a business meeting at most.

But seeing him again after so many years triggered a montage of images and a flood of desire and regret. The first time they'd met, almost five years ago, he'd been standing on the other side of her door. The memory always made her heart flutter just as it had that day. He'd moved into the apartment down the hall from hers and had gotten her mail by mistake. Their postal carrier had continued mixing up their mail like a determined matchmaker. After their third exchange, he'd asked her out. The next seven months had been the best time of her life. Mal had been kind, funny, attentive. And sexy, incredibly sexy. Leaving him had felt like losing part of herself.

"So do you." Mal's words were friendly enough. However, his eyes—those incredible eyes—smoldered with suspicion and resentment. "Is this where you moved to when you left?"

She stiffened. Was it possible? "Yes, it is. How long have you been here?"

"I moved back almost four years ago." His voice lacked inflection, but his words shook her foundation. "I left Chicago shortly after you did."

"I see." Her lips were numb.

They'd been living in the same city for the past four years and neither of them had known. Granted, almost two million other people also made their home in Columbus. But still. Why hadn't she realized this could happen; that he could move back? He'd mentioned more than once that he was from Columbus and his family lived here. She'd never thought she would see Mal again. Now, seated across the table from him, all she could think about was them.

What would it have felt like if they'd found each other again under different circumstances? Could she have reached across the table and cupped his hand with hers the way her palms were itching to right now? Grace clenched her fists and looked away. This was the reason she'd left Chicago—and Mal. He was too much of a distraction from her plan.

"But that's not why we're here, is it?" The coolness in his tone made her shiver. "Why are you hacking Buckeye Dynamic?"

"They hacked me first." Her cheeks heated. She sounded so childish. She took a breath and started over. "Why are *you* helping them? Do you work for Buckeye Dynamic?" *Are you behind the hack?*

"They're a new client. My brothers and I co-own our family's business, Touré Security Group."

"I remember." Grace regretted her interruption when the flash of resentment returned to Mal's eyes.

But she did remember. She remembered everything they'd ever talked about. He'd told her his parents had built the security firm after leaving the military but before starting their family. He and his brothers—the oldest, Hezekiah, Zeke for short; and the youngest, Jeremiah, Jerry for short—had grown up in the business. The firm had started by providing security procedures, systems, and personnel. As the brothers had grown, the company had expanded to include cyber and personal security. Things had been going well until tensions between Zeke and Jerry boiled over. That's when Mal had taken a job with an internet-security company in Chicago—and an apartment down the hall from hers.

"Buckeye Dynamic approached us when they weren't able to trace you." Mal held her eyes. She felt like she was drowning. In the past, she'd loved feeling that way with him, but he'd never looked so angry. "And then I found you going through their network."

"Correction: *I* found *you*. And the only reason I was in their network is that they hacked *my* system and stole *my* files."

Surprise nudged aside the resentment in his eyes. "What was stolen?"

He'd phrased his question carefully: *What was stolen?* Not *What did they steal?* He didn't believe her. That distrust wasn't all due to loyalty to his client. Some of it had to do with their past. As their conversation progressed, she sensed his mood entering different stages: surprise, resentment and now anger. She understood, but it still broke her heart. Grace hadn't liked the way she'd left him, but at the time, she'd thought it was for the best.

She took a breath and collected her thoughts. She

needed to focus on their discussion, not his appearance or the memories of how he'd made her feel. Were those just memories, though? Seated across from him, she was experiencing some of those feelings right now: breathless, restless and warm.

She held his eyes, bracing herself for his cool curiosity. "Five days ago, someone hacked my system and accessed several of the files on my hard drive. Those files pertained to a very sensitive formula I'm in the process of developing. I tracked the hacker to the defense contractor's building. Someone with that contractor stole research documents from my computer. I want to know who, why and how they intend to use my formula."

For long moments, Mal held her eyes in silence. She never looked away, but she had no idea what he was thinking. He had to believe her. Just as she had to believe he didn't have any part in the theft. He was just a security contractor with bad taste in clients.

Finally, he sat back. "That's *your* story. I need to speak with my client and get her response to your accusation."

"Great." Grace leaned back on the booth's bench seating. "I'll go with you. I'd love to hear what she has to say."

Mal shook his head as she spoke. "No, I'll speak with her alone."

Grace leaned over the table. "Your client has already lied to you by presenting my actions as some kind of unprovoked cyberattack. I'm telling you that she—or someone she works with—stole my files."

Mal pulled out his cell phone. "How do I know *you're* not lying to me?"

Grace gasped. His words cut so deep. "How could

you say that?" Her voice was a whisper. "I've never lied to you, Mal."

His jawline tightened. "You may not have lied, but you led me to believe plenty of things that turned out not to be true."

Her heart punched against her chest. His accusation was unfair. But this wasn't the time or the place to defend herself. "Mal." She cleared her throat and started again. "Mal, I need to know what your client says..This isn't a disagreement over twenty dollars. This formula is very sensitive. In the wrong hands, it *will* be dangerous. Please make it clear to her that she must agree not to pursue the formula. Otherwise I'll have to report her."

Mal searched her face. Could he tell she wasn't bluffing?

He gave a short, sharp nod before tapping a number into his cell phone. Grace could hear the recipient's phone ringing. A voice greeted him on the other end.

"Verna, it's Malachi Touré." A pause was filled by the faint voice again. "No, I don't have a resolution yet, but something's come up. When can we meet?" He checked his watch. "You're working from home? I can be there in thirty minutes. Thanks." Mal ended the call and stood. "Give me your number. I'll call after I speak with Verna."

So he'd deleted her number. It had been four years. Grace wasn't surprised. She'd deleted his, too.

"I'd rather come with you." She had to give it one more try.

"No."

With a sigh, she pulled a napkin from the dispenser on the table and dug a pen from her knapsack, which carried her smart tablet and thumb drive. She paused before writing her number. "Do you have a card?" She smiled when he hesitated. "Whether you believe me or not, I'm sure you realize you and your client have more to lose than I do. If I don't get her cooperation, I *will* go to the authorities. So you're going to need my number."

Mal hesitated a moment more before reaching into his front pants pocket. He pulled out his wallet and offered her a card. Grace took it before he changed his mind, then wrote her number on the napkin. "I'll be waiting for your call."

A cloud passed over Mal's lean features. It pierced her heart. Without a word, he turned and strode out of the café.

Four years ago, after her sister had died, she'd written Mal a letter, saying goodbye and wishing him well. She'd thought she was doing the right thing for the greater good. Their relationship had distracted her from her medical research. But her actions had hurt them both, and what did she have to show for it? A potentially dangerous formula that could fall into the wrong hands, threatening the greater good she'd been fighting for.

"How's your search for the hacker going?" Grace's grandmother, Melba Stall, had been asking some variation of that question for the past four days.

She'd hated worrying her grandmother, but with her mentor's death, she needed someone to confide in. Her grandmother had proved to be the perfect choice: empathetic, encouraging and stubbornly optimistic. She'd also extended her cheerleading squad to include Gilda Reynolds, her closest friend at her retirement community in Coconut Creek, Florida. Of course, they hadn't told Gilda everything about the security breach.

"There've been some interesting developments." Grace was taking her grandmother's call at the coffee shop while waiting for Mal's update. A glance at the clock in the lower right corner of her computer screen showed he'd been gone less than ten minutes. After he'd left, she'd moved to a more isolated booth. She scanned the café. The Tuesday-morning coffee crowd had thinned. It was just her and five or six other people. Still, she had to be careful of what she said.

"Good developments, I hope." Melba's voice was cautious.

"The company brought in a cybersecurity expert." Grace told her grandmother about identifying Mal in cyberspace and meeting with him at the coffee shop. "He's supposed to call me after speaking with the company's representative."

"That's great progress, although I agree with you. It would've been better for you to be present while he spoke with his client. Then everything would be out in the open."

"That's what I thought." It gave her a sense of validation that her grandmother felt the same way. She studied her now-empty porcelain coffee mug. *Were four cups too many?* Maybe she'd get one for the road. And a chocolate chip cookie. She deserved the treat. It had been a hard few days. "He probably thought I'd make a scene."

"How could he know you so well in such a short span of time?" Her grandmother's tone was dry. "Wait, did you say his name's Malachi Touré? Isn't that the man you'd been dating in Chicago?"

Grace swallowed a groan. She'd had a feeling her grandmother would remember. Malachi Touré was a memorable name. And she was certain she'd mentioned him on dozens of occasions to her grandmother and sister. "Yes, he's *that* Malachi Touré."

"Oh, sweetie." Her grandmother's empathy was like a warm blanket wrapping around her through the long-distance phone line. "How're you doing?"

"I'm OK, Gran." She managed the lie without tripping over her words.

Her grandmother wasn't buying it. "When you're ready to talk, I'm always here to listen."

She swallowed the lump in her throat. "I know. And I love you for that."

There was a pause before Melba continued. "How did he seem?"

"Honestly?" She sighed. "Shocked, resentful and angry. In that order. And I can't say I blame him. I mean, if the situation had been reversed, I probably would've walked out of the café, even though I thought I'd done the right thing at the time."

"What do you think now?"

"If I had a second chance to choose, I'd make the same decision." Grace's heart felt like it was tearing all over again. "I'll always choose my family."

"I don't think Pam would've wanted you to make that choice the first time. She wouldn't have wanted you to sacrifice your happiness for her memory."

Grace thought of her beautiful, loving older sister. Pam had been six years older than her. She'd known her sister had been struggling under the burden of her diabetes, but she hadn't been aware of how much of a fight it had been.

One of the reasons she'd gone into medical research was to find a cure for diabetes, or at least a better, more affordable treatment protocol. But then, four years ago, before Grace could find that cure, Pam had died from complications due to the disease. And what had Grace been doing while her sister was struggling to pay for her life-saving medicine? She'd been enjoying Mal's company. The company of an intelligent, exciting and very attractive man.

After being laid off, Pam hadn't been able to afford her medication. So she'd gone without. She hadn't told anyone about her situation, not even their grandmother. Why not? Had it been pride? Shame? Had she just given up?

For pity's sake, Pam. Why didn't you say something, anything?

"I wish she'd told me. I would have helped her." Words Grace had been saying off and on for the past four years. They never fixed anything. They didn't even make her feel better.

"How would you have helped her?" Her grandmother's response was firmer each time they had this conversation. "You had your own money problems, paying off your student loans."

"I would've been happy to go without something so my sister could afford her insulin." Although there really hadn't been much, if any, excess in her life in Chicago. The occasional drinks with friends, a few movie nights. And then there had been Mal. He'd insisted on paying when they went out, but a few times, she'd convinced him to split the bill.

"Grace, I know you feel bad that you didn't know. I feel bad, too." Her grandmother's voice was strained, making Grace feel even worse. "I'm her grandmother and I didn't know. You were in Chicago, but I was right

here with her in Florida. We both have to work on for-
giving ourselves. Pam wouldn't want us to spend even
a day feeling guilty."

"I know you're right, Gran." Grace massaged her neck,
trying to ease the tightness there. "I'll try harder, but it's
a struggle."

Her sister's death had torn at her soul. It had also
given her a horrible sense of failure. She felt as though
she'd betrayed someone she loved with every beat of her
heart. All she'd been able to think about was finding a
way to make things right. To keep her promise to Pam.

After her sister's funeral, she'd flown back to Chicago, broken her lease, packed her apartment and left
that note for Mal under his apartment door. Back in
Florida, she'd helped her grandmother move into a
comfortable senior-living residence while applying for
medical-research positions at every lab in the country.

And like a coward, she hadn't responded to any of
Mal's texts or voice mail messages. It was a horrible
thing to do. She wouldn't have wanted someone to do
that to her. But maybe part of her blamed him for being
such a distraction, which was also a horrible thing to do.
Her breaking her promise to Pam hadn't been his fault.
But on top of grieving her sister, Grace had struggled
with guilt for not doing more to help keep her alive. She
hadn't had the strength or clarity to explain all this to
Mal. She didn't have the words to make him understand
she couldn't see him anymore. So she'd kept silent.

"If you want to do better, you can start by rejoining
the living. I know you're determined to find a cure for
diabetes, but you've been spending all day, every day in
that stuffy little home office with your research. That's

not healthy. And it's not what Pam would've wanted for you."

Her home office wasn't a "stuffy little" room, which her grandmother knew very well since she visited every spring and summer. "I go into the lab several days a week. And I'm out in the real world right now, people-watching." She watched two more people leave the café. Now it was just her and two other customers in the dining area.

Her grandmother snorted her disdain. "When is the last time you actually went out with other people?"

"Just this morning, remember? I was with Mal in the coffee shop."

"That doesn't count. It was a business meeting. But at least you're moving in the right direction. I'm serious, Grace. You're not doing Pam's memory justice by shutting yourself off from the world. She wouldn't want that for you and neither do I. You have to create a balance between your work and your personal your life."

"I'll try, Gran." An image of Mal flashed across her mind. She had a strong sense that ship had sailed. She wasn't going to get a second chance with him. "I'd better go. Mal should be calling soon."

"All right, sweetie. Keep me updated."

"I promise. I love you."

"I love you back."

Grace smiled as she disconnected the call. Her grandmother could lift her spirits in any situation. Her smile faded as she stared at the face of her cell phone. She prayed Mal would be able to convince his client to cooperate. Otherwise, she didn't think anything or anyone could lift her spirits.

* * *

Police cruisers and uniformed officers surrounded Verna Bleecher's red brick Tudor home in Bexley, a wealthy suburban city about three and a half miles east of Columbus. Mal's skin went cold. He slowed his SUV to a crawl before parking in the first open spot he found at the curb. He stepped out of his car and grabbed his sports coat from the back seat before activating his vehicle's security alarm. Shrugging into his jacket, Mal took in the activity around him.

Curious neighbors out for a jog or walk on this late Tuesday morning—some with dogs, some with babies, some with both—were gathering on the sidewalk on the other side of the wide tree-lined asphalt avenue. They wore wide-eyed expressions of dread and interest.

At the Bleecher family residence, crime scene technicians walked in and out of the home. They were identifiable by their uniforms and the evidence bags they carried. Police officers were posted behind the bright yellow tape that read Police Line Do Not Cross. The tape had been tied to two trees growing on opposite sides of the avenue. It moved lethargically in the light, cool breeze sweeping through the crowd.

Mal suspected the two men and one woman consulting with each other near a cluster of cars haphazardly parked in front of the house were detectives. But from which division? Robbery? Or Homicide? He scanned both sides of the street again but still couldn't find Verna. She wouldn't have been allowed to remain in her house if Forensics was collecting evidence and taking photographs. So where was she? He was more than a little reluctant to learn the answer.

"Cy!" Mal hailed one of the officers he spotted check-ing the front yard.

He and Cyrus Fletcher had run track together in high school. More recently, they'd participated in various fun runs and charity races.

Cyrus lifted a hand in greeting before joining him near the police tape. He nodded to one of the younger cops stationed near the tree. "I know him." He smiled at Mal, but his blue eyes were clouded with grief and con-cern. "It's good to see a friendly face, but what are you doing here?"

Mal felt the tension surrounding his friend. Cyrus had aspired to be in the police force since they were in high school. He'd wanted to protect neighborhoods, prevent crime and patrol the streets. But Cyrus had said some of the things he'd seen on the job made him question whether he was making an impact. It was as though he took every criminal act in his community as a personal failure.

Mal jerked his chin toward Verna's home. "I had an appointment with Verna Bleecher. Her company, Buck-eye Dynamic Devices, hired us. What's going on?"

Cyrus sighed, planting his hands on his slim hips. "Looks like someone broke into Ms. Bleecher's home. The perp must not have realized anyone was there. The house was tossed. Ms. Bleecher must've surprised them and they killed her, but not before she triggered a secu-rity alarm. That's what alerted us to the break-in and murder."

"Murder?" The news scrambled Mal's thoughts scat-tered into the wind. He forced himself to focus. "But I just spoke with her."

Surprise cleared the lines of tension from Cyrus's face. "When?"

Mal checked his watch. "About twenty minutes ago. A little before ten. She gave me her address and said she'd be waiting for me."

"One second." Cyrus looked over his shoulder. "Detectives." The three plainclothes officials answered his summons. He gestured to each of them in turn. "Detectives Guy Klein, Taylor Stenhardt and Eriq Duster, this is Malachi Touré. He co-owns Touré Security Group. Mr. Touré spoke with Ms. Bleecher twenty minutes ago about work he's doing for Buckeye Dynamic Devices."

Three very interested sets of eyes fastened onto Mal.

"Where were you when you called?" In his mid to late thirties, Guy was the youngest of the trio. He was several inches shorter than Mal's six foot three and carried a few extra pounds around his midsection. He'd swept his thick dark blond hair back from his forehead and suppressed it with a generous amount of product.

Mal frowned. What did that have to do with anything? "At a coffee shop about fifteen miles away."

Guy looked up and down the street. Was he looking for Mal's car? "Can anyone verify that?"

Mal was torn between insult and amusement. "I have a time-stamped receipt."

He looked toward the Bleecher residence. This couldn't have been a robbery gone wrong. A silver Lexus sedan stood at the end of the long, spacious red brick driveway. Curtains over the front windows were open, allowing an unobstructed view from the street into the home. What kind of criminal breaks into a residence when someone was obviously home? A murderer.

"When did Verna Bleecher hire you?" Eriq interrupted Mal's thoughts. He appeared to be the oldest of the group. He gave the impression of someone who'd seen everything. His graying dark brown hair was in need of a cut. His ebony eyes were jaded. His bolo tie was a statement.

"Yesterday." Mal had the sense the older man was sifting his words through his internal lie detector.

Guy grunted. "That seems kind of quick."

Mal exchanged a look with Cyrus. What was Guy implying? Cyrus shook his head as though assuring Mal no one took the other man seriously.

Taylor's attention remained on Mal. "How did she seem when you spoke with her?"

Mal took a few moments to recall her words and tone. "Distracted. At the beginning of the call, it seemed like she was doing something else while she was speaking with me. Otherwise, she seemed the same—pleasant and easygoing."

Eriq glanced at the other two detectives before speaking. "Thank you, Mr. Touré. We'll be in touch if we have any other questions."

"Thanks, Mal." Cyrus started to leave.

"Cy." Mal stopped his friend. "How was she killed?"

Cyrus faced him again. His shoulders seemed to slump. "Shot. Four times. One in the stomach, two in the back, one in the back of the head."

Mal closed his eyes briefly. A vicious attack; the killer had wanted to make sure Verna was dead. Why? "No one heard the shots?"

Cyrus shook his head. "Officers are still going door-to-door. I spoke with the nearby neighbors, but they hadn't heard anything. You know the governor's mansion is two blocks from here." He inclined his head in the direction of the Tudor revival–styled home. "The media's going to go wild. The department will be under even more pressure."

All true. Homicides were hard enough without the added scrutiny.

Mal shoved his fists into his front pants pockets. First, Grace had claimed Buckeye Dynamic Devices hacked her system for information on a potentially lethal formula; then the company's chief technology officer was murdered. He didn't want to believe the two occurrences were connected, but he couldn't afford to believe they weren't.

Mal gestured toward the Lexus in the driveway. "A robber who enters a residence when someone's obviously home, armed with a gun that may have been fitted with a silencer? That doesn't sound like a random burglary to me. It sounds like a hit."

Cyrus frowned, looking away as he considered Mal's pronouncement. "Those are good points." He lifted his eyes. "I'm sure the detectives have that covered. Tell Zeke and Jerry I said hi." He returned to his search of the grounds.

Mal wished he shared his friend's confidence, but the detectives' line of questioning gave him doubts. If they were looking for something other than a robbery gone wrong, why had they questioned him as though he were a suspect in the break-in? Why hadn't they asked him any questions about his work for Buckeye Dynamic Devices? Granted, due to the confidentiality clauses detailed in their client contracts, he wouldn't have been able to answer any of them, but that shouldn't have stopped the detectives from asking. No, he had a bad feeling about this.

He started back toward his car. With every step, his sense of foreboding grew. He deactivated the alarm and found his cell phone and Grace's number. Mal settled onto the driver's seat before placing his call. She answered on the second ring.

Mal rubbed his fingertips against his forehead. "We have a problem."

Chapter 3

Grace was waiting for him in the coffee shop's parking lot late Tuesday morning. She must have heard the tension in his voice when he'd called her twenty minutes ago to say he was returning for her so they could update his brothers on the case. She could've stayed in the café. He would've parked, then gone in to meet her. But that would've taken time, and Grace didn't like to wait. It had been one of the many things they had in common when they'd dated in Chicago. He didn't like to wait, either.

Mal pulled his car beside her. He started to get out, but Grace had circled the trunk and let herself in through the passenger door before he'd put the car in Park. No, she definitely wasn't one to waste time.

"Your client was murdered?" She set her knapsack between her feet and buckled her seat belt. "I was sure she was the hacker. Do you think she was killed because of my formula?"

Mal made a loop in the lot, then stopped his car. The anguish in her voice tore him up inside. He needed to reassure her. "The police think the homicide was a break-in gone wrong."

"But you don't." It was a statement, not a question. Her troubled cinnamon eyes searched his.

"No, I don't." He spoke gently, trying not to upset her more. "I think there's a connection between her murder and the hack. But you're not responsible for Verna's death, Grace. The killer is."

Grace nodded, but Mal couldn't tell whether his words had helped. He merged into traffic, pointing his SUV toward the interstate. It added a couple of miles to the drive to his office but would cut precious minutes from their trip. His skin warmed where her eyes touched him.

"You said the police think a burglar killed Verna. Did you tell them about the hack?"

Her soft, light fragrance filled his car. Mal tried taking shallow breaths. They didn't help. "Can't. Our contracts have a confidentiality clause. Besides, they didn't ask."

"Hmm." Grace's tone was noncommittal.

Mal took the on-ramp to the interstate. In his peripheral vision, he saw Grace frowning through the windshield. He could almost feel her thoughts churning, trying to connect the pieces of the puzzle they had and make them make sense.

He broke the silence. "What're you thinking?"

"It doesn't seem logical that someone would murder her—unless she had a partner."

"Possible, but I don't see it. I don't think Verna was involved in the breech."

"Maybe her partner was the hacker and shot her." Grace expelled a heavy breath. "But we keep coming back to motive. Why would they kill her?"

She massaged the side of her neck, another gesture that was achingly familiar. His palms tingled as he remembered how soft her skin had beenbeneath his hand when he'd rub her neck. Take her arm. Hold her close.

Mal gave himself a mental shake. They'd spent less than half an hour together, between their first meeting at the coffee shop and this commute so far to his office. Yet in that time, he felt the years of her absence and his resentment fading under her closeness and memories of a past he'd worked so damn hard to forget.

He remembered her voice with its hint of her Chicago roots in her accent. The way she pursed her lips when she was thinking. Her act-first-and-worry-about-the-consequences-later attitude, which had led her to hack Buckeye Dynamic Devices.

Mal shifted on the driver's seat. "Let's hold our theories until we get to the office. We're almost there. I don't want to have to repeat everything for my brothers."

"You're right." Grace turned her attention back to the scenery along the interstate. "I just wish I were meeting your brothers under better circumstances."

Mal's eyes strayed back to her. His heart contracted once, twice. *So do I.*

The Touré brothers should have come with a warning label: "Exposure will cause loss of breath, weak knees and racing hearts." Grace walked into the Touré Security Group's conference room late Tuesday morning and was struck by the strong physical family resemblance between the three men. Just as noticeable were their personality differences.

Zeke projected strength and authority from his position on the left side of the long, rectangular glass-and-sterling-silver conference table. Beside Zeke, Jerry gave the impression of a long coil of energy, wrapped and waiting for an opportunity to spring. In contrast, Mal allowed himself to blend into the background. He was the observer, taking in everything, both what you wanted him to see and things you didn't want him to notice. A careless person could forget he was there. And that's what made him the most dangerous one in the room.

The space's chalk-white walls showcased bold watercolor paintings in black metal frames. The subjects were well-known Ohio landmarks, including the Ohio Statehouse, the Cincinnati Observatory, the Paul Laurence Dunbar House, the Rock & Roll Hall of Fame and The Ohio State University's oval.

The back of the room was a floor-to-ceiling window overlooking the front parking lot. It offered a wealth of sunlight. It also framed the treetops and a distant view of the city's outer belt, Interstate 270.

Both of Mal's brothers stood as he led her to the right side of the table, opposite Zeke. He gestured toward each of them. "Dr. Grace Blackwell, my brother Zeke. He's in charge of corporate security. My brother Jerry's in charge of personal security."

Mal held out her chair as she settled onto the cushioned black seat and placed her knapsack on the floor beside her. His actions brought back memories of their time together. He'd always held her seat, even when she cooked for him at her apartment. At first, she'd thought he was trying to impress her. Then she'd realized his gallantry was as much part of him as his dark eyes. His brothers reclaimed their seats after she was settled. Manners were a family trait. Grace was impressed.

Mal hooked his jacket on the back of his chair and addressed her. "Start from the beginning so we have a better idea of what we're dealing with."

She looked from him to Zeke and Jerry as she collected her thoughts. "I've been working on a version of a medication for diabetes treatment that's more effective and affordable than our current form of insulin. I've had some success, but the formulation's unstable."

"What do you mean by 'unstable'?" Zeke had a way of focusing on someone with an intensity that reminded her of Mal. In a navy suit and bold paisley tie, the older brother was the most formally dressed of the three.

"I accidentally discovered that by adding another chemical to the formula, it could become a toxic agent." The admission left a bad taste in Grace's mouth. It was the reason she'd tried to deal with the hacker on her own rather than going to the authorities. "It could be an effective diabetes treatment. Or it could be the basis of a low-cost, highly toxic chemical weapon."

The brothers exchanged a look of surprise and dread. Grace imagined she'd had a similar expression when she first discovered the problem.

"Have you contacted Homeland Security?" The concern in Zeke's voice increased Grace's anxiety.

She gripped her hands on her lap. "Midwest Area Research Systems is a small, emerging pharmaceutical-research company. Technically, we aren't required to report security breaches within the same timeframe as larger facilities. We're hoping to handle this quietly so we don't make our investors nervous. But we're up against the clock."

"How much time do we have?" Mal's voice was devoid of inflection.

Grace rubbed the side of her neck. "Two weeks at the most."

"Who else knows about the hack?" Jerry's business attire was the most casual of the men, black pants and an emerald jersey. The gleam in his midnight eyes gave her the impression he was well aware of the effects of the Touré good looks and charm.

Grace drew a shaky breath as she fought back a wave of grief. "Besides the chief science officer and my grandmother, who lives in a senior residential community in Florida, the only other person who knew about this problem was my former grad school professor, Dr. Bennett MacIntyre. I'd asked for his help in coming up with a solution."

"Your mentor *was* the only other person? What happened to him?" Jerry was also impatient.

Grace paused, struggling to keep her voice from breaking. "I believe he was murdered."

"Murdered?" Zeke straightened on his chair, exchanging a look with his brothers.

"What makes you think that?" Mal's voice was measured, as though he was making an effort to keep everyone calm.

She met his eyes and saw curiosity as well as strength and compassion. "I received an email from him. It was time-stamped Friday morning. The email had an attachment that was a Trojan horse. It took over my hard drive. I was able to stop it but not before it accessed several of my research files."

Mal inclined his head. "The hack you traced back to Buckeye Dynamic."

"That's right." Grace wrapped her arms around her waist. The room was chilled—or was it her? "When I called Dr. B to ask about the email, his administrative assistant told me he'd had a fatal accident Thursday night."

"Thursday?" Jerry frowned. "Before sending you the email with the Trojan horse?" He sat back, crossing his arms. "No wonder you don't believe his death was an accident."

"Have you shared your suspicions about his death with the police?" Zeke asked.

Grace nodded. "And his widow. Of course I didn't divulge what I thought the hacker was seeking. The fewer people who know about the formulation, the better. The police didn't seem interested, though, and Tami became very agitated." It had broken her heart to upset Dr. B's widow, but she couldn't keep her suspicions to herself. He deserved justice.

Zeke inclined his head toward his brothers. "We have some contacts in the department. We'll follow up with them about Dr. MacIntyre's murder."

Grace felt as though at least some of the weight had been lifted from her shoulders. "I'd appreciate that."

"Why did you initially think the email was from Dr. MacIntyre?" Mal asked.

Grace winced. "It greeted me with a nickname only he used. Most of his students call—*called*—him Dr. B. When I earned my doctorate, he started referring to me as Dr. B, and that's how the email addressed me." She shivered just as she had the first time she'd realized the salutation was a deliberate effort to make her believe the sender was someone else.

Mal frowned. "Two suspicious murders that appear to be connected to your computer hack and the theft of your formulation."

First her friend and mentor, now Mal's client. Never in her life had she imagined she'd be caught up in a homicide, much less two. She struggled to pull herself together. "They didn't get the actual formulation, just research articles and notes about the disease. I use an old laptop to connect to the internet and a separate one for my work. But my formulation, I keep on a jump drive. Those articles won't help them recreate it."

"That's smart." Jerry uncrossed his arms.

"And a relief," Zeke added.

Mal nodded his agreement.

"What're you going to do now?" Grace looked around the table. "Buckeye Dynamic hired you to identify their so-called hacker. You've done that. But someone in the company hacked my system. I need to know who and why."

Were they going to sell it to the government? Or some shadowy organization? How much trouble was the public in because of her mistake?

"I believe the person who hacked your system murdered our client." Mal turned to look at his brothers. "We can't close this account. We have to find our client's killer. It's the right thing to do. If we don't do anything, our lack of concern will send the wrong message about our company."

"You're right." Jerry smoothed his hand over his tight curls. "If we walk away now, we'll look scared and—worse—untrustworthy."

"As though we don't care about our clients' safety or justice." Zeke pinched the bridge of his nose. "We're all in agreement: we have to help solve Verna Bleecher's murder."

The tensed muscles in Grace's back and shoulders eased slightly. Her lips parted with relief. "I'm really happy to have your help. What's our next move?"

"'*Our* next move'?" Mal's smooth bourbon voice made her lightheaded.

Grace saw the determination in his eyes and cleared her mind for battle.

Mal couldn't say which part of this case disturbed him more: the fact two people had been murdered and Grace was a strong candidate to be the third, or being in close proximity to her. The first, he and his brothers could address with the police's help. The second, he had no idea how to handle. Both factors were reason enough to take her off the assignment.

But the greatest objection he had to working with her was that her unexpected and unapologetic return proved how stupid he'd been to have ever believed he'd gotten over her. And every minute spent in her company— feeling her warmth and absorbing her fragrance into his pores—made him question whether he'd be able to forget her. Ever.

Mal hid his conflict behind an expressionless mask. "Thanks for bringing us up to speed on the case. We'll take it from here."

Her heart-shaped lips tightened, forecasting a building storm. "You'll need my help if you're going to find your client's murderer this decade. We've already established that the same person who killed Dr. B likely killed Verna Bleecher. I know Dr. B and the people who worked with and for him. I probably already know the killer. I just need to identify them."

Mal started to shoot holes into her argument, but Jerry spoke first. "She's right, Mal. Her help will speed things up."

He glared at his younger brother. Jerry shrugged.

Zeke interrupted. "The killer must've known the professor well enough to know about his nickname for Grace. It stands to reason they also know her."

Mal stood to pace the narrow room. "And it stands to reason her life's in danger." He walked past the window, ignoring the view of the tree-lined boulevard and corporate parks beyond the asphalt parking lot. "We need to talk about protecting her, not involving her in our investigation."

"It's my investigation, too." Grace's long-lidded eyes tracked him as he crossed back to the wall behind her.

"Why don't *you* protect her?" Jerry's idea came out of nowhere.

"What?" Mal narrowed his eyes at his brother, questioning his sanity—and not for the first time.

"She can stay at your house." Jerry sounded pleased with his plan. "You can work the case together and protect her at the same time."

Mal shot a look at Grace. Did he have the same deer-in-the-headlights expression? He rubbed his fingers across his brow. Tension was building. "You should stay with your grandmother in Florida until we've caught the killer."

Grace lifted both hands, palms out. "Gentlemen, I appreciate your concern, but I'm not staying with you, Mal, and I'm not going to Florida, either."

"You said yourself we're up against the clock." Zeke looked from Grace to Mal. "Jerry's right. Having the two of you in the same place, working together, will save time. Mal, you have plenty of space."

He pictured their family home, which now belonged to him. The guest bedroom was down the hall from his, and the guest bathroom shared a wall with his master bath. Zeke was wrong. He didn't have enough space.

"I'm sure Mal and I can maximize our time without moving in together." Grace's voice was tight. She collected her knapsack and stood. "Thank you for your concern, but I'll be fine in my own home. My town house complex has a guard station and regular security patrols." She faced Mal, her eyes wavering before meeting his. "Could you please take me home? I want to put together a list of acquaintances I had with Dr. B. It's a pretty long list. Once I've narrowed it down, I'll call you."

Mal took a hesitant step forward, then stopped. He wanted to tell her his brothers were right. A killer had worked their way into her social network, and he needed for her to be safe. But with their shared history, he also needed to worry about his own protection.

He glanced at Zeke and Jerry. He could read their thoughts in their intent stares. *Convince her to stay with you so she'll be safe.* He almost laughed in their faces. What made them think he had the power to convince her to do anything? He hadn't been able to convince her to stay four years ago.

He grabbed his jacket from his chair. "Let's go."

Mal led her down the three flights of stairs and across the lobby. His SUV was waiting in the parking lot's front row. He deactivated the alarm and held the passenger door open for her.

"Thank you." She sent him an uncertain look from beneath her thick, long eyelashes before sliding onto the passenger seat.

As he settled behind the steering wheel, Grace gave him her address. With a brusque nod, he put the car in gear and navigated out of the lot to merge with the traffic moving toward the northbound interstate.

Once again, her scent filled the space between them. On the drive from the café to the office, the traces of roses and powder had brought back memories that caused the muscles in his abdomen to tighten. Seated beside her at the conference table, the torture had continued. After she'd left Chicago, it had taken months to get her fragrance out of his mind but just moments for it to become familiar again now that she was with him. Once the killer was caught and they went their separate ways, how long would her scent linger on his mind this time?

"Your brothers seem nice." Her statement broke the heavy silence.

"They are." Mal's lips curved into a smile before he remembered to keep his guard up. He couldn't allow her to get close again.

"Do they know about us?"

He didn't know about them. "If you're asking whether they know we met in Chicago, the answer's yes. I called them on my way back to the café."

"Oh." She nodded once. "I sense you're not happy they want me to help investigate."

Mal drew a calming breath that filled his molecules with her fragrance. For a moment, he lost his train of thought. "I'm concerned you're not taking this threat seriously. Two people who are somehow connected to your formula were murdered. What will it take for you to realize you need to remove yourself from this situation and let us handle it?"

"Like I said, the town house complex has security patrols. I'll be fine." She let the silence linger for several moments. "I was surprised to see you again." Her words were abrupt, as though she hadn't meant to say them out loud.

"I don't know why. You knew I was from Columbus, that I still had family here. I never made any secret of it." It was small of him, but he couldn't resist the dig.

"You seemed happy in Chicago."

"So did you." His fists clenched around the smoke gray vinyl steering wheel. "I don't understand why you didn't at least *say* goodbye instead of pushing a piece of paper under my door." The memory still hurt like a knife being twisted in his chest.

She pointed out the windshield. "We're coming up on my exit. I explained in my letter. After my sister died, I needed to be with my grandmother."

"I understood that." Mal hit his signal and checked his blind spot before shifting into the right lane. A thought occurred to him. "Did you think I'd try to talk you out of leaving? I wouldn't have."

"I know that now."

"Then why did you tell me not to contact you?" Mal gritted his teeth to stop the flood of words rushing from his heart.

"I thought it would be easier that way." She gestured toward the entrance of a large, sprawling town house complex on their left.

Easier than what? "I'm glad it was easy for *you*." He flipped the left-turn signal and waited for the few cars in the opposing lane to crawl past.

He regretted engaging in this conversation. It was pointless. Grace had made her feelings about their relationship clear four years ago. He wasn't going to make the mistake of falling for her again.

She directed him to her unit, and he pulled in front of her single-car garage. She climbed out of the vehicle before he could come around to assist her. Mal followed her up the walkway to her town house. An uneasy feeling came over him steps from the back door.

"What…?" Grace froze. The word was a breathy surprise.

Her door was open.

Mal swallowed a curse. He stepped in front of Grace, guiding her off the sandstone walkway and shielding her with his body. A quick scan of the surrounding area didn't reveal anyone nearby.

"Wait here." He approached the town house, walking at an angle to the backdoor. If an armed intruder was lying in wait, he didn't want to be an easy target.

Mal sensed Grace at his back. He'd told her to wait. They were obviously having communication problems. He couldn't deal with that now. He stilled beside the door, straining to catch any sound coming from inside. Nothing. No whispers, no movement, no breathing. He eased the door open farther. There weren't any suspicious shadows shifting along the eggshell walls or across the thick tan carpet. Grace pressed against his back as though trying to see around him. He felt her heart galloping against his spine.

Catching her attention, he mouthed the words *Stay here.*

Her eyes returned to the backdoor without acknowl-
edgment. Mal squelched his impatience. If she wasn't
going to follow his instructions, at least she wasn't lying
to him. This time.

He pushed the door open wider, ready to shove her
out of harm's way if shooting started. Nothing.

Bracing himself, Mal crossed the threshold. The
backdoor had led him into a half dining room with a
circular blond-wood table and four sturdy matching
chairs. A short, wide dark wood bookcase stood behind the table, tucked into a corner. The kitchen was
to the right of the door. Both spaces had been trashed.
In the dining room, books and knickknacks had been
thrown to the beige carpet. In the kitchen, pots, pans
and silverware had been scattered across the white linoleum. Drawers were open and cupboards were empty.
Their contents had been dropped onto the white laminate countertops.

"I'm so sorry, Grace." Mal didn't know what else to
say.

Looking past the archway to the rest of the house, the
same devastation waited for them in the living room.

"Mal?"

He turned to her. "Yes."

She met his eyes. "Can I change my mind about staying with you?"

Chapter 4

"Until we find the killer, Grace is staying with me." Mal spoke from his seat beside Grace at his kitchen table Tuesday afternoon.

Zeke and Jerry were grim. He turned his attention to Grace, lingering on her delicate features. Beneath the anger tightening her full lips and narrowing her wide eyes, she seemed…shattered. Mal understood. Someone had hacked her computer and murdered her best friend. They'd broken into her home. Suppose she'd been there? She could've been hurt—or worse. His muscles clenched with fury and fear.

Before they'd left her town house, Mal had called his brothers to update them and Grace reported the break-in to the police. One officer had searched the rooms for clues he and Grace may have missed while the other asked the standard burglary questions: What time had they come home? Had they noticed anyone or anything suspicious in the area? Was Grace certain she'd locked her doors and windows?

Having a record of the crime and preserving the scene was important for their investigation. If nothing else, the report could provide additional evidence against the killer/hacker. Playing fast and loose with procedures now could trip them up later. That fact had kept Mal seated and focused during the almost-hour-long process instead of tearing the city apart, looking for whoever was after Grace. His former lover had been back in his life less than a day, but already every protective instinct he'd ever had for her had reawakened with a vengeance. He was starting to feel again.

"Was anything missing?" Jerry was seated across the table.

"Fortunately, they didn't get my thumb drive." Grace nodded toward her knapsack, which sat beside her chair. "I keep that with me at all times. But they tore apart my townhouse looking for it. They tossed everything." Her voice wavered. Was it with anger or fear? Perhaps both. She shot a quick look at Mal beside her.

Her home had looked like a tornado had gone through every room, drawer and closet. The intruder had left no corner untouched. It was as though they'd taken out their anger and disappointment over not finding what they'd come for on Grace's belongings. Mal had put to rights the kitchen, dining area and living room. He'd left Grace alone on the top floor to take care of her more personal belongings.

Seated beside Jerry, Zeke's coal eyes darkened with concern. "Grace, I'm glad you weren't alone when you got back to your place."

The thought of Grace confronting that scene by

herself—whether or not the intruder had still been there—turned Mal's guts to ice.

Grace glared at the table's round, blond-wood surface. "I should've known better than to have trusted the townhome-complex manager when he said the facility offered twenty-four-seven, three-sixty-five security for its residents." She snorted. "Some security."

Mal frowned. This wasn't the first time he'd heard her make negative comments about trusting people. She'd made similar remarks when they were dating. What had happened to make her so suspicious? Had that experience been the real reason she'd ended things between them so abruptly?

Zeke continued. "Was anything left behind?"

Grace's rounded eyebrows knitted. "They came to *take* something. Why would anything be left behind?"

Zeke spread his hands. "They may have left a note or some kind of threat, something that points us to the intruder or could link them to the murders?"

"No, nothing that I noticed." Grace turned to Mal.

Mal pulled his eyes from her. He shook his head. "I didn't find anything that seemed out of place, and I was looking. The police didn't, either."

"I'm positive they were after the files." Grace massaged the side of her neck. "It can't be a coincidence that right after the client that hired you to catch me is murdered, my home is broken into. Can it?"

Zeke were steady on hers. "We don't believe in coincidences. It's not safe."

"No, it's not. We have to take control of this situation." *And keep you safe.* Mal had been putting a strategy together since he and Grace had contacted the police. "We need a list of suspects who have a motive to get their hands on Grace's formula. Once we have that list, Zeke, I'll need you to do a background check on those names. Everything you can find on them."

Zeke inclined his head. His eyes gleamed with satisfaction. "I'll be ready."

"Thanks." Mal turned to Jerry. "I need you to circle back to the detectives in charge of Verna Bleecher's murder investigation. I spoke with them today—Eriq Duster, Taylor Stenhardt and Guy Klein. Cy knows them."

"Fletcher?" Jerry typed the names into his smart phone. "Any idea who's taking lead?"

"No, but Klein doesn't seem like he's been on the job long. I'd start with Duster or Stenhardt." Mal caught the glint in Zeke's eyes. "What?"

"Nothing." His older brother shook his head. "It's just good to have a solid plan."

Mal frowned. "It's a start. The break-in was a wake-up call. We have a lot of catching up to do."

He could hear the clock ticking. They'd only just gotten started and already they were running out of time.

The doorbell interrupted their meeting.

"That'll be the pizza." Jerry jumped up from the table and strode to Mal's front door.

Grace glanced at her silver Timex watch. It was a few minutes past noon on Tuesday. Pizza for lunch didn't sound half-bad. Her stomach hummed in agreement. It was time to supplement the plain toasted bagel and four cups of coffee she'd had today.

"What pizza?" Mal's confused question went unanswered as Jerry disappeared down the hall.

Zeke looked similarly baffled. Grace felt the first stirrings of amusement she'd had all day. Probably all week.

Moments later, Jerry returned with what appeared to be an extra-large pizza box, which he set at the center of the table. Grace breathed in the aroma of oregano, seasoned sauce and extra cheese. Jerry made himself at home, collecting plates and silverware from various cupboards and drawers.

"What do you have to drink?" Zeke crossed to the refrigerator to answer his own question.

Mal followed his older brother. "When did you order a pizza?"

"On my way over." Jerry pitched his voice above the sound of Zeke filling four glasses with ice from the automatic machine in the refrigerator. "You never think about food when you're working. Not everyone can skip meals like you do. I need fuel to think."

Grace smiled as Jerry's words invoked fond memories. She slid four of the navy mats from the center of the table to each of their seats, creating their place settings. Her words came without thought. "He used to skip meals in Chicago, too. I'd bring him carryout sometimes when he worked late."

The sudden silence chased away those happy images. Grace looked over her shoulder toward the brothers. Zeke carried two glasses of iced tea to the table. His dark eyes sparkled with curiosity. Jerry winked at her as he distributed the cream porcelain plates. Avoiding her eyes, he handed her a glass.

Grace's face heated. *Awkward.* She took a long drink of her iced tea.

Jerry opened the lid to the pizza box. Hot, spicy, cheesy steam escaped, reminding Grace how hungry she was.

Zeke broke the uncomfortable silence. "Grace, how soon can you get us a list of suspects?"

She swallowed a bite of pizza. "Within an hour. I'll start right after we eat."

"We know there's a connection between the university and Buckeye Dynamic." Mal's measured words belied the tension radiating from him. "The email you received from Dr. B's university account led you to the defense contractor."

Grace fought to ignore the discomfort between them. "Somehow the killer discovered Dr. B knew about my formula and hacked his system to get to me."

"That should narrow the list." Jerry freed a second slice of pizza from the box. "We can focus on those people Dr. B knew who also have a connection to Buckeye Dynamic."

Something didn't feel right. "But how could they have learned about the formula?"

Zeke paused with his glass halfway to his full lips. "Could Dr. B have told someone?"

She shook her head vehemently. "He promised he wouldn't and Dr. B always kept his promises. *Always.*"

"Then someone must've overheard a conversation between the two of you." Mal didn't sound convinced. "Grace, I still think it would be safer for you to leave Columbus. You could stay with your grandmother in Florida until all of this is over." He gestured toward his brothers. "I give you my word this investigation will be our top priority. Not only is solving this case important to protecting your project and your life, it's important to protecting our reputation and getting justice for our client. But we have to take you out of harm's way."

A chill ran down Grace's spine. *Out of harm's way.*

Jerry's words were muffled by the buzzing in her ears. "Mal, we could use her help with this investigation."

Zeke's response was like a whisper. "She could give us information and access to the people—"

"Grace, what's wrong?" Mal's question drew her from the fog.

"Harm's way." Her eyes locked with his. "Could my grandmother be in danger? The killer knows where I live. They probably know where I work. What other information do they have on me? I can't assume they don't know about my grandmother."

Mal's chiseled features tightened. He turned to his brothers. "New plan: Jerry, we need you to secure Grace's grandmother."

Grace's cheeks stung as the blood drained from her face. "She lives in a senior residence in Florida. How will you protect her there? Should we relocate her? Where would—"

Jerry set down his pizza and held up his right hand, palm out. A confident smile brightened his sharp sienna features, which so closely resembled Mal's. "We'll keep your grandmother safe with the help of our security resources. But first, let's get the residence manager on the line and explain the situation to them. Then we'll talk with your grandmother."

Grace looked to Mal beside her. His determined expression convinced her knees to stop shaking. She dug her cell phone out of her knapsack and found the listing for the director of her grandmother's senior residence among her contacts.

She cleared her throat. "I don't know what to say."

Mal touched the hand that held her phone. The warmth from his fingers radiated up her arm, easing her tensed muscles. "Keep it simple. Explain that your grandmother will need additional security for a period of time, and we'll take it from there."

Grace gave him a grateful look. She pressed the icon to dial the director's number and put the phone on speaker.

"This is Lisa Mylar. May I help you?" The director's greeting managed to be brisk but welcoming. Her innate warmth was one of the things that had convinced Grace to support her grandmother's desire to move into the residence. That and the fact that three of her friends were already there.

"Lisa, this is Grace Blackwell." Her mind was rushing to find a nonthreatening way to explain that, because of her, a killer could be after her grandmother. She squeezed her eyes shut, thinking of the danger she was bringing to the residence's door.

A smile entered the other woman's voice. "Hello, Dr. Blackwell. To what do I owe the pleasure of your call?"

Lisa's friendly greeting made the need for the call even more uncomfortable. "I'm here with Mal, Zeke and Jerry Touré of the Touré Security Group. I'm afraid I have some difficult news. Because of my work, I'm worried my grandmother will need some additional security measures."

Lisa spoke after a brief, shocked pause. "I'm sorry, Dr. Blackwell, but are you saying your grandmother's *life* may be in danger?"

Grace swallowed the lump of fear in her throat. Her voice was husky. "Yes, that's what I'm saying. There are people who are after one of my formulations. Two people have already been killed."

Mal jumped in. "Ms. Mylar, this is Mal Touré. Our

security firm has experience handling dozens of cases like this one over the years. We have a plan."

"With respect, Mr. Touré, has your firm ever provided protection at a retirement residence?" The director's tone was skeptical.

Mal seemed undeterred. "No, but we've successfully protected people at similar facilities. My brother Jerry's in charge of our personal protection services. He'll walk you through our procedures."

"This is Jerry." The youngest Touré gave the cell phone his winning smile. "May I call you Lisa?"

Within the hour, the Touré brothers had reassured Lisa and, with her help, developed a strategy that would increase protection not only for Grace's grandmother, Melba, but all the residents and staff at the facility.

Lisa wrapped up the call. "So you'll explain this process to Ms. Stall?"

"We'll do that now." Grace sent her grandmother a text asking if she was available for a videoconference with her three male colleagues. Melba requested a few minutes so she could get back to her room.

"That's good, then." There was a nod of approval in Lisa's voice. "And, Jerry, I wish we were meeting under more pleasant circumstances, but I'll expect your arrival tonight."

"I wish that, too, Lisa." Jerry paused as though once again considering the gravity of their situation. "I'll text you as soon as I have my arrival time."

Grace recovered her tablet from her knapsack. "My grandmother should be ready for our videoconference." She looked around the kitchen table. "I know I don't need to say this, but doing so will make me feel better. Please don't scare her. Gran's tougher than she looks, but she's still my grandmother."

A murmur of understanding whispered around her. She launched the computer program, angling the screen to include Zeke to her left, Jerry to her right and Mal, who stood behind her. Within moments, Melba appeared. She looked so much like Grace, with her wide brown eyes, delicate nose, bow-shaped lips and heart-shaped brown face.

Grace's smile was spontaneous. "Hi, Gran."

"Hi, honey." Melba's greeting was cautious. "Who are those men with you? They look very somber." The hint of a protective mama bear was in her tone. Grace could almost hear her underlying question: *Do you need me to come to Columbus?*

"These are the Touré brothers of the Touré Security Group." She gestured toward each brother. "Zeke and Jerry. Mal's standing behind me."

Zeke smiled. "Ms. Stall, it's a pleasure to meet you."

Jerry waved. "Hi, Grace's grandma!"

Mal nodded at the screen. "Hello, Ms. Stall."

"Mm-hmm." Melba's eyes moved around the screen, considering the three men. Her attention returned to Grace. "How bad is it, honey?"

Grace's chest tightened. She blinked to ease the sting in her eyes. "It's not good, Gran."

After giving her the latest update, it took all four of them more than fifteen minutes to talk Melba out of flying to her granddaughter's side. Then it took more than half an hour to convince her to trust Touré Security to protect Grace and not get Homeland Security involved.

"Gran." Grace tried to interrupt her, but it was like trying to stop a hurricane when it's already on its way.

"I'm not going to let you go through this alone." Melba stepped out of the screen.

"Gran, please sit back down and listen." Grace strained to control her impatience. "We've already gotten approval from Lisa Mylar for our plan."

Melba's face reappeared on the screen. "You spoke with Lisa?"

"Yes, ma'am." Jerry sounded dazed. Grace worried he was having second thoughts about accepting this Coconut Creek assignment. "We'd like to tell you about it as well."

Melba sat down. "Go on, then."

Jerry and Zeke exchanged worried looks before Jerry laid out their plan for her. He detailed the steps they'd take to tighten security procedures at the residence, brief the staff, and hire additional security contractors for round-the-clock protection inside and outside the building. "The fact that it's just one building makes it a lot easier to secure."

Melba arched an eyebrow. "And what makes you qualified to be someone's bodyguard?"

Jerry flashed a grin that showed he wasn't offended by her question. "I have CPR, weapons, boxing and martial arts training. I have more than nine years of experience protecting individuals and families, including captains of industry, government officials and the occasional celebrity."

From the tone of his voice, Grace had the impression his celebrity details were his least favorite.

Apparently satisfied, Melba sniffed. "And you'll be arriving tonight, and you're supposed to be my godson, visiting from out of town?"

Jerry nodded. "That's right, ma'am."

"Mm-hmm." She looked around the screen again. "And who'll be protecting my granddaughter?"

"I will, ma'am," Mal responded without hesitation.

Melba gave him a long, steady stare. "She's very precious to me."

"She's…" Mal cleared his throat. "I understand, ma'am."

Melba smiled for the first time during this entire exchange. She addressed Jerry. "I guess I'll see you tonight…godson."

Jerry chuckled. "Yes, Aunt Melba."

Grace exchanged a few more details before ending the session. She turned to Jerry. "Please, please take good care of my grandmother." Her voice cracked. "She's all I have."

Jerry put his hand over hers on the table. The muscles in his throat worked before he spoke. "I give you my word I'll protect her as though she was my mother." His lips curved. "Well, my mom but without the combat or weapons training."

Grace gave a weak smile. Mal had told her his parents had met while serving in the Marine Corps.

Zeke patted Grace's left shoulder as he stood. "There's no one better qualified than Jerry to keep your grandmother safe. We stake our reputation on that."

Grace heard the pride in the eldest Touré's voice. That along with Jerry's words eased her worries—or at least most of them. She followed the men to the front door.

Mal turned to Zeke. "Could you deal with Jerry's travel arrangements? I'm going to help Grace get settled."

Humor and affection brightened Zeke's eyes. "It's good to have the old Mal back."

What did that mean? Grace watched Mal lock up behind his brothers. From his closed expression, she didn't think this was the right time to ask.

"It's been a long day. Do you want to take a break before settling in?" Mal searched Grace's eyes, and the tension that had tightened around him with every twist and turn in their day eased. It was late afternoon. He took his first easy breath since that morning. She was safe and he would make sure she stayed that way.

Grace stepped away from the door, breaking the spell Mal was under. "You're right. It's only Tuesday, but it feels like we've been through an entire week." She reached for her suitcase, which they'd set beside the stairs when he'd first brought her to his home. "I'm fine. The sooner we start looking into the people who could've...hurt Dr. B and Verna Bleecher, and hacked my system, the sooner this nightmare will be over and we can return to normal."

He didn't know how she defined *normal*. After their unexpected reunion, he didn't know whether he'd ever feel *normal* again.

Taking her suitcase from her, Mal mounted the staircase. "I'll show you the guest room."

He hadn't taken the time to go through the niceties of showing Grace around when he'd first brought her to his home. He'd been focused on developing a plan of action he could share with Zeke and Jerry. In that respect, Zeke was right: leading their strategy session had felt like old times. It had been years since he'd been hands on with the company—four years, in fact. He'd never been *in charge*. That's not the way he and his brothers handled their business. But he'd been deferring to Zeke and Jerry. He hadn't been interested in making major decisions, not even the one Zeke had asked for regarding their company's future. Mal realized now that was bad for the business. It was bad for him. And judging by the escalating tension between Zeke and Jerry, it was bad for them. He needed to assert himself more, starting now.

At the top of the staircase, Mal turned right. "This is the guest room. I'll make up the bed after I show you around."

He stepped aside so she could enter first. She stopped in the middle of the spacious square room.

Mal had always been tidy, which was fortunate since, when he'd woken up that morning, he hadn't known he'd be moving an ex-girlfriend turned client into his home. If this had happened to Jerry, for example, things could've been embarrassing. Jerry was a slob. He knew it but didn't care.

Sectional rugs in rich jewel tones had been placed on the polished hardwood floor around the queen-size bed. The dressing table and matching nightstands were made of teak wood. The two windows allowed plenty of natural light, making the room bright and welcoming.

"It's lovely." She turned to smile at him. "I'm very grateful, and I can make the bed." Grace stopped abruptly and walked to the closet as though the framed colored-pencil image on the wall beside it had lured her closer. "This is wonderful. It's Antrim Lake, isn't it?" She squinted at the artist's signature. Her eyes widened in surprise. "Zeke drew this?"

"He drew all of these and the charcoal sketches in our office." Mal heard the pride in his voice. His brother was a wonderful artist. He set Grace's suitcase on the floor at the foot of the bed and gestured toward the two other drawings on the wall across the room. One was of the rose garden at the Park of Roses. The other captured the Scioto River.

Grace crossed the room. "Wow, he's very talented. Thank you for letting me use this room."

Mal nodded, taking pleasure in her appreciation of his brother's gift. "You're welcome. This used to be Zeke's bedroom. Jerry's old room is across the hall. It's now the smaller guest room. I moved into my parents' room after Mom died and use my old room as a home office."

"So this is your family home." A hint of a smile curved Grace's lips. She seemed to look around with new eyes. "It's lovely. You've maintained it well."

"Thank you." He appreciated her comment. He hoped his parents would also be proud of the way he was caring for this part of their legacy. "I'll show you the rest of the house."

"It's nice that you and your brothers had your own rooms." Grace's smile grew with her memories. "My sister and I shared a room, but that was nice, too. I always had company, a friend nearby."

"Zeke, Jerry and I had to have separate rooms to keep the peace." His tone was wry. Mal led her back into the hallway. He felt her warmth behind him. "This is the guest bathroom. You'll have plenty of privacy. My room has an adjoining bathroom. I'll get you fresh towels."

Grace ran her fingertips over the turquoise walls and her eyes across the blue ceramic tiling. "I like the color scheme."

"That's my room." Mal tipped his head toward the end of the hall. The door was open. Fortunately, he always made his bed as soon as he woke.

"So you and your brothers had to share this bathroom." She jerked her thumb toward the guest bathroom. "What was that like?"

"It was a nightmare." Mal chuckled as he was pulled decades into the past. "Zeke is a compulsive neat freak, even worse than me. Jerry's a born slob, except when it comes to his appearance. He'd spend hours staring at himself in the mirror."

Grace's face brightened with surprised laughter. "Really?"

Mal grinned, enjoying her amusement. "He still does." He led her back down the hall and opened the door to the last room. "This is my home office. You can work at that second desk. It's probably a good idea for you to telecommute until we close this case. Will your boss to agree to that?"

"I'm sure certain of it." There was a note of dread in Grace's voice. "I'll discuss it with him, the chief science officer, in the morning. He knows about the hack. If I don't identify the hacker soon, we're going to have to report this breech to Homeland Security. He doesn't want it to get to that far. Neither do I."

Neither did Mal. If two murders weren't enough, Grace's pronouncement was additional proof that this case was a serious threat. And Touré Security Group was at the center of it.

He captured Grace's hypnotic eyes. "My brothers and I feel the same way. The security breach will reflect badly on your lab, and it'll hurt our company. We're committing everything we have to keeping you, your grandmother and the public safe."

Grace nodded. "I'm grateful for everything you're doing."

He stopped beside a short, black metal filing cabinet. An iPad lay on top of it. "This is connected to a twenty-four-hour home security system that monitors the perimeter of the house. You'll need to be familiar with it for those times you're in the house by yourself."

He took a few minutes to review the login information and the system's various features. The computer screen displayed real-time video feeds from six cameras strategically placed around the house. It seemed to only took a few minutes for Grace to feel comfortable with it. Mal was confident she could handle the program on her own.

Their next stop on his tour was his basement. "Washer and dryer." He gestured toward the laundry units in the corner, then swept his arm to encompass the treadmill, elliptical machine, old-school weight bench and black vinyl boxing bag. "Exercise equipment. Do you still run?"

They'd participated in several fun runs and charity races together in Chicago.

"I do." Her tone was cautious. "Why do I have the feeling you're going to tell me I can't run outside for the foreseeable future?"

"It's for your safety."

She spread her arms. "Intellectually, I know you're right. But the idea of that level of hiding doesn't sit well with me."

"That's fair." He inclined his head. "The idea of your being in danger doesn't sit well with me. I'm sure your grandmother feels the same way."

Grace's eyes flared. "You're playing the Gran card?"

"Yes."

"Fine." She spun on the heel of her pointed-toe black

flats and marched back upstairs. She stepped aside while he closed the basement door. "Thank you very much for opening your home to me. I wouldn't have been comfortable on my own. I hope I don't have to impose on you for long."

"Grace." He cleared his throat. "Keeping you safe is not an imposition."

She gave him a soft smile. "You and your brothers are wonderful people. I wish I'd known your parents. I would've liked them."

She turned away. Moments later, he heard her footsteps on the stairs.

Mal exhaled. "They would've liked you, too."

Chapter 5

"You need to stay with me in Florida until this murderer is caught." Melba wasn't making a request.

"No, Gran." Grace was respectful but firm even as her heart broke a little. Should she go to her grandmother to help keep her safe? No, she had to help find the killer. That was the best thing she could do to protect her Melba. "I'm sorry you're upset, but I'm needed here to help with the investigation."

After Mal's tour of his home Tuesday evening, Grace had returned to the guest room he'd given her to speak with her grandmother in private. She was using her wireless earbuds so she could unpack while they talked.

She hadn't brought many clothes. She hadn't known what to take with her. The break-in and its implications had frightened her more than she'd admitted even to herself. How had the hacker known where she lived? Had they been surveilling her? Were they tracking her now? What else did they know about her? How many people had she put in danger? That last question turned her blood to ice.

"Do they need your help? Or do you feel obligated to get involved?" Melba's voice pulled her from her dark thoughts. "You're not responsible for any of this. You don't have to put your life at risk."

The group videoconference had been necessary to update Melba on the situation and the measures the Touré brothers were putting into place for her safety. But Grace needed this private time with her grandmother to admit her fears and express her concerns. Her grandmother needed it, too. She'd listen to whatever Melba had to say, but she would not hide in Florida. Bottom line: running from the investigation wasn't an option. There was too much at stake, including their lives.

"The hacker-turned-killer put my life at risk, Gran." *And yours as well.* Grace's hands shook as she returned to her unpacking. "But the Touré Security Group is helping me. You know what they say about there being safety in numbers."

That partnership came with its own risks, though. She thought of Mal, and her heart skipped a beat.

"They do seem to be capable. And experienced." Melba's words may have been grudging, but they were still an endorsement. Grace would take it.

"And we're working with the police."

"But this is the twenty-first century. If the Tourés need your help on the case, they can call, text, email or videoconference you." Melba was getting testy. She was moving quickly through her five phases of negotiation: reasoning, coaxing, testiness, demanding and silence.

Melba had never made it to silence in the past. Grace didn't have a reason to believe today would be different.

"Gran, I can't introduce them to the suspects via text, and we can't question them via email. This is a hands-on situation."

"I don't want anything to happen to you." Melba's grumble was barely audible.

"I don't want anything to happen to either of us." Grace grabbed two fistfuls of white-and-gray ankle-length tube socks and stuffed them into a drawer.

She jogged every morning. The activity helped her stay in shape, but it also cleared her mind and helped her focus on her tasks for the day. Mal could be right, though. It may not be wise to exercise outdoors for a while. As clean, comfortable and well equipped as his fitness room was, the thought of running on a tread-mill for the foreseeable future was depressing. The list of reasons to capture this hacker/killer quickly continued to grow.

Melba huffed. "We don't know that I'm in danger. Staying here with me in this residence could be the safest place for you."

"We don't know that you're *not* in danger." Grace's tone was hard; she wouldn't apologize for that. "I'm not going to be cavalier with your safety. If the killer touched one hair on your stubborn head, I'd wrap the formula in a bow and deliver it to them personally on a platter. Knowing that about myself makes *your* safety *my* top priority—or do you want to be responsible for a dangerous formula getting into the hands of a murderer?"

Tension strained Melba's sigh as it traveled through the line connecting them. "No, I don't."

"Thank you." Grace rolled her head clockwise, then counterclockwise, attempting to ease the knotted muscles in her neck and shoulders. "Jerry and his team will be there to keep you safe. I'd appreciate it if you'd cooperate with them."

"And I'd appreciate it if you cooperated with Mal."

Grace shoved her exercise bras into the same drawer with her socks. "I promise."

It was a difficult promise to make. Grace had been raised to be independent and self-sufficient. It was a tough concession for her grandmother as well. After all, Melba had raised her.

Her grandmother abruptly introduced a new line of questioning. "Are you absolutely certain you'll be safe staying in that house alone with Mal Touré? I don't know him, and you haven't seen each other in four years. He's practically a stranger."

Malachi Touré? A stranger? Never. "Yes, I can trust him. He's an honorable person, and that will never change."

No matter how many years, miles or hurts separated them, Mal would never be a stranger to her. From the beginning, she'd recognized their connection. He'd gone from her neighbor to her obsession in a matter of weeks. When she'd realized how completely enthralled she'd become, she ended their relationship cold turkey.

She took her blouses from her suitcase. She'd thrown them into her bag without removing their hangers. As she carried the garments to the closet, memories played across her mind like a slide show. It was the little things Mal had done while they were together that revealed how important her safety was to him. He'd walk on the outside of the sidewalk. He'd pick her up from her apartment, and he made sure she locked her door at the end of their evening. She was safe with him.

A faint woodsy, pine smell drifted from the closet and wrapped around her. *Mal.* It came from the winter coats and sweaters he'd left on the top shelf. She closed her eyes for a moment and just breathed. She could swear Mal was standing beside her. She shook her head to clear her mind.

"Could I tell Gilda about my round-the-clock security surveillance?" Melba seemed to have accepted the situation. At least for now. Grace felt her tense muscles ease.

Gilda Reynolds and her grandmother had been friends for years, even before they'd moved into the retirement home together. They'd shared each other's secrets and sorrows. Gilda had been there for her and her grandmother after Pam had died. And Melba had helped her friend through the loss of her sister. Grace was confident her grandmother's friend was trustworthy and that her grandmother wouldn't tell Gilda the critical details of the formulation. But as for sharing information about the surveillance, that decision wasn't up to her.

"You should ask Jerry. That's up to him, although Gilda knows you don't have a godson." Grace turned to collect her pants and skirts from the case. "Whatever you do, please don't tell anyone why someone's after the formula."

"I know, sweetheart. I don't want you to be in any more danger than you already are." Melba sounded fretful. "I know you've promised to be careful, but that doesn't change the fact that someone's plotting to get your files, and that person has already killed two people."

Grace wished there was something more she could do

or say to comfort her grandmother. That was the tricky part. She didn't want to make assurances she might not be able to keep. "I'll check in with you at least once a day. And I'll give you Mal's and Zeke's cell phone numbers in case you need to get in touch with them."

"That's a good idea. Thank you."

Grace ended their conversation. Her mind wandered as she finished unpacking. She'd told her grandmother she'd be physically safe with Mal, and that was true. But what about her heart? There already were signs it was in danger. Had the years given her the strength she needed to resist him?

Did she want to?

Mal had never noticed before just how small his kitchen was. Still, he did his best to avoid touching Grace as she helped him clean up after dinner Tuesday evening. The aromas of the seared chicken breasts, wild rice and garden salad he'd made lingered in the air. Beneath those scents, he caught wisps of Grace's fragrance—roses and powder. This task. Her closeness. Their movements in the kitchen. They combined to drag him back into four-year-old memories of similar evenings together. They'd cook, talk about their day and then clean up. And afterward...

Was she remembering, too? Did their time together mean anything to her? Or was it just another part of her past?

"It feels like we met with your brothers days ago instead of hours." Grace carried the empty pitcher of iced tea to the sink. Her voice was casual, as though being near him didn't cause anywhere near the turmoil he was experiencing.

"I was thinking the same." He sounded grumpy. Mal resisted the urge to clear his throat and try again.

Before dinner, he'd spent a few hours on his other cases. He planned to work into the night. This murder investigation was his top priority—his other assignments weren't matters of life and death—but he didn't want to break commitments to other clients.

"I can do that." Mal tried to stop her from loading his dishwasher.

Unsurprisingly, she ignored him. "You cooked dinner. I'll clean up."

He started to argue but then remembered kitchen duty was one of his least favorite things. "If you insist." He heard her chuckle as he crossed back to the kitchen table. "What did your supervisor say about you working remotely for now?"

They'd spent most of dinner on a conference call with Zeke and Jerry. Jerry had been at the airport. He'd bought a ticket for the last flight to Coconut Creek and planned to call once he was with Melba.

Grace closed the dishwasher and turned her attention to scrubbing the pots and pans in the sink. "The chief science officer agrees it would be for the best. But we're running out of time. As I explained, MAR Lab is an emerging pharmaceutical-research company. If our investors learned about this security breech, it would destroy us."

He took a seat facing Grace and reached for the sheet of paper she'd left on the table. "Is this the suspect list?"

"That's what I've come up with so far." She pitched her voice above the sounds of the faucet.

"'So far'?" Mal frowned. She'd filled both sides of a page from a standard white writing tablet. There was one name per line with a brief description beside it. "There must be at least fifty names here."

"Fifty exactly. Dr. B knew a lot of people."

His mind reeled. "We need a list of murder suspects, not Christmas card recipients."

Grace frowned as though confused. She gestured toward the paper. "Those *are* suspects."

Mal's eyes widened with incredulity. "You really think there are fifty people who'd kill your friend and my client for your formula?"

There was a moment of silence while she seemed to give his question serious consideration. "Money's a strong motivator. So is power. In the wrong hands, this product would give someone both."

"I know but…" He considered the list. "How do you function, thinking everyone around you is a potential murderer?"

He'd suspected Grace had trust issues when they'd dated in Chicago. She hadn't been jealous or suspicious of him, but she'd been cautious about opening up. He'd respected that. He'd felt their relationship was worth the time and effort, so he'd let her set the pace. And then she'd disappeared.

Her back still to him, Grace shrugged. "How do you function, thinking they're not?"

Mal returned his attention to the list. According to the descriptions, she'd included some of Bennett Mac-Intyre's students, past and present. There were also members of the university, including colleagues, the president, executive committee members, donors and the board of trustees. Grace had even mentioned her colleagues and her boss.

Incredible. "You included your boss?"

"Everyone's a suspect. Isn't that what they always say on those police procedurals?"

Mal massaged his forehead with his fingertips. "If your boss really wanted that formula, couldn't he just ask you for it? Would he go so far as killing Dr. B and Verna?"

Grace hesitated as she dried one of the pans. "I suppose he could. He knows I'm concerned the formula could be weaponized, but he's never asked for the components. It's as though he doesn't want to know."

"OK, then. We could take him off—"

"Or he could be a very good actor." She hunted around the kitchen, the pan still in her hand.

And we're back to Wariness World. Is she even taking this exercise seriously? "You're very distrusting."

She straightened, arching a rounded eyebrow at him. "And you're very trusting, which is odd for someone in security."

Should I ask? "How is that odd?"

She paused as though considering her answer. "If we didn't have to worry about people doing bad things, we wouldn't need security. So, in fact, your industry should be indebted to people like me. Without people like me—who have a healthy level of skepticism—you'd be out of business."

No, I shouldn't have asked. "The pots and pans go in the lower cupboard beside the stove." The lightweight material of her black slacks tightened around her posterior as she bent over to put away the pans. Mal's palms tingled. He dragged his attention back to the sheet of paper in his hand. "This isn't useful. You've cast too wide a net."

She sat beside him at the table. "Better too wide than too narrow."

They could argue about that for days. She'd even included a couple of people without descriptions. He wasn't going to go there. "Let's take a different approach. Let's focus on the people who were in a position to know how close you and Dr. B were. Who knew he also referred to you as Dr. B?"

"I didn't think anyone had." A cloud passed over Grace's delicate features. She must've really cared for Bennett MacIntyre. She must have trusted him. *Lucky man.* "That's why I thought the email was from him."

"But then, how did the hacker know to call you that?"

"I have no idea." Grace took the paper from him. "But you're right. It would take too long to investigate all of these people. I'll prioritize it, putting at the top of the list people who were connected to both me and Dr. B." She grabbed her pen from the table and used it to put an asterisk beside several names. "These are our top suspects."

Mal noted three names now had asterisks beside them. "Both of his research assistants and a Buckeye Dynamic bioscientist."

Grace's nod was decisive. "I've met all of them. They could benefit professionally and financially from my mistake. We can start by interviewing these three. If they don't pan out, we can move down the list."

Mal gave her a considering look. "Grace, I'm still not convinced it's a good idea for you to be present for these suspect interviews. One of them could be our killer."

Grace's eyes hardened with determination. "I have to take that risk. The suspects know me. They don't know you. They'll open up with me, whereas they probably won't even speak with you."

She had a point. But… "You've never interviewed suspected murderers before."

"Neither have you." She gestured toward him. "Your company provides security services, not investigative services."

She was guessing. She was also right. And although he'd had decades of training to protect himself and others, the situation was still risky. "There's a killer after you. Bringing you to them wouldn't be smart."

"But you'll be with me. I won't take any chances and you'll keep me safe. I'll follow your instructions—unless you try to investigate without me."

"I don't—"

Grace cut him off. "We'll get started tomorrow. I received an email about Dr. B's wake. I want to pay my respects to his family. And I'm sure several of the people from our list, including our primary suspects, will be there."

Mal sighed, rubbing his forehead again. "All right. You've made some good points. But I'll hold you to your promise to follow my directions."

Grace gave him a relieved smile. "Thank you, Mal. I'll keep my promise—as long as you don't try to leave me behind."

His muscles tightened. That's what he'd spent the last four years trying to do: leave her in his past. He just realized how badly he'd failed at that.

"She has trust issues." The comment burst from Mal as he and Zeke began their final lap around the perimeter of Antrim Lake Wednesday morning.

The sun was beginning its ascent. The sky had been dark when they started, gradually lightening into gray. Mist floated above the water as the temperature rose. He smelled the musty, damp earth beneath his running shoes and the sharp, dew-laden grass that rimmed the pond. At this time of day, there was only a handful of people at the park. Other joggers and several walkers—some with dogs, others with strollers and a few on their own—were enjoying the fresh air. Grace had been using the treadmill when he'd left. She hadn't seemed happy about exercising indoors, but she agreed it would be best if whoever was stalking her didn't see her spending her entire day with the Touré brothers.

Usually, Jerry joined them for their morning workout, but he'd arrived in Coconut Creek last night to help guard Grace's grandmother. He'd arranged for two additional agents to ensure Melba would have round-the-clock personal protection in addition to the guards at the residence.

"Grace? What makes you say that?" Zeke glanced at him before returning his attention to the path ahead.

The dirt trail gave way to an asphalt surface. Rows of trees arched over the rolling footpath on both sides. Those on the left bordered the pond; those on the right shielded the woods beyond the lake.

"Let's start with her suspect list. She gave me fifty names." His mind still reeled.

"What?" Zeke stumbled on the path. "She thinks there are fifty people who'd want to kill her?"

"Money and power are strong motivators. Her words." Mal's tone was dry. "I convinced her to cut it back to a more reasonable number. She's 'prioritized' the names, so we're starting with three people of interest. They'd all benefit professionally, not just financially, from getting the formula. Two are Dr. B's research interns. The third is a former intern, now a bioscience researcher at Buckeye Dynamic."

"Those sound like solid candidates." Zeke nodded his satisfaction. He slid a look at Mal. "You two dated in Chicago. How did you meet?"

They'd turned the first corner in the path, entering the section sheltered by trees. Superimposed over the view were Mal's memories of all but gushing to his parents and brothers about Grace when they'd first started dating. And then the strained silences after she'd disappeared.

"I told you, she lived down the hall from me." Mal used the back of his wrist to swipe the sweat from his upper lip. "I got home from work one evening to find the postal carrier had put her electric bill in my mail slot. When she opened her door, she gave me this little smile. I felt like someone had sucked all the air from my lungs. I gave her the envelope. She thanked me and closed the door in my face."

"Oh, harsh, player." Zeke stopped jogging and bent over with laughter.

"It wasn't that funny." But looking back, Mal had to chuckle, too.

"We have to tell Jerry." Zeke started jogging again. "So what did you do?"

"I tried to forget about her but couldn't. I managed to accidentally on purpose run into her a couple of times, but she'd just smile and keep walking. She has a great smile."

"Yes, she does."

"I got desperate, so I put my mail in her mailbox."

"Smooth." Zeke nodded his approval.

"I thought so." The memory brought him back to that evening. The excitement of knowing he wasn't only going to see Grace again, but this time he'd have a chance to speak with her. He'd worried about what he'd say. He had to make a good impression. "But when she returned my mail, she didn't actually stop. It was more like a drive-by. 'Knock-knock. Here's your mail.' And she was gone."

"Brutal." Zeke's voice was thick with amusement.

"Like a kick to the gut." Mal blew out a breath as he remembered the pain of his disappointment. "I gave it another try, this time on a Saturday. I made coffee and cookies—"

"You baked?" Zeke's thick, dark eyebrows couldn't rise any higher on his forehead.

Mal muttered his embarrassment. "Well, they were frozen. I warmed them in the microwave."

He ignored Zeke's snort of laughter as the memory played across his mind.

"The carrier gave me your mail again." Grace's full, pink lips parted to reveal the tips of perfect white teeth.

"Again?" Mal stepped back, pulling his apartment door wider. *"Can I make it up to you with coffee and cookies? I'm trying something new and would appreciate an unbiased opinion."*

Yes, it was misleading, but that's how desperate he'd been.

"Well, I..." She hesitated with his heart in her hands. *Finally, her smile widened, and she crossed his threshold. "Sure. Thank you."*

Zeke's expression was judgmental. "Frozen cookie

dough? Not even from a mix. Just frozen. Yeah, we're definitely telling Jerry."

Mal was defiant. "It worked. Make sure to tell him that."

Zeke raised his eyebrows before looking away. "How do you feel about her now? Is your past going to be a problem?"

They closed in on the next turn on the path around the pond.

"No, it won't be a problem." Would it? Were these feelings echoes from the past—or something more?

"Mom was sure you were in love."

It was Mal's turn to stumble on the path. "Like you said, my relationship with Grace is in the past. My personal feelings won't interfere with this investigation. There's too much at stake for our company and for Grace."

"I'm concerned about the company's bottom line. We can't take any more hits. But I'm not worried about you." Zeke's frown cleared. "Like I said yesterday, it's good to have the old Mal back. Chicago changed you. You've been taking a back seat to me and Jerry. The company needs more from you. *We* need more from you."

"No, you don't." Mal struggled against a stirring irritation. "The way you and Jerry argue, you have more than enough of each other."

Zeke was silent for several strides. "You're right. I don't know how to stop it. I know that's the reason you left the company—"

"That's in the past. I'm back and the two of you are still arguing." Mal led them around the final turn on the jogging path. "We need to keep our focus on three things. Stopping you and Jerry from fighting. Getting the company out of the red. And most importantly for now, finding the person who killed Verna and Dr. B, and is threatening Grace."

It was a lot—enough to distract him from whatever he was feeling toward Grace. He hoped.

Chapter 6

Why do we wait until a loved one dies before celebrating their life?

Grace stood beside Mal in the funeral home's lobby early Wednesday evening. A crowd of mourners had attended Dr. B's wake. The event was a wonderful gathering of family and good friends, sharing heart-warming and humorous anecdotes about the brilliant scientist, dedicated educator, loving family man and caring person.

An image of her older sister, Pam, took shape in her mind. She'd been the best big sisters. Grace was never far from those memories. She swallowed to ease the obstruction in her throat. If she could turn back time, she'd do more to let Pam know how much she'd treasured their relationship. She would have done more to find a treatment—if not a cure—for her sister's diabetes.

She wouldn't have let anything—or anyone—distract her from that priority.

She breathed through another wave of grief, noting the slight lavender fragrance that floated around the spotless room. During the formal part of the event, Grace hadn't gone to the podium to share her thoughts about Dr. B. She hadn't been brave enough. But the stories others had recounted reinforced what a good friend Dr. B had been to so many people. Had she done enough while he'd been alive to let him know how much she'd valued and appreciated him?

Forcing the question aside, Grace scanned past the cherrywood Queen Anne furnishings. She searched the crowd of mourners drifting in and out of the room assigned to Dr. B's wake, looking for their primary suspects. Most of the attendees seemed to be consoling one another, but a few seemed to be networking. Odd. She'd never thought of a funeral as an opportunity to advance one's career. She looked away.

Her eyes landed on Mal. He was attractive in his understated black suit and tie. She wasn't the only one who thought so. He'd received several admiring and curious looks. Either he wasn't acknowledging them or he hadn't noticed.

"Dr. B was very popular." Mal turned from examining the mourners. His eyes fastened onto hers. "I'm very sorry for your loss."

Grace pulled her gaze away, swallowing twice before she could answer. "Thank you. He'll be missed." Her wandering eyes found a familiar face. "There's Jill Streep, one of Dr. B's research assistants." And one of their three primary suspects.

She led Mal across the lobby. Despite the crush of

mourners, the room felt chilly. She put her hand on the graduate student's shoulder to claim her attention. "Jill."

The young woman turned to her. "Dr. Blackwell. It's good to see you again." There was relief in her voice. The full-figured blonde looked as though she'd been crying. Her blue eyes were rimmed red, and the tip of her short white nose was pink.

Grace's heart contracted. Without thinking, she reached out to the shorter woman to envelope her in a hug. "I wish it were under better circumstances."

Jill tightened her arms around Grace. "Me too." Her words were choked. Stepping back, she cleared her throat.

Seeking privacy, Grace guided her a short distance from the other mourners. Jill's attention was drawn to Mal. A spark of interest brightened her eyes.

Grace swallowed a sigh. She ignored a stir of what felt a lot like jealousy. She put her hand on Mal's arm, telling herself she wasn't staking a claim. "Jill Streep, this is my friend Malachi Touré."

Mal inclined his head. "I'm sorry for your loss. Grace told me Dr. MacIntyre was your mentor."

A cloud passed over Jill's round peaches-and-cream face. "He was. I was so honored when he tapped me to be one of his research assistants. It really boosted my confidence." She slid Grace an amused look. "And the pay that came with the position was a big help, too, you know?"

Lowering her voice, Grace searched the younger woman's face for signs of subterfuge. "Dr. B told me you were a promising student. He was very concerned the tuition could cause you to drop out of the graduate program."

Would you steal my research to pay your tuition, Jill? That formula could set you up for years—perhaps decades. Is that your plan?

Jill gave a resigned nod. "I was kind of thinking of that when Dr. B offered me the position. It's like he was giving me a lifeline. No one had ever taken an interest in me like that during my whole academic career." She blinked quickly, seeming to fight back tears. Grace knew how she felt. Dr. B had done the same for her. "And then he told me about this grant, the Bishop Foundation Grant for Future STEM Leaders. It's for grad students in the sciences. I wasn't even going to apply. I didn't think I could get it, you know? I didn't think I was qualified. But he sort of pressured me. He even got my adviser to help me fill out the application. I found out Monday that I'm a finalist." Her blue eyes sparkled with emotions of happiness, relief and pride.

Grace's heart filled with joy for the young woman. "Jill, I'm so excited for you. I'd received that grant, too. It changed my life. When will they announce the recipients?"

"A week from today." Jill bounced on her toes as waves of apprehension broke free. She looked over her shoulder toward the room where mourners lingered, though Dr. B's wake had ended. "He'd died before I could even tell him he was right about my applying for the grant. I know I haven't gotten it yet. But without his encouragement, I wouldn't even have applied, right?"

Grace looked over her shoulder at Mal behind her. "He would've loved hearing that."

His responding smile mesmerized her, temporarily putting her under his spell. Jill's self-conscious laugh broke it.

"I wish I could talk with him." She shared a look with Grace and Mal. "My parents are great, but they're not scientists. And I've got tons of friends in the program, but they don't know any more than I do. Dr. B had decades of hands-on experience in the field. When he reassured me, he put it in terms that meant I could actually see myself working in a lab."

"He did the same for me." Grace reached into her purse and dug out her business card. She offered it to Jill. "I'm not Dr. B, but if you ever want to talk, please call me."

Jill's eyes lit up. "Thank you." She scanned Grace's business card, then slipped it into her purse.

Grace drew a breath. "Do you remember where you were Thursday night? The night Dr. B…died?"

A cloud dimmed the graduate student's blue eyes. "I was with my study group. There're four of us. We'd signed out a room in the library for the quiet. We also wanted to use their laptop and screen. Do you remember where you were?"

Grace made a mental note to check the library's meeting room and equipment sign-out sheets. "I was working late."

Mal scanned the room as he spoke. "Is Dr. B's other research assistant here?"

Like Jill, Trenton Mann was in his second year of the three-year biosciences graduate program.

"He probably thought he had something better to do." Jill's tone had a bite.

Grace gave her a closer look. Was it a simple sign of healthy competition between the two assistants or something more? "I only met Trent a handful of times, but he didn't seem like Dr. B's usual assistants."

Mal cocked his head. "In what way?"

Grace tried to describe her gut feeling. "Dr. B's assistants were usually students who had a passion for science but who were curious about other things fields of study as well."

Jill nodded her agreement. "He likes his assistants to have a wide range of interests outside of bioscience. He says diversity of thought brings new perspectives to research."

"Exactly." Grace had found Dr. B's selection of Trent odd because the graduate student seemed too self-absorbed to be intellectually curious. But she'd never found the time to ask her mentor about his decision.

Jill's eyes darkened with disapproval. "Trent didn't like Dr. B."

"Why not?" Mal asked.

"They were always butting heads." Jill shrugged her right shoulder. "It was like Trent thought he knew more than Dr. B." She leaned toward them, lowering her voice. "I dunno, but I think Dr. B had had enough of Trent's attitude and was going to pull him from the research project."

Mal's eyebrows stretched up his smooth forehead. "What makes you think that?"

Jill shrugged again, keeping her voice low. "Last week, I went to the lab. It was the morning of the day Dr. B died." Her face started to crumble with emotion. She caught herself, drawing a breath. "He was at one of the tables, reading a report Trent had given him. I sensed he was frustrated with it, you know? He must not have heard me come in. He was speaking under his breath, but I heard him say something like, 'Trent, I don't think this program's the right fit for you.'"

Mal and Grace exchanged a look. She could tell they were thinking the same thing: they had a motive for Trent.

"Jill Streep's study group gives her an alibi." Mal kept his voice down. "Her grant takes away her motive since it would cover her tuition."

He was close enough for Grace to catch his scent of soap and pine. It gave her comfort in an otherwise stressful situation.

"She doesn't have it yet." Grace glanced at him. The clean lines of his profile were too distracting. She returned her attention to the room. "We should confirm both of her claims. She says she was with a study group. At CCSU, to reserve a study room with equipment, students have to sign the room out and give everyone's name."

Mal frowned. "Why?"

"If something happened to the equipment or if students don't show up to claim the room, everyone would be held responsible, not just the student who made the arrangements."

"How do we verify that?"

Grace felt his eyes on her. She resisted his pull. "We'll ask the librarian whether Jill signed in before using the room. As for her grant, it's awarded by the Bishop Foundation. We can check its website to see if the foundation has announced its finalists."

"You said you'd also received this grant."

"Yes, Dr. B encouraged me to apply for it." She finally turned to him. "I was amazed when the organization awarded the grant to me. Thank goodness Dr. B convinced me to believe in myself enough to apply for it. If Jill's telling the truth, I'm so sorry he isn't alive to know another one of his protégés is a finalist."

Mal looked around as though making sure no one was close enough to hear their conversation. "If you feel that way, how could you consider her a suspect?"

Grace felt her smile fade. "Too many times in the past, I've trusted people, only to be disappointed. Someone killed a very good person who was dear to me. It doesn't matter whether I personally like them—everyone's a suspect until I can prove to myself that they're not."

Mal searched her face in silence. A glint of respect brightened his dark eyes. "Bennett MacIntyre was lucky to be able to call you friend."

Grace turned away before she launched herself into his embrace to hide from the horrible situation she'd found herself in. Although she'd spent the morning working on the formula, she wasn't any closer to correcting the flaw that made it so easy to weaponize. She was dealing with too many distractions. A killer who was after her formula had murdered her best friend and an apparently innocent person. Her grandmother, her ex-boyfriend and his brothers were in danger. All because of a mistake she'd made. She had to fix this, both the formulation and the threat to their lives.

"I was the lucky one." Grace glanced at her watch. The wake had ended fifteen minutes ago, but there still wasn't any sign of Dr. B's family leaving the funeral home. "It's getting late. Let's see if we could get a private moment with Dr. B's widow before she leaves."

She felt Mal behind her as she cleared a path across the lobby to the room reserved for Dr. B's wake. They'd paid their respects when they arrived, but Tami MacIntyre had been surrounded by well-wishers. Neither of them had wanted to bring up their investigation in front of an audience. But as his wife, Tami could provide valuable insight to their inquiry.

She sat in the first row, but she wasn't alone. Dr. B's three adult children from his first marriage were beside her, silent. They looked shell shocked, as though they thought they were trapped in a bad dream. Cancer had stolen their mother from them far too soon. Now their father had seemingly died in a freak accident—or so they'd been told.

Grace hesitated. Did she really want to bring up the possibility of foul play in their father's death? Here? Now? Mal's hand was firm and warm against the small of her back. She squared her shoulders and continued forward.

She inclined her head toward Dr. B's children. They were all tall, brown-eyed brunettes like their father. They returned her gesture with empty eyes that broke her heart.

Grace stopped in front of his widow. "Excuse us, Tami. Mal and I are getting ready to leave."

Tami's thin lips quivered in a smile. Vivid red curls framed her pale diamond-shaped face. Her gray eyes were damp and pink. "Thank you for coming." Her voice was almost robotic.

Still hesitant, Grace bit her lip. Tami and Dr. B had just celebrated their second wedding anniversary. Now she was sitting at his funeral. Her eyes stung as she glanced at Mal. He gave her an encouraging nod.

Grace took a breath and continued. "We wondered if we could ask you some questions about the last couple of days and Dr. B's work?"

Tami's smile disappeared. "Is this more about your

foolish notion that someone killed my husband?" She
hissed the question. "His death was an accident. A tragic
accident. Everyone loved him. Students, colleagues,
alumni—*everyone*."

Grace sensed Dr. B's children's attention lock onto
her. She rushed to soothe the widow. "We know Dr. B
was beloved by everyone who knew him. But there are
things about his death—"

"Drop this ridiculous story about someone killing
my husband. Now." Tami spoke through clenched teeth,
her eyes narrowed.

On her left, Mal leaned toward the agitated woman.
"Ms. MacIntyre, we just want to make sure we—"

Tami talked over him. "If you aren't here to pay your
respects to my husband, then I want you to leave."

Doris Flank, Dr. B's administrative assistant, appeared on Grace's right. She put a gentle hand on her
shoulder, claiming Grace's attention. Beyond her thick,
gray-rimmed glasses, her gray eyes—almost the exact
shade as her hair—were troubled. "I'm so sorry, Grace,
but maybe it would be best if you give Mrs. MacIntyre
space for today. This really isn't a good time."

"You're right, Doris." Grace stepped back. "I'm so
sorry to have upset you, Tami." She once again inclined
her head toward Dr. B's children. Their eyes had gone
from empty orbs to gems of curiosity and concern.

With her hand on Doris's elbow, Grace drew the
other woman aside, gesturing for Mal to join them.
"Would it be possible for you to let us into Dr. B's office at the university this evening?"

Doris's eyes bounced between Grace's and Mal's.
"Today?"

"Would you mind?" Grace wondered if she sounded

sufficiently wheedling. She didn't have much practice. "I'd like to see it one last time. And we won't be long. This will probably be my last chance to see it."

Doris expelled a breath. "I've already packed all of his things. There's nothing of his in his office left to see."

She put more effort into her wheedling. "Please? Just a few minutes, for old time's sake."

"Oh, all right." Doris's tone was disapproving. "I want to spend some time with Tami first, though."

"Thank you, Doris." Grace's muscles relaxed. She was surprised at how tensed they'd been. "Take your time. We'll meet you there in, say, ninety minutes."

The other woman's nod was curt with displeasure.

Mal gave her an approving nod. "Good thinking to check his office, but what are we searching for?"

Grace slid him a look. "What do they say in the movies? 'We'll know it when we see it.'"

"Dr. Blackwell." The voice came to Grace from the crowd on her right.

The woman approaching seemed friendly and familiar. Grace struggled to pull her identity from the recesses of her memory.

"Ms. Mann." Relief flooded her as the other woman's name and the circumstances of how they'd met popped into her brain. She shifted direction, catching Mal's hand to bring him with her.

Martina Trenton Mann was the mother of Dr. B's missing research assistant, Trent. They'd met during Central Columbus Science University's annual Spring Science Fundraiser. Dr. B had purchased a table for six and invited Martina because she was a member of the university's board of trustees.

"Please, call me Martina." She gave Mal a curious and admiring look.

"Thank you. And please call me Grace." She gestured toward Mal. "Martina Mann, my friend Malachi Touré."

Martina inclined her head. "Malachi. That's a strong, biblical name. How do you know Grace?"

Mal's smile was a little stiff around the edges. "We're old friends."

"Not that old." Grace hoped the banter would make their relationship seem more natural to those on the outside looking in.

Martina turned back to her. She gave the impression of rigid perfection. Her posture was military straight. Every strand of her chestnut hair was in place and rested gracefully on her narrow shoulders. "I was pleased to see you again, although I'm sorry it's under such sad circumstances."

"Of course." Grace breathed through another wave of sorrow, inhaling more of the lavender scent permeating the lobby.

"Dr. MacIntyre's death is such a great loss, not only to his family and friends but for the university." She folded her thin hands in front of her hips. Her nails were perfectly manicured and polished a darker shade of blue than her two-piece skirt suit. She had a runner's build, long and lean. "As a member of the institution's board of trustees, I can say we all admired him and thought very highly of the work he did with the students."

Grace nodded. "I had the privilege of being one of his research assistants. I learned a great deal from him.

I'm sure your son, Trent, has learned a lot in the program as well."

Martina's smile glowed with maternal pride. "He's had a lot of wonderful things to say about Dr. MacIntyre. With him, it's always, 'Dr. B this' and 'Dr. B that.'"

Grace exchanged a look with Mal as she fought to mask her surprise. Had he caught the inconsistency as well? Martina's response contradicted Jill's confidences about Trent and Dr. B's relationship. Jill had painted a contentious picture of their interactions. In contrast, Martina's description made it seem as though Trent had a case of hero worship.

Mal's question ended her speculations. "Is your son enjoying the program?"

Martina's smug smile indicated maternal pride. "He enjoys the challenge. He's doing well, but there's always room for improvement."

Mal nodded as though in understanding. "What does he want to do with his degree?"

Martina gestured toward Grace. "He plans on going into research, like Grace."

Grace spoke to Mal. "The program will give him hands-on experience and boost his confidence."

Martina gave a dainty shrug of her slender shoulders. "Getting into the program was his first hurdle. He'll have to excel if he wants a position with a prestigious lab. One can't rest on one's laurels. Medical research is a very competitive field."

Grace thought she heard a trace of defensiveness. Perhaps Trent wasn't doing as well as his mother wanted them to believe. "It sounds like he's getting a lot out of the program, though."

"That's our dilemma." Martina spoke with care. "With Dr. MacIntyre's passing, the university doesn't have anyone to administer the program."

That problem had occurred to Grace. Dr. B had managed the university's student scientific-research program for more than a decade. Recently, he'd started wondering who'd replace him when he retired. He'd wanted to find the right person before he stepped down. His goal had been to train them and get them involved in a couple of cycles of the program to ensure a smooth transition. But Dr. B had believed his retirement was still a long, long way off. Grace had, too.

She stiffened as a troubling thought occurred to her. "I agree Dr. B will be difficult to replace, but I hope the university will remain committed to the program."

"Of course." Martina spoke quickly. "In fact, I'm even more committed to the program now that I have personal experience through my son's participation."

Grace exhaled with relief. "I'm glad. It's a very valuable experience, and it gives CCSU an edge, not just in recruiting STEM students but also in placing alumni in scientific facilities across the country."

Martina looked satisfied with Grace's response. "The board is well aware of the value Dr. MacIntyre's program adds to the university. That's why we're committed to continuing the program with someone who would bring to it the same passion, dedication and drive he brought. I was hoping you'd consider the position."

"I'm sorry. What?" Grace looked from Martina to Mal and back.

Martina smiled. "Doris Flank raves about you. She insists you're Dr. MacIntyre's most successful mentee.

And I saw firsthand during the gala how well you interacted with my son and Jill, Dr. MacIntyre's other research assistant."

Grace's brow furrowed. Why was Martina proposing she take over the research program when the university had other science professors who could step in? "Thank you for thinking of me. I'm flattered. Teaching is an honorable profession—that can't be overstated. But I'm very happy and fulfilled with my career."

"You're a *medical* researcher, is that correct?" Martina asked.

Grace nodded. "That's right, and I'm very satisfied with my work."

"I'm sure you are." Martina's eyes widened as she tried to convince Grace. "Dr. MacIntyre continued his research projects even as he taught. Those projects were the impetus behind his student research program."

"I'm not Dr. B." Grace stepped back. "We should get going. I'm sorry I didn't get a chance to speak with your son. I thought he might be here."

"So did I." There was a note of irritation in Martina's voice. Was the cause of her annoyance Trent's absence or Grace declining to become Dr. B's successor?

Martina glanced over her shoulder toward the funeral home's entrance before she faced Grace and Mal again. "I'm surprised he didn't make it. I don't know where he could be. We talked about attending the wake together, but he said he had something else he needed to do first. I took that to be code for not wanting to be seen attending the function with his mother."

Mal chuckled. "We all felt that way when we were younger, but as we get older, things change." He inclined his head. "It was good to meet you, Martina. Please excuse us."

"Of course." Martina turned again to Grace. "I hope you'll reconsider my proposal."

"I enjoy what I do." Grace hoped her smile would soften her response. "I'm not interested in giving it up. But, again, thank you for thinking of me." She walked with Mal out of the funeral home and around the building to its rear parking lot.

Mal's hand was warm and reassuring at her back. "Asking you to take over Dr. B's position is more than a great compliment. It sounds like a great opportunity."

Grace's hum was noncommittal. "For someone else. It's not what I want to do."

"I know your research is important to you, but Martina said you could continue it as you teach. Apparently, Dr. B did."

She could feel him searching her profile as they walked. What was he looking for? "I know he did. We talked about his research. But I'm not going to take his place. I can't."

Mal stopped, taking her arm to claim her attention. "No one's asking you to take his place, but perhaps you could consider continuing his legacy?"

"Someone else can do that." Perhaps her voice was firmer than she'd intended. "I have to focus on finding a better treatment for diabetes, if not a cure. Once we solve this case, I'm returning to the lab. I can't allow anything to distract me from that."

Mal's hand stiffened before dropping from her arm. Without his touch, Grace felt cold. And alone. She thought about what she'd said and wanted to take the words back, but how could she? If she wanted to be successful, she had to commit to something—either her research or their relationship. It was one or the other; it couldn't be both. Could it?

Chapter 7

"Grace! Grace! Wait!" A woman's voice, breathless and tense, hailed her as she and Mal advanced on his SUV.

Grace turned to see Dr. B's youngest child, Alana MacIntyre, jogging toward her. The environmental lawyer's three-inch black stilettos impeded her progress. Her scoop-necked, long-sleeved black sheath dress skimmed her slender figure, ending just above her knees.

Her siblings, Elsie and Toran, jogged in almost a straight line behind her. They all appeared to have overcome their frozen bonds. Their faces were flushed. Was it with exertion or emotion? Their dark eyes burned with intensity.

The pulse in Grace's throat jumped with alarm. She glanced at Mal. His brow was creased with curiosity.

She stepped forward, addressing Dr. B's youngest by

the nickname he'd always used. "Lana, what's wrong?" Her eyes swept over his other two children.

Dr. Elsie MacIntyre, the eldest, was an oncologist, a profession Grace was certain had been inspired by her mother's death from pancreatic cancer. She wore a simple A-line black dress with a boat neckline and pleated skirt that swung around her mid-calf. Both women had pulled their chestnut hair back in simple ponytails.

Their brother, Toran, was the middle child. The investment banker was dressed in a plain black suit with matching tie and snow-white linen shirt.

"Is it true?" Lana squeezed Grace's left hand. "Did you tell Tami someone killed Daddy?"

Elsie's dark brown eyes were wide and frightened. "Do you really think our father was murdered?"

Toran frowned. Lines of pain and confusion creased his pale forehead and bracketed his thin lips. "Why would someone—*anyone*—want our father dead?"

Their collective pain struck her like cannon fire. Under its force, Grace stumbled back on her heels. Mal's long, strong arm caught her waist, drawing her close to shelter against him.

His voice was firm as he addressed the MacIntyre offspring. "How much has your stepmother told you?"

The trio's attention swung to him.

"She hasn't told us anything." Lana's voice sounded on the verge of hysteria.

"Malachi Touré, right?" Toran's dark eyes scanned Mal as though trying to decide if they could trust anything coming out of his mouth.

Feeling unaccountably insulted, Grace started to straighten away from Mal's embrace to launch into a defense of his character. Mal's arm tightened around her, anticipating her tirade.

His calm response stopped her. "Call me Mal."

"I'm Tor." He gestured toward his siblings. "My sisters, Elle and Lana."

"What happened to our father?" Elle's words were tight, as she struggled to remain composed. "Why do you think his death wasn't an accident?"

Mal glanced over his shoulder toward a knee-high red brick wall fencing off the landscaping from the sidewalk along the parking lot. "Let's sit."

His hand on Grace's back guided her to their destination. Thank goodness he was with her. It may be cowardly, but she couldn't explain their concerns about Dr. B's death to his children on her own. She was too emotionally tied to this case. The idea that someone pushed her friend—a father figure—down a flight of steps to his death shattered her. How could she tell his children? They would need her to be strong, and she couldn't be. They were his entire life. And the handful of times she'd seen them with him, she knew he was everything to them.

Mal waited until Grace was seated beside Dr. B's children. "Grace noticed a few inconsistencies that make us suspicious." He shared a look with the trio as though trying to gage whether they were prepared to hear everything he had to say. "First, it appears your father sent Grace an email the morning *after* his death."

The siblings reacted in unison. "What?"

Lana leaned forward, looking past Elle beside her and Tor to catch Grace's eyes. "Are you sure you didn't *receive* the email after his death? He could've sent it *before* the accident, but it only appeared in your inbox *afterward*."

Grace shook her head. Her shoulders were heavy with the burden of speaking the truth. "His email was dated and timed minutes before I opened it Friday morning, not Thursday."

The blood drained from Lana's face. She, Tor and Elle exchanged a look of shock and fear.

Grace briefed them on the rest of the case: the email's reference to two "Dr. B's," the attempted hack of her system, Doris informing her of Dr. B's death, and Verna's murder.

"You told Tami all of this?" Tor shared a look between Mal and Grace.

"She didn't say a word to us about any of it." Lana's voice shook with outrage. She launched herself from the brick half wall and paced beside the landscaping. "We have a right to know about these inconsistencies."

"She doesn't believe Dr. B was killed." Grace acknowledged the admission was a weak defense of their stepmother. Like Lana, if her parent's death was considered a possible homicide, she'd want to know.

"And you're investigating because you think the hacker killed our father?" Elle looked from Grace to Mal. "Do you have any leads?"

Mal responded before Grace could. "We were hoping to get some ideas from the people who attended your father's wake. Can you think of any reason someone might want to harm him? Had he been worried about anything recently? Do you know of any tensions he may have had with colleagues or even students—anyone?"

"Oh, yes." Lana stopped pacing. "Tami. Maybe the

real reason she doesn't want you investigating Daddy's death is because she's behind it."

Elle frowned. "Come on, Lana."

Tor shook his head. "That's crazy."

"Is it?" Lana crossed her arms. "Their arguments started as soon as the honeymoon was over."

"But she wouldn't've killed him." Elle turned to Tor, seeking confirmation.

"Of course not." Tor looked around the parking lot and sidewalk in front of the funeral home before lowering his voice. "I don't like her, either, but Dad loved her. Still, if we seriously thought she was capable of killing him, we wouldn't have let him marry her. I'm certain of that."

Grace was, too. Dr. B had told her funny anecdotes about the way the trio fussed over him. She'd even witnessed their protectiveness firsthand. Dr. B knew his children weren't Tami's biggest fans, but he appreciated the fact that they treated her with kindness and courtesy for his sake.

Lana spun on her heels to face Mal and Grace. "What can we do to help with your investigation?"

Mal glanced at Grace. "If you think of anything that could help us identify the hacker who could be behind his death, please let us know."

"Of course." Lana gave them a distracted nod as though her mind raced with possibilities. Grace wondered whether Tami was still on that list.

Elle stood, drawing Grace's attention to her. The other woman put a gentle hand on Grace's shoulder above the cotton fabric of her simple black dress. "Dad spoke very highly of you. You went from being one of his star students to being a very thoughtful and caring friend. For that reason, we'll always be grateful to you."

Grace blinked back tears. "Your father helped me realize my dream."

Tor stood beside Elle. "Please be careful. We know your investigation isn't just about Dad, but he wouldn't want you putting yourself in danger."

"Don't worry." Grace glanced over her shoulder at Mal. "There are a lot of good people watching over me."

There are a lot of good people watching over me.

Grace's words helped heal the four-year-old wound her leaving had caused. They implied she trusted him. But as his mother always said, actions speak louder. Grace's words said she trusted him, but her leaving said she didn't.

"I hope Doris doesn't leave before we're able to meet her at Dr. B's office." Grace's tense observation interrupted Mal's thoughts.

He stopped at the red light before the entrance to Interstate 270 . "I didn't see her in the parking lot."

"Neither did I, but she could have left while we were speaking with Martina Mann." She stared through the windshield as though willing the traffic light to change. It didn't.

"Thank you for what you said back there, about my brothers and me helping you with the case." Maybe he was making more of her response than he had a right to. She had faith in him, Zeke and Jerry to find the murderer, and keep her and her grandmother safe. That was it. Nothing more.

Grace looked surprised. "I couldn't do this without you and your brothers. Thank you for coming with me to Dr. B's wake. It was hard enough dealing with his death. Questioning the other mourners, especially Tami, made it worse."

Hearing the pain in her voice, he wanted so badly to reach out and hold her hand as it rested on her thigh. Instead, he tightened his grip on the steering wheel and ignored the scent of her swirling around his head.

Mal guided his car through the green light and onto the ramp for the Outerbelt. "I'm sorry you had to go through that."

He checked his mirrors and blind spot before merging with the interstate's rush hour traffic. It would take another thirty minutes to get to the university in the southeast part of the city. Like Grace, he hoped Doris waited for them. If not, they'd have to reschedule with her for another day. And the clock was ticking. They couldn't afford to postpone any part of their investigation, not with Grace's life, Melba's life and their company's reputation on the line.

Grace's seat made a rustling sound as she shifted her position. Mal felt her eyes on him. "Roberta George, Dr. B's former research assistant, wasn't at the wake. She now works for Buckeye Dynamic, so she's connected to both the university and the research institute where the hack originated."

Mal considered that. "There were a lot of people at the wake, though. Maybe we missed her. Or maybe she's working. Let's not jump to conclusions."

"I know you don't agree with me, but there are a lot of potential suspects among the university's staff, students, alumni and trustees, not to mention his colleagues in the biosciences field." A note of stubborn defiance entered her words. "And now, based on what Lana said, we also have to consider his widow."

Mal frowned, keeping his eyes on the traffic in anticipation of dangerous rush hour feats. "I don't know if I agree with Lana's theory about her stepmother. She knows Tami better than I do, but I think Tor's right. Those three love their father too much to let him marry a psycho."

"Maybe they didn't know she was a psycho in the beginning." Her seat rustled again as she faced forward. "I keep asking myself who would benefit from getting their hands on my formulation. The answer is anyone in a position to sell it to buyers who would pay to weaponize it, like our government or foreign countries."

Mal changed lanes to get around a driver determined to maintain a speed twenty miles per hour under the limit. "Someone at Buckeye Dynamic would have those connections or know how to get them."

"Several people connected with Buckeye Dynamic attended his wake. And several people who work for the university have connections with Buckeye Dynamic. So, again, we are surrounded by suspects."

Mal moved into the lane to exit from the interstate. "But who was in a position to know Dr. B had spoken with you about your formula and what you'd told him?"

Grace expelled a breath. "I've been racking my brain over that. We didn't discuss the formula in the open. I went to him because I was desperate. I still am. I wanted to consult with him in case he had any thoughts on a solution. But we only discussed the situation three times: once over the phone when he was in his university office, once in person in his university office and once in his home office."

"Could someone have overheard him in his office?" Mal met Grace's eyes briefly before returning his attention to the traffic.

Grace shrugged. "We need to find out. If someone overheard him, then we're back to looking at—"

"I know. Faculty, staff, students and trustees." Mal shook his head again. "You have a lot of trust issues, Grace."

She looked away. "That's what happens when enough people disappoint you."

Mal settled back into silence as they continued the long drive to Central Columbus Science University, but his mind was shouting questions he didn't want to voice.

Who hurt you, Grace? Are they the reason you ran from me?

Rushing footsteps advanced on Mal and Grace as they walked the third-floor hallway of McWorter Hall, Central Columbus Science University's academic building, Wednesday evening. Mal turned to confront the arrival, shifting his stance to shield Grace.

Doris came to a breathless stop less than an arm's length from him. She adjusted her glasses. "I didn't want to keep you waiting."

Grace stepped out from behind him. She gave the older woman a gracious smile. "We were afraid *you* were waiting for *us*."

There was a chill in the disinfectant-laden air. Mal didn't think it was all coming from the university's HVAC system.

Doris smoothed the skirt of her black suit and adjusted its jacket. "I was delayed. It took longer than I'd anticipated to calm Tami." She gave Grace a pointed look.

Grace's smile remained in place. "As Mal and I explained, we didn't want you to rush."

Doris glanced at Mal before narrowing her eyes at Grace. "Have you just arrived? What delayed you?"

"Traffic," Grace lied without batting an eyelash.

Mal masked his surprise. Was this another example of her inherent trust issues? What had her mentor's admin done to earn her suspicion?

Doris set a brisk pace down the hall to Dr. B's office. Grace's two-inch heels drowned the sound of Doris's modest black flats as they tapped against the black-and-brown-speckled tiling.

Doris tossed a glance at Mal from the other side of Grace. "Is this your first time at CCSU, Mr. Touré?"

"It is and please call me Mal." He scanned the hallway. It was spotless, but there were signs of wear and the stench of age. "I graduated from Ohio University."

"Oh?" Doris's response was noncommittal. Mal couldn't tell if she was impressed or offended. "What was your area of academic study?"

Mal gave her an amused smile. She was fishing for information. Fair enough. If he and Grace wanted information, they'd have to share some as well. "Computer science. I also have an MBA."

All three Touré brothers had earned an MBA. Mal's emphasis was in accounting. He was more comfortable with numbers than people. Zeke's was in management. He had a talent for seeing the bigger picture. And Jerry was an extrovert, which made him a natural marketer.

Unlike Mal, Zeke and Jerry were alumni of The Ohio State University. Mal didn't know why the two had thought attending the same university would be a good idea. They'd been arguing since Jerry could talk.

Although OSU had almost seventy thousand students when Jerry had attended, the campus hadn't been large enough to separate them. Mal had heard all about their arguments during school breaks and holidays. Fortunately, since Zeke had been in graduate school by the time Jerry had started at the university, they hadn't overlapped for long.

Mal brought his thoughts back to the present. It was after five o'clock. The building seemed empty—at least, the third floor of the three-story building was deserted. But he and Grace had walked right in. What were the safety protocols?

"What time does the university lock this building?" He glanced at Doris.

"Seven p.m. sharp." Doris didn't pause or turn to face him. "That's when dinner ends and the cafeteria closes. Security does a thorough sweep of the building from this top floor to the basement. Then everything's locked up until six a.m. the next morning."

Mal stopped himself before placing his palm on the small of Grace's back again. Instead he shoved both hands into his front pants pockets. In the two days since they'd been reunited, he'd returned to his habit of touching her while they walked. He needed to stop that now, otherwise it would become another ache to fill when she left.

He returned his attention to Doris. "Was the building unlocked when Dr. B's body was found at seven?"

"That's right." Doris's voice was soft. "A guard found him during her rounds. I'd already left for the day. The formal announcement was made Friday morning before the start of classes."

Dark wood door frames with beveled glass windows

interrupted the worn chalk white walls. Tan bulletin boards were covered with well-organized flyers. Some announced events that had recently occurred. Others promoted upcoming activities, including graduation, which was scheduled for next Saturday, the first weekend in May.

Doris stopped in front of an office beside one of the bulletin boards. She unlocked the door, then stepped aside so they could enter. "I don't know what you hope to find here. As I told you, I boxed up all of Dr. MacIntyre's personal belongings."

Mal frowned. The musty smell of age was stronger here. Divots damaged the plaster walls and scratches marred the wooden door frames. Grace cleared her throat. "You'd worked with Dr. B for almost three years. It must have been hard to pack up his office."

Doris adjusted her glasses. "Yes, it was difficult. But my pain was nothing compared to Tami's or his children's."

Grace seemed to brace herself before entering the room. Mal broke his promise to himself; he rested a supportive hand at her waist. He wanted her to know she wasn't taking this next step alone. The muscles in her back relaxed against his palm.

Briefly closing her eyes, Grace needed a moment to prepare before entering the suite of rooms in which Dr. B had his office. The warmth from Mal's large hand came through the cotton fabric of her black dress, releasing the strain building in her lower back. The tension creasing her brow and pulling on the muscles in her face eased. She looked at him over her shoulder. His eyes were dark with concern. She gave him a small smile, thanking him for his support. She blew a thin breath, then stepped forward into the narrow reception area.

The thin gray carpet silenced her steps. Three tall maple wood bookcases lined the far chalk-white wall. They held office supplies—reams of papers, boxes of pens, pencils, manila folders, staples and rubber bands. A long rectangular table pressed against the wall to the left of the door. Catalogs and brochures promoting the university's science programs fanned across its walnut-wood surface. Comfortable gray, blue and tan cushioned chairs had been arranged around the area.

Grace pointed toward a large, heavy oak desk to their right. "That's Doris's desk." She swept her right hand past four closed doors. "These are the offices of other science professors." Finally, she pointed to the last and presumably largest room in the suite. "That's Dr. B's office. He was the chair of the Division of Math and Science. I suppose someone in the lobby could have overheard conversations in his office."

"That's not possible." Doris's objection was firm. She crossed the lobby and marched to her desk. "Especially when his door was closed, which it always was if he was on the phone or in a meeting. Surely you remember that, Grace."

Doris was right, but Grace wasn't ready to give up on this theory. How else could someone have learned about the formulation? Dr. B was the *only* person with whom she'd shared the details of the flaw. Her chief science officer knew the product was unstable, but he didn't know the manifestation of that instability. It wasn't until after Dr. B's death that she'd confided in her grandmother, Mal, Zeke and Jerry.

So how else could someone have known to hack her

system in search of her project folder? They must have overheard her mentor speaking with her about it. But how?

Grace considered Dr. B's closed office door. "Just because his door was closed doesn't mean no one could hear him."

Doris crossed her arms and shrugged her solid shoulders. "I never did. What do you think they heard?"

Grace held the other woman's eyes. "Something that upset them enough to attack him."

"This again?" Doris dropped her arms. "Dr. MacIntyre tripped on the stairs. He wasn't pushed. No one killed him. I'm as heartbroken over it as you are. Possibly more so since I worked closely with him every day. We both have to accept the fact of his untimely death."

Mal strode across the reception area. He tried Dr. B's doorknob, then turned to Doris. "Do you have the key to his office? We could test the theory."

Doris threw up her hands before digging into her gray purse for a set of keys. "If you must."

Grace followed Doris's brisk pace to Dr. B's office. The administrative assistant unlocked the door, then gestured for them to precede her.

Mal turned to Grace. "You play Dr. B. Close the door, then sit behind his desk and pretend to be speaking with someone in a normal voice. I'll see if I can hear you from out here."

Grace closed the door against Doris's skeptical expression. She scanned the familiar space and its mismatched furniture. It was so empty. She'd never seen it this way. The books and mementos he'd crammed into his cherrywood bookcase were gone. She walked to his oak desk. It was swept clean of everything but his desk phone and inbox.

She lowered herself reluctantly onto his black faux-leather executive chair. She didn't belong there, but Mal was right. They needed to test their theory. What was she supposed to say?

"What should we talk about, Dr. B?" She leaned back against the seat. It squeaked. A burst of surprised laughter startled her as she remembered one of Dr. B's favorite dad jokes. *My seat's in a chair band.*

She repeated her response from memory. "Dr. B, that joke's incredible...ly...bad."

He'd given her an unrepentant grin.

"Do you remember how you'd responded?" she asked the room. "With another dad joke, of course. 'Why did the farmer become a musician?' Against my better judgment, I'd asked why and you'd said, 'Because after the harvest, he'd had a bunch of sick beets.' Urgh!" She laughed, loving the memory of his delight at the ridiculous jokes. "You had a million of them. No, seriously, there must've been one million. I felt so sorry for Elle, Tor and Lana." Her eyes stung. "Actually, no, I didn't. They'd had a great dad and they knew it."

A knock startled her. Mal opened the door. "We can't hear you. Were you talking?"

She stood quickly, turning her back to the door to wipe her eyes. "Yes, I was. You were right, Doris. No one could've overheard him." She followed them from the office, avoiding Mal's all-seeing gaze. "Could you show us where Dr. B was found, please?"

Doris gave her a sober look. "Of course, dear, if that will help you with your grieving process."

The administrative assistant secured Dr. B's office, collected her purse and then locked the door to the suite before leading them to the staircase at the closest end of the hall. Squaring her shoulders, she gestured toward the stairs. "The authorities believe he tripped on his way down this first flight, tried to catch himself when he reached that landing and then stumbled and fell to the second-floor landing."

Grace's throat burned with tears. She nodded wordlessly.

"Thank you for all of the time you've given us this evening." Mal's words were quiet and respectful. "We hope we haven't inconvenienced you too much."

"Not at all." Doris adjusted her purse on her shoulder. "If you have any other questions, please let me know. Have a good evening."

Doris strode down the steps and through Grace's mental image of Dr. B, stumbling to his death.

"Grace?" Mal's hand was gentle on her shoulder.

Her voice shook. "I know I'm right. Someone somehow overheard us talking about the formulation, either over the phone or in his office."

"Neither Doris nor I heard you while you were in his office." Mal offered her a handkerchief.

"Thank you." Turning from him, she dried her cheeks and dabbed her eyes. "I'll get it back to you."

Mal's words were hesitant. "Perhaps Dr. B mentioned the difficulty you were having to someone he thought he could trust, someone he thought would be able to help."

"He'd promised me he wouldn't. Dr. B was a man of his word." Suddenly, she was so tired. "They threw him down the stairs. Like he was garbage." Her voice caught. She struggled on. "Like he didn't have family. Friends. People who loved him. Would miss him. Like he didn't have value. We have to find whoever did this. They have to be punished."

Chapter 8

"I told Aunt Melba she could sit in on our meeting." Jerry remained in character as the videoconference began Wednesday evening. His gunmetal-gray jeans and black jersey seemed incongruous against the overstuffed floral-patterned armchair.

"It's *my* living room. Why shouldn't I be here?" Melba spoke from her matching armchair beside him. Her citrus jersey and ocean blue yoga pants were striking against the upholstery.

Mal struggled against a smile as he watched the videoconference feed. Like grandmother, like granddaughter. He sat beside Grace in the Touré Security Group conference room. Zeke sat to his right at the head of the table. He and Grace had just returned from Dr. B's office.

"That's fine, Gran." Grace exchanged looks with him and Zeke as though she'd entertain their opinions. He didn't buy it.

"Of course, Ms. Stall." He straightened on his seat. "This involves your safety as well."

Grace's grandmother gave him a pleased smile. "You can call me Melba."

"Thank you, Melba." His smile spread. Watching Grace's grandmother was like seeing Grace in the future.

Mal summarized the details they'd gathered from the mourners at Dr. B's wake, including his widow, children, research assistant Jill Streep and board of trustees member Martina Trenton Mann. Grace provided context for the information. They also described their sound test at Dr. B's office.

Mal rubbed his forehead as he concluded their update. "There doesn't appear to be any way someone could've overheard Dr. B in his office talking about the formula."

Jerry frowned in thought. "Maybe someone hacked *his* computer."

"They wouldn't have learned about the formulation that way." Grace shook her head. "We didn't discuss it via email, and I didn't give him any of my notes, either in hard copy or electronically."

Melba addressed Grace. "I know you trusted Dr. B. He was a great mentor and an even better friend. But it's possible he told his wife about the formula." She lifted a hand as Grace started to interrupt her. "At least think about it. Sometimes if you tell a married person a secret, unless you specifically tell them not to tell their spouse, they will. I did that all the time with your grandfather. He never said a word."

Mal thought it sounded plausible—but then, he'd never been married. His eyes drifted toward Grace.

While they'd been dating, he'd shared secrets with her. Had she confided in him? He didn't think so. Hadn't she trusted him? Was that why she'd left so abruptly?

Mal put the past away and returned his attention to the laptop and its image of Melba and Jerry. "I can't see Tami MacIntyre pushing her husband down a flight of stairs at the university. Her grief seemed genuine."

Melba shrugged. "Maybe she's a really good actress."

Jerry ran with Melba's theory. "It would be easier to cover her tracks if she pushed him at the school rather than at home."

Zeke shifted on his seat. "Grace, what do you think? You know Tami MacIntyre better than we do. Is she capable of killing her husband?"

Grace glanced at Mal before turning to Zeke. "I don't know. Dr. B's children said he and Tami argued a lot. Perhaps she'd decided to leave him and knew the formulation could be a source of revenue. She'd need the money. After they got married, Tami quit her job and started doing a lot of charity work. But like Mal, I can't imagine her killing him. I can't imagine anyone killing him."

Mal shook his head. "Especially after all the praise people gave him during the speeches we heard at the wake. Students, faculty, alumni and staff only had good things to say about him."

Jerry grunted. "With all due respect, those were only the people who spoke. What about the ones who didn't speak?"

"A lot of people shared their memories of him." Grace seemed enveloped in a cloud of sadness. "I wasn't comfortable going to the podium, but if I had, I would've only had good things to say as well."

Melba spread her hands. "Tami may not be the killer. But she might be the leak we're looking for. Maybe Dr. B told his wife, as married people do, and Tami mentioned it to someone else."

Frown lines disappeared from Grace's forehead. She exchanged another look with Mal. "That could lead us back to the faculty. Tami might have mentioned the formula during one of their gatherings."

Mal inclined his head. "I'd rather narrow the list than grow it, but you have a point."

Grace gave him an obstinate look. "I'm keeping Tami on the list."

Mal swallowed a sigh. "We'll need a list of faculty members Tami knew well enough to mention your formula to—someone who has connections to make stealing it worthwhile. We'll work on that tonight."

"Once you have the list, I'll help with the background checks." Zeke shifted his attention to the laptop screen. "How are things on your end?" he asked Jerry and Melba.

"Everything's quiet so far." Melba turned to Jerry. "What do you think, Jerry?"

He gave a sober nod. "I've checked in with the residence's administrative team and guards. They've all been told to be aware of unfamiliar faces trying to gain access to the buildings, or loitering on or around the property."

Melba's nod emphasized Jerry's statement. "I've already noticed the guards paying more attention to visitors and doing additional rounds inside and out."

"That's wonderful." Grace spoke on a sigh of relief.

Jerry continued. "I've also brought in two contractors to help with round-the-clock personal security. May

Storm and Summer Darling are working undercover to supplement the residence's staff. They can check out some spaces I wouldn't have access to."

"He means the bathrooms." Melba's tone was dry.

Grace addressed Jerry. "Are you sure they can be trusted?"

"Absolutely." Jerry nodded. "We've recently vetted them. They come highly recommended from a reputable security company in Florida."

Mal recognized the two contractors' names from their files. "It's a good thing we had that list for this emergency." He looked at Zeke. "Maybe your expansion plans weren't premature."

Touré Security Group didn't often need out-of-state assistance, but as part of Zeke's plans to grow the company they'd started building a list of contractors from across the country that they regularly vetted and updated. At first, he and his brothers had feared they'd overreached their capabilities too soon but it appears they were right on time.

Jerry's voice was gentle with understanding. "Remember, I promised to treat your grandmother as though she was my mother. I keep my promises."

Mal sensed Grace relax beside him. He gave his younger brother a smile of gratitude.

Melba grunted. "Several of the residents are already talking about fixing up my 'godson' Jerry with their granddaughters. They're sizing him up to be their new son-in-law. They don't even care that he doesn't live in Florida."

Was Jerry blushing? Mal shared a grin with Zeke.

Zeke laughed. "Just let us know if you're going to

stay in Florida and raise a family. I'm sure we can make arrangements for you to work remotely."

Jerry gave them a half grin. "Shut up." He grew serious. "The residence already has tight safety measures. There are strategic security doors, guest sign-in sheets and badges. You selected a good residence. I'd be comfortable with our parents living here if they were still alive."

Melba snorted. "We're paying them enough."

"Gran, please be careful." Grace's voice trembled just a bit, tying Mal's stomach in knots. "Make sure you're never alone or with people you don't know."

"I will. Stop worrying." Melba offered her granddaughter a reassuring smile.

"I'll stop worrying as soon as this is over. Until then, get used to it." Grace's smile didn't mask her concern.

Mal looked forward to resolving this case, too. But then he'd need another way to hold on to Grace—if that was even possible.

As she helped Mal clear the table after dinner Wednesday night, Grace felt as though she was slipping between the past and present. It was unnerving how easily they'd returned to the same rhythm they'd used to cook together in Chicago. Through unspoken agreement, he'd prepared the pasta. She'd made the salad and set the table. It helped that his kitchen in his family home was organized the same way he'd arranged the one in his apartment in Chicago.

Memories flooded back. Easy conversations, laughter, looks, caresses. Kisses. Grace fought to stay in the present. Then a look or a touch would send her years back in time, and she'd have to fight her the present. *Stay focused!* She needed a clear mind and a plan to resolve this case.

It had helped to once again review everything they'd seen, heard and felt during the day's events as they ate dinner. But they weren't any closer to unmasking the murderer than they'd been that morning. Grace's frustration was driving her to desperation.

Mal's voice broke into her thoughts. "You don't trust people easily. But you confided in Dr. B about the issue you're having with your formula." He met her eyes. "Why were you so certain he'd never betray you?"

Grace paused as she thought about her relationship with her former graduate school professor, mentor and dear friend. "We'd known each other for years. He hadn't been my graduate-program adviser. I'd chosen a lousy one." She could chuckle now, but at the time, she'd been angry with herself and concerned about her future. "I'd been anxious to identify an adviser for my course files and the professor had been only too happy to be just a name on a piece of paper. But Dr. B had reached out to me. He'd said he'd been impressed with my work in his class."

"And you believed him?" The amusement lurking in the dark depths of Mal's eyes indicated he knew the answer to his question.

Mal knew her so well, even after all this time. "Not at first. But he was offering me hands-on, real-world lab experience through his research program."

Mal washed the pan and laid it on the cream-colored vinyl drain board beside the silver sink. "And you decided it was worth the risk to participate in the program."

"I don't trust blindly." She retrieved the dish towel,

which hung on a peg near the sink, and dried the pan. "I asked a couple of alumni who'd gone through the research program. They said it had helped jump-start their careers after graduate school."

"And through the program, he'd earned your trust." Mal made it a statement, not a question. He was beginning to understand the relationship she'd had with her mentor.

"Like Jill, money had been tight in grad school." She bent to store the dried pan in the cupboard. "He encouraged me to apply for the Bishop Foundation grant, the same one Jill's a finalist for." She straightened from the cupboard and leaned her hip against the counter. "When he said he'd provide me with a letter of recommendation to submit with my application, I didn't have to remind him. He just did it. He gave me tips on evaluating labs I wanted to work for. When he said he'd give me an article to help me with my job search, I didn't have to ask him twice. He just sent it to me."

"He sounds like a remarkable professor and a great person." Mal settled back against the counter to her right.

Grace nodded. "He helped me because he believed in me. He never asked for or looked for anything in return. He became more than a professor, more than a mentor. He was like a father figure. That's why I know he didn't betray my trust. He'd probably still be alive today if he had." She swallowed past the burning lump of emotion trapped in her throat.

"His death is not your fault, Grace." Mal was adamant.

"Consciously, I know that. Subconsciously, I blame

myself. I should never have confided in him." She scrubbed her hands over her face.

"We all have to trust someone sometimes." Mal's voice was soft, preoccupied. "You said not trusting people is what happens when you put your trust in the wrong person one too many times. Who betrayed your trust?"

Grace allowed her arms to drop to her sides. Was she strong enough to have this conversation right now? She was tired and vulnerable. But she didn't want Mal to think she was some paranoid conspiracy theorist who was always looking over her shoulder. She wasn't. She was just careful. Past experience had taught her to be that way.

"My father left my mother less than two weeks after I was born." She made the statement matter-of-factly.

Mal's expression went blank with surprise. "I'm sorry. I didn't know."

She shrugged, crossing her arms. "How could you? I never told you."

"Why not?"

"Because I didn't want you to look at me the way you're looking at me now." She waved a hand toward him. "People pity me. I didn't want you to. My father walking out on my mother, my sister, and me doesn't hurt or shame me anymore. Gran took us in. I had a great childhood. And when my mother died, Pam, Gran and I were there for each other."

Mal crossed his arms. "You and your grandmother are very close."

"Yes, we are." Grace's smile faded. "But it wasn't just my father's disloyalty. Pam's husband left her less than a year into their marriage. He decided he didn't want to be monogamous anymore."

Mal closed his eyes briefly, feeling the pain in her voice. "That must've been hard."

"It was." Grace's voice was distant with memories. "She'd been four when my father walked out. Gran and I think she blamed herself. And then, when it happened again with her husband, it really did a job on her self-esteem."

"I'm so sorry."

"So were Gran and I." Grace's eyes dropped to the kitchen's cream-colored laminate flooring. "Shortly after that devastating experience, I caught my fiancé cheating on me—in our apartment."

"What? Why didn't you tell me?" Mal looked shocked.

Grace sighed. "I would have. I just hadn't found the right time."

"I wish you'd told me." There was disappointment in Mal's voice.

Grace nodded. She wished the same. "Between my mother's, my sister's and even my experiences, I didn't think I wanted anything to do with relationships. My research was my life. And I was fine with that. Until our mail kept getting misdirected." She lifted her eyes. "After meeting you, I understood why someone would risk that kind of heartbreak."

"Did you trust me?" His question was quiet, hesitant.

"Yes, I did," she answered immediately.

Mal returned her steady stare. "And yet *you* walked out on *me*."

Grace felt the blade slip between her ribs. She knew she deserved the comment. He was right: She'd walked out on him. She was the one who'd done the deserting in their relationship.

She straightened from the counter. "I know and I'm

so very sorry, Mal. I shouldn't have left that way, without speaking with you. You didn't deserve that."

He nodded in silence.

Was he agreeing he hadn't deserved the shoddy way she'd treated him? Was he accepting her apology? Both?

She was too much of a coward to ask. "I hope one day you'll be able to forgive me." She crossed the kitchen with hesitant steps. Mal's gaze tracked her progress. "I'm going to read before going to bed. Good night."

Once past him, she hurried upstairs. She'd felt tired and vulnerable before she'd made her confessions. She felt even worse now: tired, vulnerable, guilty and ashamed.

She was lucky Mal had agreed to work with her after the way she'd walked out on him and refused to respond to his calls, texts or emails. At the time, she'd thought she was leaving him for the good of her research. Now she wondered. Had she been afraid he'd leave her just as her father had left her mother? Like her brother-in-law had left her sister? Like her faithless fiancé had treated her? Had she been protecting her research—or her heart?

"Before the library instituted a procedure for students to sign in and out of study rooms, often people didn't show up to claim the reserved room, or they showed up late—or even worse, they damaged equipment." Grace provided the historical information as she and Mal walked from Central Columbus Science University's visitors' parking lot to the library located on the campus's oval on Thursday.

"So the sheet is a way to force students to be more accountable. Does every student have to sign in and out?

Could another student have signed in or out for Jill?" Mal took in the pastoral surroundings. The campus was even more beautiful in the early-morning hours.

Vibrant evergreen trees and deep green barberry shrubs complemented the redbrick buildings that ringed the oval. Cement pathways bisected lush green lawns. A light late-spring breeze carried the scent of lilacs and flower blossoms past him to toss Grace's ebony tresses.

In his mind's eye, he pictured her as a student hurrying to meet her study group. Her long, toned, golden brown legs, bared in cut-off shorts, flexing and stretching as she crossed campus. She would've been unaware of the second and third looks she drew from passersby, similar to the way she was oblivious to their attention now.

Instead of the cut-off jeans of his fantasy, she was equally attractive in a simple olive green cotton dress. Its pleated skirt swung around her thighs. Her low-heeled brown flats tapped beside him on the walking path.

She paused at the library's front entrance. Her smile made him forget his question. "No one's supposed to sign for Jill. That's against the rules. But I'm sure it happens all the time."

Mal followed her into the building. It smelled old just like the academic building. It was as though the campus hadn't been updated since the 1970s.

He lowered his voice to a stage whisper. "There's our distrusting scientist."

She rolled her eyes. "This way."

Mal jogged beside her down a wide marble staircase. "There are a lot of students here for eight o'clock in the morning."

Grace led him from the steps. "Finals are next week." She shivered in mock dread.

"Oh." Mal felt sorry for the students as he recalled the post-traumatic stress of the exam period.

Grace gave the older woman behind the counter a warm smile. "Hi, Alice. How are you?"

The librarian's white face turned pink with pleasure. Her smile deepened her wrinkles. "Grace!" She spoke in hushed tones. "Or should I say, Dr. Blackwell."

Grace's smile broadened into a grin. "Oh, please. You know it will always be Grace. It's so good to see you." She put her hand on Mal's arm beneath the sleeve of his dark blue polo shirt. "Mal, Alice Dexter is one of the best librarians in the world. She was always my calm space in the eye of the storm that was my grad school experience."

Grace's warm touch against his skin was a distraction, but he didn't want her to take her hand away.

"Oh, go on with you." Alice blushed a becoming rose and waved her small right hand in a dismissive gesture.

Grace continued. "Alice, this is my friend, Malachi Touré."

"It's a pleasure to meet you, Ms. Dexter." Mal shook her hand. Grace removed her touch and he could breathe again.

She blushed. "Please call me Alice. Any friend of Grace's."

Grace's eyes searched the other woman's features. "How are you, Alice?"

The librarian's expression sobered. Her gray eyes were clouded with grief. "Dr. B's death has hit the university hard—students, staff and faculty are all devastated."

Mal felt the woman's sorrow from across the counter. "My condolences on your friend's passing."

"Thank you." Alice's response was a faint whisper. "He'd been here more than twenty years. He must've taken those same steps thousands of times."

"He'll be deeply missed." Grace reached out, covering the other woman's hand with her own as it rested on the counter. "It's not just the suddenness of his death that makes it harder to come to terms with. It's the way he died. At the university, after hours, in a freak accident."

"Yes." Alice's sigh raised her thin chest and lifted her frail shoulders. "He'd been such a pleasure to work with. That evening, he'd given Jill his next semester's documentation so she could give it to me. It was due next week but he wanted me to have it early. She was joining a study group at the library, and he was meeting with someone in his office, so she offered to bring it over." Tears rolled down her cheeks. She brushed them away.

Grace exchanged a look with Mal before turning back to Alice. "Do you know who he was meeting with?"

"Jill didn't say." Alice shrugged. "I don't think she knew. She mentioned seeing Dr. B in the hallway. Why?"

"Just curious." Grace shook her head, but Mal sensed her thoughts racing.

So were his. "Do you remember what time Jill delivered the documents?" Mal asked.

Alice took a moment to search her memory. "It was right around six. My shift was ending. She said Dr. B was anxious to get the forms to me before I left for the day."

That was around the estimated time of Dr. B's death.

"We should let you get back to work." Grace stepped back from the counter. "It was good to see you, Alice. Take care."

"It was wonderful to see you again, Grace." Alice waved. "And it was a pleasure to meet you, Malachi."

Mal offered her a smile. "The pleasure was mine, Alice."

Grace broke their tense silence as she pushed through the library's exit. "Jill may not have seen the person Dr. B was meeting with, but perhaps he'd mentioned something about his visitor. Was it another student, a faculty member, someone in administration?"

Mal kept pace beside her. "I agree. At this point, I'd take that breadcrumb. Anything to move this investigation forward. The clock's still ticking."

Chapter 9

"Excuse me, Dr. Jones." Grace started speaking as soon as she and Mal entered the graduate adviser's office early Thursday morning. Her slender body trembled with tension. "I'm Grace Blackwell. This is my colleague, Malachi Touré." She gestured toward Mal beside her.

Dr. Jenna Jones looked up from the printouts spread across her faux dark wood desk. She removed her sapphire-rimmed reading glasses. Her dark brown eyes slid from Grace to Mal and back. "I know who you are, Dr. Blackwell. It's nice to meet you, Mr. Touré. What can I do for you both?"

"We need to speak with Jill Streep." Grace put her hands on the back of one of the two gray visitor's chairs in front of Jenna's desk. "We were told you're her adviser. Could you call her, please?"

The silver-haired academic's small white face creased

in bewilderment. She gestured toward the chairs. "Please have a seat and tell me what this is about. Why do you want to speak with Jill?"

Mal held out the seat on the left and waited for Grace to settle onto it before taking the chair beside her. His mind moved quickly to come up with a plausible cover story. It wasn't a good idea to tell too many people the whole truth. The fewer people who knew details about the case and those involved, the better.

"Jill asked to meet with Grace about Dr. B's research project, but we need to reschedule." He felt Grace's eyes on him. He tried not to react. "Could you contact her for us, please?"

Jenna returned her attention to Grace. Her small brown eyes were wide with excitement. "Are you taking over for Dr. B?" A smile lit up her elfin features. "How wonderful. I was afraid Jill's and Trent's research projects would go uncompleted. With only one week left to the semester that would've been such a shame. Especially for Trent. His mother's one of our biggest donors. She's a huge supporter of STEM programs."

Grace lifted a hand as though to interrupt the other woman's enthusiastic monologue. "I'm going to meet with Jill. I'm not certain how involved I'm going to get with the research program."

Jenna's expression dimmed with disappointment. "Oh. I'm sorry. I didn't realize—"

Grace interrupted her. "But could you call her now for us, please?"

Mal tried to smooth over Grace's tense request. "We want to catch Jill before she goes to the wrong location. We don't want to inconvenience her if we don't have to. Thank you."

"Oh, of course." Jenna gave them both a vague smile before turning to her computer. She typed a couple of commands into the keyboard, then picked up her telephone receiver and punched in a number. She looked at Grace and Mal. "I'm being sent to her voice mail."

Grace pulled her business card from her purse. Mal watched her write her cell phone number on the back. "Could you tell her to call me? It's urgent."

Jenna frowned again. "Doesn't she have your—Jill, this is Dr. Jones. I'm here with Dr. Blackwell and Mr. Touré. Dr. Blackwell wants you to call her urgently. It's about rescheduling your meeting." She ended the call after reciting Grace's cell phone number.

"Thank you, Dr. Jones." Mal rose to his feet. He tried to mask his disappointment over having to wait for Jill's call.

"Thank you for your help. Have a good day." Grace stood, taking a step toward the door before stopping. "Dr. Jones, did you help Jill apply for the Bishop Foundation grant?"

Jenna beamed. "Yes, it was Dr. B's idea. Did she tell you she's a finalist?"

Grace smiled. "Yes, she mentioned it." She gave the professor a final wave before joining Mal in the hallway. "We've just confirmed that Jill no longer has a financial motive."

Mal fell into step beside her. "And we confirmed her alibi for the time of Dr. B's murder. Alice spoke with her at the library."

Grace's eyebrows knitted. "After speaking with Dr. B. I wonder if she could tell us anything about the person meeting with him. That person could be the killer."

Mal's muscles stiffened with dread. "We should ask her, but I hope she doesn't. If the killer finds out Jill has information about them, she could become their next victim."

Mal followed Grace down the stairs of the academic building. "Jill's going to be confused by Dr. Jones's message about your meeting with her, but it was the best cover I could come up with."

Grace was shaking her head even before Mal finished speaking. "No, that was good thinking. Thank you. Jill may be confused, but she'll still call. Hopefully."

Crossing the lobby, Mal reached past her to open the door that led them back out to the university's oval. The scent of lilacs and freshly cut grass hit him. It was a pleasant relief from the dust and age from the building. He blinked as his eyes adjusted to the bright early-morning spring sunlight.

He joined Grace on the walking path. A dozen or so students in shorts and T-shirts, overdressed faculty, and uniformed staff hurried around the campus. The students weren't the only ones who looked shell shocked by the pending final exams. Faculty looked dazed and staff appeared exhausted.

"With luck, we'll hear from her soon." Grace strode beside Mal. "I hate waiting."

As he moved away from the building, Mal felt an itchy sensation at the back of his neck. It seemed like a warning that someone was staring at him.

"Mm-hmm. I remember that about you." Mal surveyed the oval, searching for the source of his unease. No one seemed to be looking back. The tingling continued.

"We also need to find Trent Mann." Grace searched the walking paths as though she expected to find the research assistant nearby.

"Mm-hmm. That would be good." He glanced briefly over his shoulder. A lanky man in blue jeans, white T-shirt and navy baseball cap. He was perhaps four paces behind them. Mal had seen him before. Twice in the academic building, once in the library. His suspicions went on high alert.

"I think we should speak with Verna Bleecher's widower, too." Grace paused as she considered their next steps. "Do you think that would be possible? He might be able to help us find a connection between Verna, Buckeye Dynamic and CCSU."

"That would be good." He scanned the oval for somewhere to take Grace while he confronted their stalker.

"You seem distracted." Grace faced him. "Is something wrong?"

Mal held her gaze. "I have to get you someplace safe."

She blinked up at him. "Why?"

Mal pressed his hand against her lower back and forced a smile. "Don't stop. Act natural. Someone's following us."

Grace's lips struggled to imitate his smile. "Are you sure?"

"Good job." Mal used his hand on her back to help move her forward. Beneath his palm, her muscles were tense. "Yes, I'm sure. Thin white guy. Early twenties. Blue jeans. White T-shirt. Ball cap."

Grace's movements were stiff as she continued down the path. "What should we do?"

"I need to get you somewhere safe before I do anything."

"No, no," Grace hissed her objection. "That's a waste of time. We need to confront this guy now. Together. There's one of him and two of us."

Grace was giving signals that she was on the verge of doing something rash. In the past, her impulsiveness had landed them in the nicest places. This wouldn't be one of those times.

Mal wrapped his arm around her slim waist and pulled her closer. "I can't risk your safety in an uncontrolled situation."

She frowned up at him. "I take self-defense courses. I can take care of myself." Without warning, she whirled around.

Mal spun with her. He scanned the oval. "He's gone."

There were even more people on the oval now. Perhaps there'd been a period change. But the stalker with the blue baseball cap had disappeared.

Grace turned in a slow circle, seeming to take in the red brick buildings that rimmed the oval, the large old maple trees that cast their shade on the walking paths, the evergreen bushes and well-maintained lawns. "Do you think he realized we'd spotted him?"

"Probably." *Dammit!* They may have had the killer within reach and he got away.

But had he been the killer?

Mal took a deep breath to ease his frustration and once again inhaled the various scents that lingered over the campus. Lilacs, cut grass, moist earth and finals-week panic.

Grace set her hands on her slim hips above her dress. She lowered her voice. "The fact that the killer's following us on campus means he's connected to the university. He's seen us here before."

"Was it the killer or someone else?" Mal scanned the area.

"Who else could it have been?" Grace's frustration echoed in her question. "If it was a twenty-something-year-old man, it could've been Trent Mann."

Mal rubbed his forehead with his fingertips. Hard. "The killer went to a lot of effort to conceal their identity. Hacking your computer from a major research facility instead of their home, killing two people who could link them to the hack. Why would they do all that and then follow us all over CCSU? The campus isn't exactly teeming with people."

Grace looked over her shoulders, studying the campus from different angles. "If it wasn't the hacker/murderer, who was it?"

Mal was still irritated by his lost opportunity. "Someone who could've led us to the killer."

"You think whoever killed my wife also killed your friend?" Verna Bleecher's widower's voice was a study in pain and anger. His dead-eyed stare disconcerted Grace.

She and Mal were meeting with Robin Bleecher Thursday morning, only two days after the Buckeye Dynamic Devices's chief information technology officer had been killed in her home. Grace doubted Robin had slept since. She'd felt the middle-aged man's grief like a weight on her heart from the moment he opened the door.

Releasing her eyes from Robin's gray pallor, Grace did a visual exam of the burgundy and blue-gray living room. Warm sage green curtains were drawn against the floor-to-ceiling windows that overlooked the front yard.

They shut out the natural early-morning light of the sunny May day, leaving the room choked in shadows.

Robin sat on one of the overstuffed blue-gray armchairs. Grace was beside Mal on the matching love seat. The pillows and sheets strewn across the set's sofa gave the impression Verna's tall, slender widower had been sleeping on it. The poor man must be having trouble adjusting to being in their bed alone. Guilt nearly choked Grace. She was responsible for his heartache. Circumstantial evidence connected his wife's murder to whomever was after her formulation.

"We're looking into a possible connection." Mal's words were careful. "We'd like to ask you some questions, if you're up to them."

"I've already spoken with the detectives." Robin's voice wavered. His unspoken thoughts were clear: *I don't want to go through that again.*

On impulse, Grace leaned forward. "Mr. Bleecher—"

He interrupted. "Rob, please."

Grace smiled. "Rob, may I make you a cup of tea?" Sage green and blue-gray color theme in a living room straight out of the Georgian era. Jane Austen novels on the bookshelf. She was certain Verna was a tea drinker. Perhaps Rob was, too.

"I—" Surprised, Rob exchanged a look with Mal before responding to Grace. "Sure. That would be nice. Thank you. Let me show you to the kitchen."

He pushed himself from the chair, taking a moment to steady his legs before leading Grace and Mal to the kitchen. Grace exchanged a look of concern with Mal. When had Rob last eaten? Mal's solid presence behind her was warm and reassuring as she followed their host.

Rob reached for the teakettle. The pot shook in his grip as he turned to the faucet.

Grace put a hand on his shoulder. "I can get that. Why don't you sit down?"

Mal rescued the kettle. "Why don't you both have a seat? I can make the tea."

Grace escorted Rob to the round blond-wood table. He stood several inches above her, but his sorrow made him seem frail. Rob took the seat beside the kitchen window. Like the drapes in the sitting room, the kitchen window's venetian blinds were closed. It was as though he was hiding his pain from the world, shutting it inside himself.

Grace spoke with a gentle voice. "May I fix us a snack?"

"Where are my manners?" Rob's cheeks filled with much-needed color. "V would be so embarrassed. I think we have some tea biscuits in the cupboard." He started to push himself to his feet.

"I'll get it, Rob." Grace pressed him back into his seat. "Tell us about Verna. Did she know anyone at CCSU?"

He frowned at the table as if it hid the answer from him. "I don't think so. Are you working with the police?"

Mal managed the flame beneath the kettle before searching the cupboards for mugs. "Detectives Duster and Stenhardt know we're looking into Verna's death from a different angle. We're sharing information with them."

Rob's eyes swept the kitchen as though seeking out memories. "I don't believe she knew anyone at that university. She knew several people at Ohio State. But I don't recall her mentioning anyone from CCSU."

Grace was used to her beloved alma mater being overshadowed by the much larger state institution. "Was she involved in any new research projects with Buckeye Dynamic?"

She found red pepper hummus and flatbread in the refrigerator. Grace put a slice of flatbread in the toaster, then went in search of a plate for Rob. She and Mal had already eaten, but Verna's widower needed sustenance.

Rob's tone was more decisive this time. "V wasn't a scientist. She was in charge of the website, information technology, the institute's internet infrastructure, cybersecurity, network, and hardware and software."

Grace was impressed by how thoroughly Rob rattled off his deceased wife's professional responsibilities. "Did she talk about her work a lot?"

Rob sat back against his chair. A small smile hovered around his thin, dry lips. "Not really. She was obsessed with separating her work and personal lives. We'd talk about work while we cooked together, but once we sat down to eat, she insisted we stopped all shop talk. She'd get excited when the lab did a redesign of the website or improved security measures or upgraded software. That sort of thing. She was a techie. But otherwise, she didn't say much. She didn't keep up with the research part of it."

Mal turned off the stove when the kettle whistled. "Did she talk about the company's systems hack?"

"Whew." Rob exhaled. He stretched his eyebrows into his hairline. "She was *furious* about that. To her, it was a direct attack against her professionalism. She told me she'd hired your company to find the hacker. Touré Security Group had come very highly recommended by several of her colleagues at other firms."

Rob's words filled Grace with pride even though she didn't have anything to do with Mal's company's stellar reputation.

"I appreciate that. Excuse me." Mal pulled his cell phone from the front pocket of his dark gray slacks. He scanned the face of his phone, then typed a quick message before returning his attention to brewing the tea. "Sorry for the interruption." He carried two mugs to the table, giving one to Rob and the other to Grace.

"You're fine." Rob took the mug Mal offered him. "Did you ever identify the hacker?"

Grace turned from adding a tablespoon of hummus to his plate to meet Rob's eyes. "It was me. I hacked Buckeye Dynamic. My system had been hacked, and I traced it back to the company."

Rob's bright blue eyes came to life with curiosity. He swallowed some of his hot tea. "*You* did? You must have great computer skills." He grinned. "V was so angry with you."

"I didn't want to do it, but someone had been after information on my computer." Grace placed Rob's plate on the table. "I need to know who that was. They may be responsible for Verna's death."

Anger stirred in the depths of Rob's expressive eyes. "You think someone who worked with my wife killed her?"

"That's what we're trying to find out." Mal gestured toward Rob with his mug. "Was Verna concerned about any projects or people at the company?"

Rob frowned at the cream and blue-gray linoleum flooring. "No—but as I said, she didn't talk much about work."

Mal pushed. "True, but she would've told you if

something was troubling her. She might have said something at least in passing while you were preparing dinner together."

Rob stood from the table, bringing the mug of tea with him. He ignored the hummus as he cradled the hot drink between his palms. "Last week, she was uneasy about a board of directors' vote. The board was nearly unanimous in their decision to revoke access to the lab's research projects from one of their members. V said the board had reason to believe the member was shopping their intellectual property."

Grace and Mal exchanged looks. Mal turned back to Rob. "Which member?"

Rob shook his head. "It was a confidential matter. V wasn't supposed to be discussing it at all, not even with me, but as I said, she was very upset. She was careful not to mention personal information about the member. I don't even know their gender." His blue eyes were dark with pain and anger. "Do you think this member killed my wife?"

Mal held his eyes. "We're going to find out."

Verna wasn't involved in hacking her system. Grace was now certain of that. But if she didn't know anything about it, why would someone kill her? She must have known something without realizing it. What could that have been?

Chapter 10

"Zeke texted me while we were speaking with Rob." Mal checked traffic before pulling away from the Bleecher family home late Thursday morning. "He wants to speak with us."

"In person?" Grace's optimism stirred after days of lying dormant. "Has he learned something new?"

"He didn't say what he wanted, but he sounded concerned." Mal came to a halt at a stop sign.

Optimism went back to sleep but not before waking Anxiety. "Is my grandmother all right?"

Mal's smooth bourbon voice was warm with reassurance. "I'm sure this doesn't have anything to do with her. If it did, he would've called. He wouldn't have kept that from us."

Grace exhaled. "You're right."

It would've been cruel and insensitive to delay giving Grace critical information about her grandmother.

She hadn't known Zeke or Jerry long, but she knew Mal. He was neither cruel nor insensitive. And he obviously loved his brothers, no matter what was going on between them on the business side. For that reason, Grace knew she could trust them.

Mal interrupted her silent pep talk. "We can take Verna off the suspects list."

"I agree." Grace tried to get comfortable on the passenger seat. It was a difficult task, as her head filled with thoughts of murder, cybercrimes and attempted thefts. And Mal's nearness. His soap-and-pine scent made her mind mushy. "It was interesting the way Rob kept saying Verna didn't talk about work, but he knew so much about her job. He described her responsibilities and her reactions to events at the facility. She may not have talked about her work much, but he had a level of detail that showed he'd listened to everything she'd said."

"He loved her very much." Mal's voice was low, almost offhand, as he scanned the traffic. "She may have wanted to keep her work and personal lives separate, but he wanted to be a part of everything that mattered to her. That's why he listened so closely."

Grace considered Mal's chiseled profile. "How do you know that?"

Mal pulled his attention from the traffic long enough to toss her a glance. His dark eyes were laser focused for the few moments they held hers before he returned his attention to the interstate. "Because that's what I would do if I were in a committed relationship. I'd want to know everything about that person, and I'd want that person to know everything about me. Don't you remember our long talks?"

Grace's throat went dry. She swallowed. "Yes, I do."

They'd walked and talked, driven and talked, jogged and talked. He'd always given her his undivided attention, whether she was discussing her childhood or her latest research project. He'd asked intelligent questions and made thoughtful observations. His attentiveness had been seductive. It still was. The air between them crackled with electricity. Grace knew that wasn't her imagination.

They arrived at Touré Security Group minutes later. Mal knocked on Zeke's half-open office door.

The elder brother gestured them into the room. "I didn't intend to start an argument."

Grace hesitated. What was he talking about?

"I'm not arguing." Jerry's voice came from Zeke's computer, clearing her confusion.

Zeke slid a skeptical look toward the computer monitor. "It sounded that way. We need to table this discussion. Mal and Grace are here." He adjusted the monitor so Grace and Mal could see Jerry.

From their enigmatic expressions, Grace couldn't tell what Zeke or Jerry were thinking. The fact they needed to obscure their thoughts concerned her. What was going on? She glanced at Mal, but he didn't seem troubled by his brothers' secrecy.

"Hi, Jer." Mal settled onto the farthest black cushioned guest chair closest to the office's window.

Grace followed his lead. "Hi, Jerry. How's my grandmother?" She tried to sound confident, but tension edged her words.

Jerry's smile was reassuring. "Aunt Melba's great. One of our contractors is with her. They're getting their hair done."

Salon services were part of the residence's features. Her grandmother enjoyed the weekly visits and pampering. But she'd refused to dye her gray hair. She'd insisted she'd earned every one of them.

Grace inclined her head toward the youngest Touré. "Thank you for taking care of her."

Jerry shook his head. "I enjoy her company."

Mal sat forward. "Zeke, you said you needed to see us right away. What's happened?"

Zeke shared a look between Grace and Mal. "I called Detectives Duster and Stenhardt this morning for an update on their investigation into Verna Bleecher's murder—"

Mal interrupted. "I met the detectives at the crime scene. They thought her murder was the result of a robbery gone wrong. Have they changed their minds?"

Zeke gave Grace another close look. "Apparently."

She frowned. Why was he making them pull each word from his mouth? "Have they learned something helpful?"

"There's no easy way to put this, so I'm just going to say it." Zeke leaned into his desk. "The detectives consider Grace a suspect in Verna's murder."

Grace's eyes stretched so wide they almost hurt. "How could they possibly think that?"

Mal spoke at the same time. "Why?"

Zeke locked eyes with Grace. "The detectives know Verna was looking for the hacker who breeched her company's computer system. They think you killed Verna before she could identify you."

Grace tilted her head. "How do the police know I'm the hacker?"

"Zeke told them." Jerry's voice was thick with disgust.

"You're wrong." Anger and offense pushed Grace out of her seat. "*Mal* identified me. I didn't even know Verna

Bleecher existed until he told me about her, so how could you think I had anything to do with her murder?"

"Slow down, Allyson Felix." Jerry's invoking of the US track-and-field Olympian pulled Grace up short. "We never said *we* thought you killed Verna. We're telling you the detectives do."

Grace sank back onto her seat. "I didn't even know where she lived—"

Jerry interrupted. "The detectives only have your word for that."

Grace glared at Jerry's image on Zeke's monitor. She was beginning to rethink having him protect her grandmother. She needed someone with better reasoning skills. His were suspect.

She shot a sidelong look at Mal. He was so still, alternately looking at Zeke and Jerry. What was he thinking? Why was he silent? He couldn't think she was guilty... Could he?

Anger clawed through Grace's chest, looking for a target. She directed it at Zeke. "If my justifiable distrust of Buckeye Dynamic is the best the detectives can do for a link between Verna and me, they might as well add the tooth fairy to their list of suspects. I hadn't completed my trace, so why would I suspect Verna over anyone else in that building?" She included Jerry in her accusatory glare.

Zeke spread his hands. "The way I see it, we have two choices. Either you're lying—"

"Grace is not a liar." Anger grumbled in Mal's voice.

Oh, so the mountain can *speak.* Grace stifled the sulky comment.

Ignoring Mal, Zeke continued. "Or someone's framing you."

Grace's mind was spinning. This didn't seem real. None of it seemed real. Her computer being hacked. Dr. B's suspicious death. Verna's murder. And now someone was trying to frame her. She needed to wake from this nightmare. Right. Now.

The nightmare continued. "My tracking a hacker to Buckeye Dynamic doesn't make me a murderer. It makes me a victim."

Zeke's tone lacked inflection. "They're basing their suspicions on more than the hack."

Mal asked the question on her mind. "What do they have?"

Zeke shifted his attention to Mal. "Grace's fingerprints at the crime scene."

Grace went cold. "You've got to be kidding."

"I wish we were." Zeke's inscrutable expression returned.

"That's impossible." Mal's voice was tight, as though he wanted to say more but didn't trust himself. He'd said enough. His belief in her meant Grace wasn't facing this latest test of her courage alone. "Where did they find her prints?"

Zeke shook his head. "They wouldn't say."

"We were lucky they told Zeke that much," Jerry added.

Zeke held Grace's eyes. "Where were you between nine and ten a.m. Tuesday?"

Her pulse was beating far too quickly. Was she about to pass out? "Don't you believe me?"

Jerry answered. "The detectives will ask you these questions. We want you to be prepared for them. We need you on the outside, helping us solve our client's murder. We can't protect you from a murderous hacker if you're in prison."

"Jerry." Mal chewed his brother's name through clenched teeth.

Grace's face stung as the blood drained from her cheeks. She took a moment to pull herself together. "All right. A little after eight a.m., I was at the Cakes and Caffeine Coffee Shop on Henderson. I'd just made contact with Mal through my laptop, although I didn't know it was him at the time."

"That's eight o'clock." Jerry's delivery was business-like. "What about nine and ten?"

Grace gestured toward Mal beside her. "After Mal left to see Vera shortly before nine o'clock, I stayed at the café."

"Can you prove that?" Zeke seemed intense for a fake interrogation.

There wasn't any reason to be nervous. She hadn't done anything wrong. Then why were her palms sweating? Perspiration collected across her brow. She brushed her fingertips across her hairline, then clenched her damp fists on her lap.

"Yes, I can. I have two receipts that are date- and time-stamped—one for the coffee I bought when I arrived around eight o'clock and another for the pastry I bought after Mal left around nine." She faced Mal. "I didn't kill Dr. B or Verna."

"I know." Mal's response, simple and direct, steadied her. He stood. "Let's go tell the detectives."

Grace wiped the sweat from her hands before she took his.

"Have you seen this before?" Detective Eriq Duster slid a clear plastic bag diagonally across the table to

Grace. The word *EVIDENCE* was stamped in large, red-block capital letters on both sides.

Grace sat with the veteran homicide investigator and his partner, Taylor Stenhardt, in the Columbus Police Department's local precinct's brightly lit interrogation room late Thursday morning. They'd asked Mal to wait in the break room. Grace's muscles were so stiff with tension she could barely move.

Eriq pinned her with cynical dark eyes. He had the appearance of a former heavyweight boxing champion who'd eased up on his fitness regimen. Grace guessed he was a handful of years from retirement. Would his experience help the investigation, or was he eager to wrap up his cases and walk out? His bolo tie detracted from his otherwise menacing image in his dark suit and white shirt. Grace focused on it.

She leaned over the table to get a closer look at the bag's contents without touching it. It held a thumb drive stamped with the Buckeye Dynamic Devices and Central Columbus Science University logos. Images from her alma mater's recent donor event flashed in front of her mind's eye. "This looks like the thumb drive given to guests who'd attended CCSU's Spring Science Fundraiser. Buckeye Dynamic had been the event's lead sponsor."

She shifted her attention to Taylor, who was seated across the table from her. The detective's wide jade eyes returned Grace's attention with the dispassion of a lab technician studying a specimen on a petri dish.

Taylor was an attractive woman, perhaps in her late forties. Her honey blond hair was swept back and collected into a bun at the nape of her long, slender neck.

Her drab, dark suit was reminiscent of Eriq's attire, but her jewel-toned blouse screamed individuality.

Grace gestured toward the bag. "Is this what you found at the site of Verna Bleecher's murder? Where was it?"

"Near the body." Taylor spoke without moving her eyes from Grace. It was intimidating. "When did you last use it?"

Grace shook her head. "I've never used it. In fact, I haven't seen it since the event two weeks ago. I assumed I'd left it on the table."

Eriq grunted. "Your prints are on it."

"I didn't say I hadn't touched it." Grace searched her memory. "I probably picked it up to look at it when I took my seat. But I didn't bring it home."

"You're saying someone stole it from you after you'd touched it so they could use it to frame you for Verna Bleecher's murder." Eriq sounded skeptical. "Who?"

That wasn't what she was saying—but that's what had happened.

"I don't know." Grace spread her hands. They were going to believe what they wanted to believe. All she could do was tell the truth. "Everyone who attended the event knew these devices had been given out." Her voice slowed as pieces of the puzzle moved closer together. "But your finding it at the murder scene proves I'm right."

Taylor jumped on her declaration. "About what?"

Grace gave the detective a confident look. "The hacker's connected to Buckeye Dynamic. I wasn't certain before, but this thumb drive proves it."

Taylor frowned. "How?"

Grace turned to Eriq. He sat closest to the door. "We need Mal."

Sighing and muttering under his breath, Eriq pushed himself to his feet and left the room. He returned minutes later with Mal. Grace brought him up to speed.

From his seat beside Grace, Mal turned to the detectives. "Dr. Bennett MacIntyre was the chair of the university's Division of Math and Science, and Grace's mentor. He died under suspicious circumstances last Thursday." He explained their suspicions regarding Dr. B's death and gave a general overview of the hacking of Grace's system. "Grace's computer hack links Verna's and Dr. B's deaths."

Eriq gave Grace a considering look. "So you think this killer—who's also a hacker—is trying to frame you. Who would do that?"

Grace gestured to the evidence bag. "Someone who attended the fundraiser and knew I was there also."

"How many people were at the event?" Taylor asked.

Grace tried to remember the attendance numbers the organizers had announced. "Close to three hundred."

"Who was at your table?" Mal asked.

Grace brought an image of her tablemates to mind. "There were six people to a table. Dr. B bought a table and invited me, another of his former students—who's now a bioscience researcher at Buckeye Dynamic—his two student research assistants and the mother of one of his research assistants, who's also a member of the university's board of trustees."

Eriq split a look between them. "Are you two investigating Bleecher's and MacIntyre's murders?"

Mal shifted his attention to the other man. "As well as the attempt to hack Grace's files. They're connected."

Taylor took notes. "What do you think they were looking for on your system?"

Grace kept her voice as casual as possible. "A drug formulation I'm working on. Cyber hacking isn't uncommon in the pharmaceutical-research industry."

Eriq leaned back on his chair. He gave Grace a hard look. "I realize you're working with the Tourés, but for my money, we still need to keep an eye on you. You're the best lead we have."

"Then you don't have any leads because I haven't killed anyone." Grace tamped down her temper. The detective didn't know how precious Dr. B had been to her or how devastated she was that someone was trying to turn her life-saving research into a weapon of mass destruction.

"Grace couldn't have killed Verna." Mal's voice was firm. "I'm sure she's shown you her receipts from the coffee shop, which proves she wasn't anywhere near the Bleecher's residence when Verna was murdered."

Eriq gave Grace a skeptical look. She returned it without reaction. The detective stood, tucking his pen into his notebook, and addressed Mal. "Your parents were good people. I admired them. A lot. People around here respect you and your brothers because of them."

Mal rose to his feet. "Thanks."

Eriq continued. "Your family's worked well with us in the past. So listen—keep us in the loop."

Mal inclined his head. "Definitely. And you'll do the same?"

Eriq's dark features were expressionless. "Keep us in the loop."

Taylor collected her notepad and pen before following Eriq out the door.

Mal stepped aside to let Grace precede him. She kept her silence until they were back in Mal's vehicle. "Detective Duster's noncommittal response to sharing information with us was less than encouraging."

Mal started the car. "It's the best we're going to get." He pulled out of the parking space and navigated his black SUV into traffic. "We need to interview Dr. George and take another look at Trent Mann."

Grace shifted on her seat to face him. "We also need to add Martina Mann to our list. She was at the table. She could be working with her son. And remember Rob said something about a controversy with Buckeye Dynamic's board of directors? Martina's a member."

"You're right." There was frustration in his tone as he guided his vehicle onto the interstate.

"Mal, thank you for coming with me to the precinct. I appreciate your support."

He held her eyes. "Of course. We're in this together."

Grace swallowed a sigh. *And what happens after?*

Chapter 11

"We need to put this killer behind bars so I can concentrate on my research," Grace burst out as they were cleaning up after lunch Thursday afternoon.

Mal looked over as he stacked their dishes in the dishwasher. He'd been waiting for the explosion. She'd been too quiet during their meal of clam chowder and garden salad. She'd declined the club sandwich. Instead, she'd picked at her soup and ignored her salad.

He straightened. "I told you to leave the investigation to us. My brothers and I have it covered."

Grace gave him the stink eye from the black-and-stainless-steel refrigerator. She set the wrapped remains of her untouched salad on one of the shelves, then let the door shut. "I want you to admit I've been helpful. Admit it. You wouldn't have been able to put together a list of suspects without me. And this is my formulation, my responsibility. I'm not going to delegate its safekeeping to someone else."

"Yes, you've been helpful." Mal spoke without inflection. He didn't want to admit even to himself that she was cute when she was being smug. "We couldn't have pulled together a list of suspects as quickly as you were able to, but we could have conducted the interviews without you."

Grace shook her head. "No, you couldn't have. My connection to Dr. B and the university made people more comfortable with our questioning. But that's not the point." She extended her arm like she was stopping traffic. "We need to speed up this investigation and catch this killer. We're moving too slowly. This whole thing is distracting me from my research." She let her arm drop.

"I know." Mal turned to scrub the pot they'd left soaking in the sink. "I'm handling this case and projects for several other clients. So I understand this situation is frustrating. It's difficult for me, too."

"I'm sure it is. I don't mean to imply my situation is different from yours. I'm just venting." She pinched the bridge of her nose, as though the gesture would help her focus. "My life has been upended. I've had to relocate out of my home. I'm afraid to go into my office. I'm running on a treadmill in a friend's basement while it's seventy degrees and sunny outside. I feel like a prisoner. This is such a distraction."

Mal could see his reflection in the surface of the pot he was cleaning, but he kept scrubbing.

This is such a distraction.

"Is that what I was to you? A distraction?" He turned on the faucet to rinse the pot. His movements were stiff and jerky. Mal was angry but with himself. He shouldn't have let those words past his lips. They'd revealed too much about him—more than he'd intended to disclose, especially to her. Especially now. Dammit.

They were over. *She'd* broken things off with *him*. There was no good reason to reexamine the past. Why was it so hard to remember that? He needed to let go and move on. She had.

"Mal." Her voice was tentative. "I wasn't referring to you."

Forget this. He wasn't going to be able to move on until he had some concrete answers, and the only way to get them was to ask the tough questions.

He turned to her, reading the caution in her wide cinnamon eyes. "Is that the reason you left? You thought I was a distraction? A bother? Because I thought we were in love."

"It's complicated. This isn't like two parts hydrogen and one part oxygen make water. You're looking for easy answers to a complicated situation." She paced past him.

Mal turned, keeping her in his sight. "Then explain it to me as though I was nine."

Grace squared her shoulders. Her features were sharp with tension and frustration. "You know my sister had diabetes. She'd struggled with it since childhood."

Mal nodded. "I remember."

Pam had been Grace's only sibling. Her sister had been six years older than her, but they'd been very close. Some of his temper drained as he recalled how much Grace had loved Pam. He'd heard the love and admiration in her voice. He'd seen it in her eyes whenever she talked about her sister.

Grace continued. "Pam did her best to manage her illness through diet and exercise, but she'd still needed insulin. And the cost kept getting more and more expensive."

Mal knew the seriousness of the situation and the importance of her research. He'd read a recent study that cited diabetes as the seventh-leading cause of death in the United States. One in ten people had diabetes and knew it. About a quarter of the population wasn't aware they had the disease.

Grace wrapped her arms around herself as she paced the length of the white-and-yellow kitchen. "I saw how much stress the situation was causing her. She needed insulin to stay alive, but all the drug manufacturers seemed to care about was profits. They wanted to make as much money as they could to keep their board members happy. It's shameful. So I made my sister a promise. I went into bioscience intending to create an alternative treatment for the disease that would be easier to deliver and much, much less expensive."

"Your sister's death devastated you." Mal's heart hurt as though the pain had been his. "I can only imagine your grief. I'm so sorry you weren't able to complete your research before Pam died. But to your credit, you've continued your work, and once you're successful, your formula will help millions of people in Pam's memory."

Grace stopped pacing. Her eyes swam in tears. "Thank you for saying that."

Mal swallowed the lump in his throat. "Did you ever think of finding me when you came to Columbus?"

She took a step toward him. "I honestly thought you

were still in Chicago. You seemed so happy and settled there. It never occurred to me you'd left."

"I'd been happy there—with you." He watched her close the gap between them. Every step she took seemed to speed up his pulse. "After you left, I didn't have a reason to stay. And I missed my family."

She stopped within an arm's length of him. Her warmth embraced him. Her scent—roses and powder—filled his mind. "I wish I'd known you were here, too. I missed you."

Those words cleared his senses. She'd missed him? "Then why did you leave?" Crap! He hated sounding so needy, but he had to know.

Rubbing the side of her neck, she turned from him. "I don't know."

Was she kidding? "You broke my heart and you don't know why?"

Her voice was distracted, as though she'd traveled back in time to the place she'd been when she'd left him. "I was in a fog. I'd failed my sister by not focusing on my research. I hadn't realized how sick she was or the financial trouble she was in. I should have, but I'd been thinking only of myself. When she died, I was consumed with guilt. All I could think about was running away."

Mal stepped forward, cupping his hand over her shoulder. "Don't blame yourself. Pam didn't tell you she was in trouble because she didn't want you to worry about her. She wanted you to be happy, Grace."

Grace turned to him. Pain and grief clouded her eyes. Her lips parted as though she was going to say something. Mal felt the pull of her like an invisible hand drawing him forward. He gave in to the urging, leaning forward. Slowly. Giving her the chance to turn away. One taste. It was all he wanted. Was it what she wanted? He brushed his lips across her. Lightly. He looked into her eyes. Need swirled in their bright depths. It was an echo of his feelings. He covered her mouth with his. Comfort and longing. Her taste was sweet. Her scent was soft.

Memories merged the past and present, pushing and pulling him. He hadn't realized she'd tugged his shirt free of his pants until he felt her soft, hot hands curve over his pecs. He felt heavy with desire, but a warning sounded in his head.

"Grace." He stepped back, drawing her hand away from him. "I don't just want tonight. Are you willing to give me more than that?"

Her eyes glowed with desire. But beneath the heat, he saw clouds of confusion. Closing his eyes briefly, Mal gritted his teeth. He had his answer.

He stepped back and turned away. It took everything he had to keep walking.

The coffee shop was in the heart of Bexley and short driving distance from Central Columbus Science University. Late Friday morning, it was stuffed with the over-caffeinated twenty-something heirs to the Columbus suburb's wealthy families. The opening chords of Elton John and Dua Lipa's duet, "Cold Heart," came over the sound system.

Mal held fast to Grace's delicate hand as he made a path from the door to the center of the café. He was sure the students—a few more than a dozen in a near-equal mix of men and women—were harmless, but he didn't want to lose her. He also wanted every excuse to touch her since this was apparently all he could have.

According to Jill Streep, their target, Trent Mann, Dr. B's second research assistant and the son of CCSU board of trustees member Martina Mann, came to this coffee shop with friends on his way to class every morning. Grace had located the young man seconds after they'd walked through the door.

Trent and three of his friends—two women and a man—sprawled on cushioned armchairs grouped in a circle near the center of the cafe. Their knapsacks were strewn around them. Mal cataloged the research assistant's appearance. His cotton short-sleeved caramel V-neck T-shirt and designer jeans looked new. His brown loafers probably cost as much as a car payment.

As Mal drew closer, he heard Trent's voice above the sound of the pop song, clattering porcelain dishes and other conversations.

"So his mother gave him a choice: a summer job at her law firm or his own car." Trent paused to laugh. "He took the job. What an idiot."

A young woman with auburn hair that waved down her back and a heavy hand with expensive-looking makeup was curled in a chair to Trent's right. "Wait, I'm confused." So was Mal. "Wouldn't he have to get a job anyway? I mean, that was the point of her offering to buy him a car, right? So he could get a job for the summer?"

Trent looked at her in disbelief. "Come on, Ruby. You take the car. You always take the car. Then you can spend the summer 'looking'—" he made air quotes with his fingers "—for a job."

A chorus of agreements rose from the other two members of the group. Ruby was quiet, but she didn't look convinced. Good for Ruby. Mal had hope for her.

He started to interrupt the group's conversation, but Grace spoke first. She released his hand.

"Hello, Trent. Do you have a moment?" Her tone was casual. Her expression was friendly, but determination gleamed in her bright eyes.

The young man looked up at the sound of his name. The gel that molded his thick dark brown hair kept the strands in place. "You're Dr. Blackwell." His attention turned to Mal. "Who's your friend?"

"Malachi Touré." He'd just met the research assistant and already didn't like him.

Humor flashed across his brown eyes so like his mother's. "Very biblical. I gave at the office."

While two of his group laughed their appreciation of Trent's wit, Ruby considered Mal and Grace with open curiosity. "What's this about?"

Mal held Trent's attention. "Dr. Bennett MacIntyre's murder and the possible motive."

Their audience responded with an abrupt stillness.

"Murder?" Shock wiped the smug gleam from Trent's eyes. "I thought the old guy had fallen down some stairs."

Grace's features tightened. The research assistant's dismissive tone angered him as well.

Mal nodded his head toward the café's side exit. "Let's discuss this outside."

Trent's practiced look of cynicism fell away. His eyes were wide. The uncertainty in them made him look younger than his twenty-two years. "Are you guys cops? You can't think *I* had anything to do with this."

Grace gestured toward the nearby door. "Will you come with us, please?"

The chemistry senior glowered at her before pushing himself up and out of the overstuffed brown corduroy chair. His gait was stiff as he marched to the exit and shoved the door open. Mal stood aside to let Grace exit first.

Trent spun to confront them. "Let me see your badges. You have no right to harass me. I don't know anything about Dr. B's death."

Mal could almost smell the younger man's panic. "We were told you and Dr. B didn't get along."

Trent retreated a step. His scowl deepened. "Are you a cop?"

Mal paused a few beats. It was an interrogation technique he'd learned from his military officer parents. "I'm an investigator, working with the police on this case. Tell us about the tension between you and Dr. B— or would you rather the homicide detectives bring you in for questioning?"

Trent's face flushed an angry red. He stretched his neck forward. "Who told you I had a problem with Dr. B? Was it Jill, that nosy—"

Mal cut him off. "Answer the question. Or do you have something to hide?"

Trent turned with agitated movements. He ran his hand over his sculpted hair, then over his right hip as though wiping gel from his palm. "Yeah. Sure. Dr. B and I got into it a couple of times." He faced them. "His standards were unreasonable. No one could meet them. They were too high."

Grace narrowed her eyes as though she'd detected a

lie. "Jill didn't have trouble completing her assignments for Dr. B's project."

Trent's thin features darkened with increasing fury. "Good for her, but he was harder on me."

Somehow, Mal doubted that. The exchange he'd overheard between Trent and his friends had revealed the college senior's lack of ambition. If he'd expend that much energy plotting ways of moving ahead rather than scheming to cut corners, who knew what the young Mann could accomplish?

"Is it true Dr. B planned to remove you from the program?" Mal asked.

Trent looked away, shaking his head. "Wow. You guys have spent a lot of time looking into me. Should I be flattered?"

"Is it true?" Grace prompted.

"Maybe." Trent turned to her. His voice had cooled, but anger still smoldered in the dark depths of his eyes. "But if that's the best you and Rent-A-Cop could do for a motive, you've failed your assignment. I told my mother two weeks ago I was dropping out of the program. That's *before* you claim Dr. B had been murdered."

Grace's eyes grew distant, as though she was searching her memory. "We saw your mother at Dr. B's funeral. She didn't mention your dropping out of the research program."

Trent's shrug was an impatient flex of his muscles. "Yeah, well, she was hoping I'd change my mind. But I won't. *She's* the frustrated scientist in the family, not me. She pulled some strings to get me into the program. Something she never seems to get tired of reminding me. She doesn't care that I had zero interest in it. If she could've, she'd have enrolled herself."

It frustrated Mal, but everything the arrogant junior said had a ring of truth. Still… "Do you have an alibi for Thursday evening?"

"I sure do." Trent's tone was full of forced cheer. "It was fifty-cent wing night at the bar near campus. I watched the Cavs beat the Nets on their big-screen TVs."

Mal arched an eyebrow. The kid was annoying. "Can anyone corroborate that?"

"Sure can." Trent marched past him and Grace on his way back into the café. "My friends were with me. Let's ask them."

Once again, Mal stepped aside for Grace but this time, Trent held the door for them. His manner was gratingly facetious. He led the way back to his circle of friends. The trio was in agitated conversation. They looked up as he approached. Their eyes were wide with concern.

"Is everything all right?" Ruby looked from Mal and Grace to Trent.

Trent flopped back onto his puffy armchair. He folded his arms behind his head and gave Mal a superior smile. "Ruby, tell these nice people where we were Thursday night."

Ruby's smooth, creamy forehead furrowed in confusion. "We were at Burgers, Wings and Beer. It's a bar near campus. It was fifty-cent wing night, and the Cavs played the Nets."

Did Trent realize how fortunate he was to have someone of Ruby's caliber in his life? Doubtful.

"Thank you, Ruby." Mal turned to Trent. "We'll be in touch if we have any other questions."

"You do that." Trent's taunt followed Mal as he turned to leave the café.

Grace glanced up at him. "Is it wrong that I was hoping he didn't have such a rock-solid alibi?"

Mal's lips curved in a slight smile. "If it was, then we were both in the wrong."

"I really thought it was him." Grace's words carried to Mal minutes later as they walked back to his car late Friday morning.

He'd parked in the café's adjoining customer lot. It was steps from the rear-exit, but the short walk and cool late-spring breeze helped clear his mind after their brief and disappointing encounter with Trent Mann.

Mal pressed his keyless-entry button to unlock his SUV. He held the passenger-side door open as Grace slid onto the seat. "I wanted it to be him, especially after he'd called me a rent-a-cop. I hate that."

Even though Trent had made a bad first impression, Mal couldn't dismiss his solid alibi for the estimated time of Dr. B's murder. One of his friends had confirmed they were miles from the university's administrative building. The other two were sure to corroborate if asked. As surprised as Mal was that Trent had solid alibis, he was even more perplexed that the junior had friends.

Grace looked up at him before he closed the door. "I can't believe people call you that."

Her tone was incredulous and, if he wasn't mistaken, angry. On his behalf? His heart beat a little faster. She still cared.

Let's not get carried away just because she wants to defend you.

Mal closed the passenger door and circled the hood to get to the driver's seat. "People don't call Zeke, Jerry or me rent-a-cops, but we've heard from our security guard contractors that some of our clients' employees call them that."

Grace scowled. "Recently?"

"Yes." Mal backed out of the parking space, then slowly made his way to the exit. "Not only is the term insulting, it's also inaccurate. Our guards don't have the authority to arrest anyone. Most of them aren't even armed. What they can do, however, is secure the building and the safety of the people inside. The clients' employees don't have to worry about encountering suspicious packages, thieves, assailants or anyone else who's not supposed to be on the premises. This leaves them free to focus on spreadsheets, marketing campaigns, legal contracts and life-changing pharmaceutical formulas."

Mal slid Grace a teasing look before merging with the still-heavy post–morning rush hour traffic on Grandview Avenue. He took a deeper breath of her scent as it floated around them.

"I never thought of our security guards as being our first line of defense while I'm up in my lab." A rustle of fabric against the dark gray cloth passenger seat alerted Mal that Grace had shifted to face him. "I feel even better about going into the office today."

Mal had been reassured when Grace told him Midwest Area Research Systems, the pharmaceutical-research company she worked for, had several guards per shift on the premises. He would've felt even better if Touré Security Group had the contract on the building. That way, they would've done the background check on each guard. They couldn't do anything about that now. Anyway, the only thing that would remove his tension would be his being with her the entire time she was in that building. But that wasn't an option. Due to the sensitive nature of their work, company policy prohibited guests from going past the first-floor conference rooms.

Minutes later, Mal pulled up outside Midwest Area Research Systems and put the car in Park. "I'll meet you right here at exactly five thirty. Watch your back. Remember, don't tell anyone where you're staying or with whom."

As he spoke, Mal's eyes scanned the well-manicured grounds. The barberry hedges were trimmed too low to provide much cover to any ill-intentioned lurkers. Nor could any threats hide behind the spindly ash trees. The glass facade of the five-story modern building was tinted top to bottom. He suspected those on the inside could see out, but anyone casing the building couldn't see in.

"I promise to be careful." Grace shrugged her purse onto her shoulder and prepared to leave the car. She offered him a smile that was meant to be confident, but Mal saw the shadows of concern in her eyes. Good. If she was worried, she'd be cautious.

He watched her walk through the front doors. Her steps were brisk. She scanned left and right. Good. Still, he wished he didn't have to leave her in someone else's care.

Chapter 12

"Trent Mann's friends confirmed he was at a sports bar at the estimated time of Dr. B's murder last Thursday." Mal propped his right ankle on his left knee. "Also, he claims he told his mother two weeks ago he was dropping out of the program. Martina didn't mention that to Grace and me, but if it's true, it removes his motive."

He and Zeke sat beside each other in the gray cushioned-and-silver-metal chairs in Touré Security Group's conference room late Friday afternoon. Zeke had placed his laptop on the large glass-and-silver-metal table so they could see Jerry as he videoconferenced in from his post protecting Grace's grandmother in Coconut Grove, Florida.

Jerry had logged on to the videoconference from Melba's living room. Grace's grandmother was having lunch with the other residents under the watchful eyes of one of their contractors and several of the residence's security guards. The number of potential witnesses—both professional and laypeople—would dissuade an assailant from moving in on Melba.

"Well, that's disappointing." Jerry was having a late lunch of cheeseburgers and frieds during their meeting."We've already removed his other research assistant, Jill Streep, from our list. We're running out of suspects."

"Grace started with a two-page list, remember?" Mal heard the grim note in his voice. "We're going to speak with one of Buckeye Dynamic's bioresearch scientists. She was one of Dr. B's former students. And she was at the fundraiser where Grace got the thumb drive that was planted at Verna's crime scene."

Zeke nodded. "Good work." He watched Mal closely, as though trying to read his thoughts. "You've got a lot on your plate. We can call in one of our cybersecurity contractors to help with your other projects."

Mal started shaking his head before Zeke finished speaking. "Thanks, but I've got it."

Zeke's eyes darkened with concern. "We know you have a hard time accepting help, but this case alone is a lot. It's all right to offload some of your projects. That's why we keep a list of qualified contractors."

Mal offered his older brother a half smile. "I've got this, Zeke. I'm on schedule with my three open cases. I closed a fourth one last night—ahead of deadline. And I've followed up with the four projects I submitted a bid on last night and this morning."

Zeke sat forward. "Mal, we have a reputation for completing projects on time and on budget—"

"Zeke, knock it off." Jerry's impatience cut the other man off. "If Mal says he's got it, he's got it."

Zeke's head snapped toward Jerry's image on the computer screen. His eyes widened with surprise at the attack. "I want to make sure he doesn't burn out."

Jerry hissed a short, sharp breath. He sat back against Melba's overstuffed floral-patterned armchair. "Why do you always act like you and you alone know everything?"

"What are you talking about?" Anger stirred in Zeke's voice. "I don't do that."

"Enough." Mal extended his hand, hoping the gesture would catch his brothers' attentions. It didn't.

"Are you kidding me right now?" Jerry spoke over him. His voice rose with incredulity. "Mom and Dad made us equal partners. You act like you're our boss."

Mal's patience frayed. He tightened his hold on it and tried again. "Let's get back to work."

"That's a lie." Zeke's temper went up in flames. Mal could almost see the smoke. "If you think I act like your boss, that's on you. It's not based on anything I've ever said or done."

Jerry's bark of laughter was forced. "I should record—"

"Enough!" Mal surged up from his chair. His voice was a few decibels lower than a roar. His muscles shook with anger. He swung his attention from Zeke to Jerry before pacing away from them. "You sound like children. For pity's sake, when will you grow up?"

He rubbed his forehead with his right hand. Their parents had never argued, at least not in front of them. And he had a hard time believing either his easygoing father or good-natured mother ever sounded like Zeke and Jerry at the height of a confrontation. Where had his parents found those two? In the woods?

"I'm sorry, Mal." Zeke's low voice conveyed his remorse. "This is what drove you out of the company and away from Columbus before. I don't want to chase you away again."

"Neither do I." Jerry exhaled a deep breath. "Something's gotta change."

Mal stiffened at the implication in Jerry's prediction. His younger brother had been seriously considering leaving their family business. Jerry hadn't shared his feelings with Zeke, though, and Mal had been sworn to secrecy. He wasn't comfortable with either situation. But that was a battle for another day. For now, he needed them to understand he wasn't going to put up with their arguing any longer.

Mal moved back to the conference table to look Jerry in the eye. "What's going to change is that the two of you will work out your differences. This time, I'm staying put. I should never have allowed your tantrums to drive me away all those years ago. Despite my visits, I lost so much time with Mom and Dad, and both of you. I regret that more than I can say. If the two of you don't learn to get along, one day you'll wake up and regret the time you've wasted being knuckleheads. You don't want that."

"You're right." Zeke looked at Jerry. Their youngest brother still appeared a little resentful, but at least he'd stopped arguing.

"I know." Mal resumed his seat. "Let's focus on work. As you know, I've got a mountain of projects to follow up on before leaving to pick up Grace at the lab."

Zeke's lips curved into a slight smile. "She's a good

influence on you. I don't think you would've expressed yourself so clearly before."

Mal's mind shied away from Zeke's train of thought. "Perhaps it's just time."

But his brother was right: losing Grace made him realize how important it was to let those you care about know how you feel. He didn't want to lose her again. But did he have the courage to put that particular fear into words?

"I read in the paper that a biosciences professor at CCSU died last week, Dr. Bennett MacIntyre. Did you know him?"

Grace looked up at her colleague, Dr. Cole Jensen, Friday evening as they walked together down the broad, winding silver-and-plexiglass staircase that curved into the lobby of Midwest Area Research Systems—MARS.

Cole was about Dr. B's age, mid to late sixties. But his dark brown skin was still smooth, and there was only the lightest dusting of gray in his tight black curls. An avid runner, Cole was tall and lean. His impeccable smoke gray suit draped his form as though it was tailor-made, even though Grace suspected it wasn't. Her colleague was too cost-conscious for that.

Cole was one of a handful of African American research scientists at the lab. He'd made it his mission to serve as a mentor to all the research laboratory's BIPOC scientists. Once he'd opened the door of opportunity, he felt it was his responsibility to keep it open for others. He was an invaluable resource to Grace as she established a space for herself at the lab.

"Yes, I knew him." Grace cleared her throat. The lobby came into view as she walked beside Cole on the staircase. "I'd earned my master's and PhD from CCSU. Dr. MacIntyre had been my mentor."

"Really?" Cole paused on one of the steps. His voice arced in surprise. "I don't remember your mentioning him."

Grace's eyes slid away from Cole's wide dark gaze. "Haven't I?" She continued down the staircase.

"I'm not surprised." Cole's amused words carried from behind her. "You're very private. I wanted to express my condolences. I didn't know him, but the article made him sound like a remarkable person and a well-regarded scientist."

A fresh wave of grief wrapped around her like a thick, wet blanket. She swallowed the lump in her throat and blinked back the tears in her eyes. "Yes, he was. His students loved him."

At least, most of us did. An image of Trent Mann popped into her mind. Ruby had confirmed the research assistant's alibi, but in Grace's mind, his resentment of Dr. B still cloaked him in suspicion.

She led Cole to the lobby. A glance at her wristwatch let her know it was five-twenty-five. Mal should be here shortly.

Her attention fell on the two young security guards on duty. One sat behind the pale quartz-and-metal counter. Her eyes scanned a trio of monitors that played images captured by strategically positioned cameras inside and outside the building. The other stood a few feet away. He appeared to be splitting his attention between the scene beyond the opaque glass front doors and the lobby.

Grace remembered Mal's observation about security guards. *They focused on our safety so we can focus on* our jobs. His explanation combined with their current situation elevated the respect she had for them.

"Dr. MacIntyre must have been very impressive to have gained your respect." Cole's comments brought her back to their conversation.

She fell into step beside Cole and offered him a slight smile. "Then you must be very impressive, too, since you've also gained my respect."

"That's very kind of you to say." Cole reached forward to hold the door open for her. His cheekbones showed a flush of embarrassment. "I trust you're planning to attend the lab's Spring Fling Fundraiser next week."

Startled, Grace's eyes flew to Cole's. So much had happened during the past week. Dr. B's death, her computer hack, Verna Bleecher's murder, her townhome's break-in, her reunion with Mal. She'd completely forgotten about the fundraiser. But on her grandmother's recommendation, she'd bought a new dress for the occasion. Melba didn't think it would be a good idea for her to keep wearing the same outfit to every event. Regardless of how attractive—or expensive—the dress was, it wouldn't be a good look to wear the same one.

Grace stepped through the door Cole held open for her. "Um, yes. I'm going." Hopefully. *If we're able to identify the computer hacker turned murderer who's trying to get my formulation.*

Cole followed her out. "Good. It will help your career and the financial support you receive from the executive leadership if they see you outside the office, socializing with our donors."

Grace winced on the inside. She'd been to every MARS Spring Fling since she'd join the lab four years ago. These events were vital to the company and her research. Grace understood that. Still, she'd much rather be in the lab—or with Mal.

She stopped just outside the door and swept her eyes across the parking lot, looking for Mal's car. "I know, Cole." She turned to him. "You give me the same pep talk every year."

"That's because I want to make sure you understand what's at stake." He gave her a sober stare. "These events provide the right environment to help management see you as a three-dimensional member of the company. You're one of our best and brightest researchers—maybe *the* best and brightest. But you need that extra networking to get their support for your projects. Not just money but buy-in. Do you understand?"

"I do, Cole. I promise. That's why I've been attending every year."

"Good." Cole finally smiled. "Have a good evening." He disappeared around the corner as he marched to the company's parking lot.

Then everything happened so fast. A white van screeched to a stop in front of the building. Startled, Grace spun toward the sound. A tall, thin figure dressed in black from ski mask to shoes jumped out of the open side door.

What the...? Who the...?

Her thoughts were jumbled except for one clear message: *Run!*

She spun around.

Get to the guard's desk!

Grace reached for the door.

Too late!

Two arms locked around her waist in a vise and pressed her to a hard torso. Male. Air shot from her lungs. *Whoosh!* A hand pressed against her mouth. She smelled old leather and too much cologne. Fear tried to paralyze her—until she remembered she wasn't power-less. She wasn't voiceless. She wasn't going without a fight.

Grace raised her legs together to make herself heavier. She sank her teeth into his palm. Her attacker grunted in pain. Vicious satisfaction rushed through her. He dropped his hand. Grace released a scream that could've been heard in the next ZIP code.

"Grace!" Mal's voice was fury and fear.

Both guards slammed through the front doors.

The would-be kidnapper dropped Grace to the side-walk. He turned to climb back into the van. Mal leaped at him, knocking him to the ground. The white van pulled away from the sidewalk and out of the parking lot.

"Call 911!" Mal commanded as he struggled with the assailant.

Grace hurried to help him as the female guard called the police. She used the belt from her spring coat to tie the criminal's wrists while Mal and the male security guard held him.

The female guard stepped forward. "The police are on their way."

Grace ripped off the villain's mask. He looked to be in his early twenties. Stringy brown hair was tan-gled around a thin white face and fell just past narrow shoulders. Angry brown eyes were set on either side of a large hawklike nose above a five-o'clock shadow.

"You!" Mal narrowed his eyes. "You were following us on CCSU's campus."

"She bit me." The attempted kidnapper glared at Grace.

She glared back. "Who are you working for?"

Thin pink lips twisted into a mocking smile. He remained silent.

Grace arched an eyebrow. "The police are coming, but your driver's gone. Do you really think *anyone's* going to help you?"

His smile disappeared.

Mal stood to tower over her assailant. He helped Grace to her feet. "That's OK. He doesn't have to talk to us. He can save it for the police."

Grace felt another surge of satisfaction at the fear in the young man's eyes.

I couldn't keep her safe.

That thought had tortured Mal since the police had arrived to take Grace's would-be kidnapper into custody. He hadn't been able to drown out the accusation.

Grace led Mal from his kitchen into his family room Friday evening. She balanced a hot mug of black tea between her palms as though she needed its warmth. "Do you think someone was waiting for me to show up at the lab, or do you think we're being watched?"

"It's more likely that someone had staked out your lab. And probably also your home, so you're definitely not going back there until the killer is caught." Mal carried his own mug of tea into the room. He took a deep drink of the beverage.

"You won't get any argument from me." Grace's tone was somber. "Thank you very much for your hospitality."

"Of course." He didn't want to think about her going through this alone. "The kidnappers were bold. They didn't hesitate to grab you right in front of the lab. They didn't care who saw them trying to abduct you. They were well choreographed and prepared."

Grace nodded. "You're referring to their masks. I agree. That could indicate they've done something like this before."

"Luckily, they weren't prepared for your ability to defend yourself." Restless movements carried Mal across the hardwood flooring. They'd finished cleaning the kitchen after a light dinner of grilled cheese sandwiches and salad. Neither of them had had much of an appetite. The aftershocks of the danger they'd faced less than two hours ago were still reverberating through Mal. Based on the way she'd played with her food, he had a feeling Grace was anxious also. What could he do to help her through this?

He didn't even know how to get himself through it. How long would it take to forever banish the memory of her being carried to an unmarked van by a masked abductor?

Grace interrupted his thoughts. "It felt wrong to withhold information from Eriq and Taylor."

Mal stood beside the dark wood fireplace. He placed his elbow on the mantel to help steady himself. "You were quick on your feet, telling Duster about intellectual property theft in the pharmaceutical industry when he asked why someone would want to kidnap you."

Grace swallowed some of her tea as she wandered away from the front entrance, which was the same dark wood as the mantel. "I was being consistent. I'd given him that reasoning when he'd asked why someone would hack my computer. Between my grandmother's life, our lives and your brothers', there's too much at stake to tell people the truth."

"I agree. Dr. B and Verna were innocent bystand-ers who were murdered because the killer thought they were in the way." Mal drank his tea. It was hot, strong and just sweet enough. Warmth was returning to his limbs.

Grace took a shuddering breath. "As frightening and terrible as this experience was, at least it's brought us closer to identifying the killer."

"But the kidnapper's lawyered up." Mal pushed away from the mantel to pace again. "Unless the police can get him to give up who hired him, we aren't any closer today to solving this case than we were yesterday."

"They'll get him to talk." Grace sounded distracted. She frowned into her mug. "His partner is free, but the detectives are holding *him* on assault and attempted kidnapping."

Mal searched Grace's delicate features. Attempted kidnapping was too close to actual abduction.

I couldn't keep her safe.

What would he have done if Grace hadn't freed her-self from her assailant? That question was going to fea-ture prominently in his series of nightmares tonight.

He'd called Zeke from the police precinct. His older brother had been concerned for Grace's safety and furi-ous that someone had tried to harm her. He'd promised to update Jerry. Zeke hadn't said anything about Mal not being able to keep Grace safe, but Mal was angry enough with himself for both of them.

He briefly squeezed his eyes closed. "I don't know if I'll ever recover from seeing someone trying to drag you into that van." His knees shook. Mal let himself drop onto the black faux-leather recliner closest to the fireplace before he fell. "I'm going to relive that waking nightmare for God knows how long."

The white van had cut him off as he'd turned into the Midwest Area Research Systems's entrance to get to Grace as he'd promised he would. That reckless act seemed to foreshadow something bad.

Then everything had happened at once. He'd sped after the unmarked vehicle, arriving in time to see the kidnapper snatch Grace from the sidewalk, intent on carrying her to the van's open sliding door. After throwing his SUV into Park, he'd raced to her rescue. He'd pushed all his strength into his limbs. Still, he hadn't moved fast enough. But Grace had freed herself. The guards had appeared. And with a final surge, Mal had stopped the kidnapper before he'd gotten back into the vehicle.

Grace crossed to the matching overstuffed sofa. "That makes two of us. I was so scared I couldn't think."

"You were doing fine." Mal rose to sit beside Grace on the sofa. He shifted to face her. "I, on the other hand, was a wreck. Seeing someone grab you right off the street was one of the worst moments in my life. I literally felt my heart stop."

Grace massaged her neck. "I'd walked out with a coworker. It was only minutes before you were to arrive. I was standing in front of the building. The guards could see me. The cameras could record me. I thought I'd be safe."

Mal shook his head, moving closer. "You didn't do anything wrong. I'm just telling you how I felt and that I don't ever want to feel that way again." His voice cracked with more emotion than he could bear.

Grace cupped the side of his face. Her palm was

warm against his skin. "I was scared, but I knew I wasn't alone. I knew you were coming to help me, if I could only hold on."

Mal covered her hand with his. "You trusted me. Thank you." Turning his head, he kissed her palm.

Grace turned his face back to hers. "Always."

The look in her eyes mesmerized him. They glinted with trust and glowed with attraction. Grace didn't give her trust easily. To know she trusted him meant everything to Mal.

"Thank you." Mal's voice was soft, hesitant to lose the moment.

He leaned toward her, pressing his mouth to hers. She was intoxicatingly sweet and soft. Her lips were warm and moist. Her scent filled his head, shutting out everything but the way she felt in his arms, the way she tasted. It blocked out the fear, anger and uncertainty.

"Mal." Grace shifted closer to him. The heat from her body warmed him.

"Mm-hmm."

Her small, soft hands slid up his torso, causing his muscles to shudder. She twined her arms around his neck and pressed even closer. Her lips opened for him. Mal swept his tongue inside her mouth. Her moan was an invitation to explore a while longer, a little deeper.

She caught his tongue and drew him in. Mal's groan echoed hers. His hand slipped beneath her linen brown skirt, over her firm thigh. He traced her rounded hip and curved over her firm waist beneath her cream-colored cotton blouse. His heart beat fast and heavy in his chest. His breathing quickened as his hand drifted farther up her torso. Her breast was soft and warm against his hand. His palm burned as he cupped its weight.

Grace moved restlessly. "Mal." She sighed his name into his mouth.

Mal drew his lips away from hers. "Mmm. You taste so good."

He trailed slow kisses down her neck. Her head fell back. The warmth of her body reached out and wrapped around him. Mal followed the arch of her elegant neck to her collarbone and beyond. He breathed in her scent. It was like a drug. Mal traced his tongue over the first soft, generous curve of her breast.

Grace shivered in his arms. "Mal."

"Mmm. Hmm."

"Mal, I need to slow down." Her words were breathless.

Six words he'd hoped not to hear. Mal leaned his forehead against hers and breathed. Then breathed again. "Of course."

"I'm sorry." Her voice was low.

"Don't be." He lowered his arms and stood. His knees were unsteady. "I'm the one who should apologize. Excuse me."

Mal turned and walked with deliberate steps to the staircase. He added another reason to the growing list of reasons for catching the killer: keeping his heart safe.

Chapter 13

"I'm all right, Grace." Melba's image on the videoconference Friday night showed her relaxed on an armchair beside Jerry in her living room. Her opening statement couldn't be a good sign.

Grace's heart pounded so hard she could hear it. "Gran, what happened?"

She and Mal were using his laptop to join the virtual meeting. They sat beside each other at his dining table.

"Jerry's team stopped an attempt to kidnap her." Zeke delivered the bombshell news in a somber tone. She couldn't tell where he was. The room he was using must be in his home.

"What?" Grace lunged to her feet. Mentally, she was making arrangements to fly to her grandmother's side. She looked down at the screen. "How are you? What happened?"

Melba made a *tsk*ing sound. "That's why the first

thing I said was 'I'm fine.' I didn't want you to worry."
She gestured toward the camera. "Sit down, sweetheart."

Grace dropped onto her chair. Her knees shook with
relief. Her grandmother was safe. But she sensed beneath her brave words, Melba was more shaken than
she was letting on. The attempt to abduct Grace had
reinforced the situation's danger for her. It must've had
the same effect on her grandmother.

"The attempt happened during dinner." Jerry's demeanor was much more serious tonight. "A woman
claiming to be you signed in at the front desk. Fortunately, the guard on duty checked your photo and realized she was an impostor. The guard asked the impostor
for identification, but she ran. That's when the guard
signaled the alarm, but the impostor had already disappeared. We've added a second guard to accompany
Aunt Melba twenty-four-seven, even inside the facility."

"I don't need *two* guards following me everywhere."
Melba crossed her arms. "I'm not the president."

Grace frowned. "Gran, Jerry's the professional. If
he says you need another guard, then you need another
guard." Even if Jerry hadn't said that, Grace would have
insisted on increasing her grandmother's protection.

"I'm sorry." Jerry expelled a breath. He looked from
Grace through the camera to Melba beside him. "I
promised to protect you as though you were my mother,
but tonight, I almost lost you—"

Melba cut him off. "'Almost.' That's the key. You
didn't lose me. Stop blaming yourself for something
you didn't do."

"Gran's right." Grace held Jerry's eyes through the
computer. "You had the foresight to give the residence's

guards photos of me, Mal, Zeke and the contractors. If you hadn't done that, tonight's impostor could've gotten through." She rubbed her arms to remove the chill. "You kept your promise. You protected my grandmother, and for that, I'm so very grateful." Tears stung her eyes.

Mal reached over, wrapping his large right hand around her left forearm. She met his eyes. Empathy and gratitude warmed them, and something else that she couldn't handle right now. She looked away.

Melba put her hand on Jerry's arm. "I'm grateful, too."

Her comment brought weak smiles to everyone's faces.

Zeke inclined his head toward his camera. "Jerry has an artist working with the guard to create a sketch of the impostor. He'll post copies of it around the center, and get some to the police and the media."

Mal crossed his arms over his broad chest. "That sounds good. Now, there's another issue to address. Grace was almost kidnapped today as well. So the question is—"

"How many people are after Grace's formula?" Zeke's voice was grim.

Melba leaned toward the monitor she shared with Jerry. Her eyes were wide with fear; her lips were parted in shock. "You were almost kidnapped? Why am I only hearing about this now?"

Grace extended her hand. "We tried to call you, Gran. You and Jerry must've been dealing with the impostor."

With Mal's help, she updated her grandmother and Jerry on her attempted abduction, which happened at the same time the impostor had arrived at the center.

They concluded their account with the kidnapper's request for a public defender.

Melba dropped her face into her cupped palms. Her voice was muffled. "Oh my Lord."

"Luckily, you insisted Pam and I learn self-defense before we left for college." Grace's voice was comforting. "And I kept up my training."

"All along, we thought we were dealing with one person." Mal's words brought them back to the case. "Apparently, there are more."

"And they're working together." Jerry balanced his elbows on the arms of his chair and steepled his hands beneath his chin.

Grace shivered at the reminder. "But if they were going to use my grandmother to pressure me into giving them the formula, why would they also need to take me?"

"To get you away from your bodyguard." The look of determination in Mal's eyes was hypnotic. "They wanted to isolate both of you, hoping that would make you more cooperative."

Grace pulled her attention from him. "It's challenging enough identifying one suspect. How're we going to find a link between both attempted kidnappings?"

Mal shrugged his eyebrows. "We already have a link between Trent and his mother."

Some of Grace's tension eased. "Good point."

Zeke inclined his head. "I may find others as I continue the background checks. Let me know if there are names I should add to the list."

They ended the videoconference with an agreement to follow up the next night.

Grace surged to her feet, stepping away from the

dining table. "My grandmother's in danger and it's my fault."

"That's not true." Mal gave a forceful denial.

Grace spun on him, struggling against the urge to start a fight. "Then whose fault is it?"

Mal swung his arm toward the front door. "The people who are trying to steal what doesn't belong to them."

Grace threw up her arms. "But they're after my formula because I created a *weapon of mass destruction*." She stormed past him into his family room and dropped onto the sofa.

Mal followed her. "You're correcting that."

"So what?" She looked up at him. "Fixing my mistake doesn't make it so that the weaponized form never existed. So we catch this serial murderer this time. How many more will there be?"

Mal shook his head, looking at her in confusion. "No one else knows about the formula."

Grace stood from the sofa and strode across the room. "Someone found out this time. How do I know it won't happen again?"

"If it does, we'll stop them, too." Mal's determination was reassuring, but Grace was only half listening. "We'll keep you safe, Grace—you and your grandmother."

She met his eyes over her shoulder. His words came so easily. Was he telling her what she wanted to hear, or did he really believe what he was saying? "For how long?"

Mal took a step toward her. "For as long as you need me."

His promise would keep him in her life. Was he saying he was willing to give her another chance? To give *them* another chance?

It felt good to have someone who believed in her. To have someone to whom she could vent her fears and concerns. The determination in Mal's eyes gave her confidence. The faith in his voice stiffened her spine. She wanted that kind of encouragement in her corner all the time. Mal had tried to give her his support four years ago but she'd mistreated him. How could she convince him that wouldn't happen again?

Grace shook her head, hurrying to the staircase. "I'm sorry. I need some time alone. Excuse me."

Grace wanted a relationship with Mal as badly as she wanted to develop a better treatment protocol for diabetes. But could she find a way to fit both into her life?

Grace opened the door of the guest bathroom late Friday night. A cloud of steam preceded her into the hallway. It carried the familiar scent of Mal's soap. As she tightened the belt of her sage green terry cloth bathrobe around her waist, she stepped into the hallway and almost into Mal's broad chest.

He caught her arms to steady her. "Careful." There was laughter in his voice.

"Excuse me." A startled smile eased her features. Then her eyes met his. Beneath her fingertips, his biceps flexed. Her smile faded, replaced by uncertainty and a stirring of need. She reminded herself to breathe. "I'm sorry about the long shower. I thought it would help clear my head."

"You don't have to apologize for taking a shower." Mal held on to her arms, keeping her close as the moist warmth from her shower swam out of the room to encircle them. "I remember you telling me they helped you think."

How had he remembered that? She didn't even remember telling him.

"That's true." Her fingertips brushed his biceps.
Intentionally? "I realized I haven't properly thanked
you and your brothers for taking such good care of my
grandmother and me. Thank you so very much. My
grandmother's precious to me. I appreciate everything
you're doing to keep her safe."

Grace leaned forward, drawn by the heat in his eyes
and the butterflies in her belly. She rose up on her toes
and pressed her lips to his cheek. A small thank-you.
His skin was warm and rough with stubble. She settled back on her feet. The yearning in Mal's eyes stole
her breath.

"You're welcome." His voice was soft, hypnotic.

Wrapping his right arm around her waist, he drew
her closer to him. Grace didn't protest. She didn't resist.
She rested her hands on his shoulders and tipped her
head back. Mal covered her mouth with his and swept
his tongue inside. Bold, demanding, searching. Grace
parted her lips and welcomed him.

An inferno exploded in the pit of her stomach. The
fire consumed her, spreading heat throughout her body
and making her skin burn. She hadn't felt this fevered,
restless hunger since the last time Mal had held her in
his arms this way.

Grace lifted onto her toes again. She needed to be
closer to him. She twined her arms behind his neck,
held on as the fire burned. Grace sent her tongue after
Mal's, sucking it deeper into her, stroking its length as
her thighs quivered. Mal lifted her higher, cupping her
derriere and pressing her hard against him. Grace felt
his need in the hard bulge beneath his zipper. She'd done

that. Grace moaned her satisfaction deep in her throat. Her toes curled. Desire burned hotter. She wrapped her legs around his narrow hips and moved herself against him.

Mal tore his mouth from hers. His dark eyes singed her. His voice was gruff. "I want you now."

"What's stopping you?"

Fierce satisfaction sharpened his expression. Two strides carried her over the threshold into his room. Mal stopped at the foot of his bed. Grace lowered her legs from his hips. Before her feet touched the ground, Mal had tugged her bathrobe off her. It pooled at her feet.

His throat worked as he swallowed. "My God. You're even more beautiful than I remember."

Grace's nipples tightened under his regard. She helped pull his clothes off between bold caresses and deep kisses. Once he was naked, she stood back to look at him. He was broad shoulders, flat stomach, slim hips and long legs.

"You're perfect." She reached out, drawing her hand over his torso to cup his erection.

Grace sank to her knees. She held Mal's gaze as she drew him into her mouth. He squeezed his eyes shut and groaned deep in his throat as she wrapped her lips around him. His erection was hard and hot. Grace worked it with her lips, hands and tongue. Mal's rapid breaths urged her on.

"Wait." He stepped back.

With one motion, he lifted her from the floor and tossed her onto the bed. She landed with a bounce. Mal knelt between her knees. He lifted her legs onto his shoulders and brought her hips to his tongue. Grace gasped as pleasure radiated up her thighs and over her torso. Her nipples puckered. Her hips pumped. Her head pressed back into the mattress. Grace gripped the bedsheets in her fists, pulling them as her body stretched tighter and tighter and tighter, until she exploded. Mal gave her one last kiss before lowering her legs.

Mal ached as he watched Grace's lithe body tremble in her climax. A thin sheen of perspiration covered her brown skin. Her puckered nipples begged for his kisses. He slid up her body, feeling her muscles trembling beneath him, and he answered their plea. Grace moaned. Mal's heart pounded in his chest.

He reached into the nightstand beside the bed and felt for a condom. He ripped open the packet and sheathed himself. Mal returned to Grace, kissing her deeply. He drew his hand over her body, pausing to stroke her breasts, tease her nipples, caress her hips. He pressed his hands between her thighs; she was still wet. Mal ended their kiss. He drew her under him. Using his knee, he separated her thighs and slid inside her. Grace gasped and lifted her hips to meet him. Mal gritted his teeth. She was so hot, so tight. So good. Her scent clouded his thoughts. He closed his eyes at the painful pleasure. He cupped her hips with his hands, thrusting deeper. The pressure was building. His pulse beat in his throat.

"Mal." She sighed his name.

"Come with me, Grace." He breathed the plea against her ear.

Mal slipped his hand between them. He touched her, and Grace cried out in pleasure. She dug her fingertips into his shoulders before drawing them down his back. Her climax broke against him, pulling him over the edge. Mal pumped his hips against her. Grace pressed her hands against his hips and arched into him. He held her close as the storm raged, wave after wave, crashing over them as they trembled in each other's arms.

Chapter 14

I'm in love with Malachi Touré. Again.

Still?

Oh. No.

The memories of his touch hadn't overwhelmed her. Passion alone hadn't made the ache to be with him so strong. She was here because she loved him. And she'd have to walk away from him again. Grace swallowed as she remembered the pain she'd felt the first time she left Mal. She didn't want to relive that. She *couldn't* relive that.

"Are you all right?" Mal's soft voice was loud in the silent darkness.

Grace jumped. "Yes. I'm fine. How are you?" She winced at her stilted response. She wanted to pull the covers over her head.

"You're so quiet. What are you thinking about?"

Oh boy. She didn't want to have this conversation.

"I don't regret what happened. Not one minute of it. But I don't think we should complicate what we have."

"What do we have?" Mal's voice lacked inflection.

Grace gritted her teeth. He was going to make this harder than it already was. She shifted onto her side to face him. She could barely make out his features in the dark room. "I think we should keep our relationship professional. We're dealing with a very dangerous situation. Tonight we learned we're facing multiple killers, not just one. We need to keep our wits about us."

The temperature in the room took a sudden drop. The rustling of sheets broke the silence as Mal shifted on the mattress and got out of bed.

He spoke over his shoulder as he strode toward his adjoining bathroom. "Speaking of keeping our wits about us, I'm hungry. We missed dinner."

It was like a wall had suddenly sprung up between them. Grace hadn't meant for that to happen. She hadn't meant to fall in love with him again, either. This time, she knew it would be even harder to walk away. "I'll help you fix something."

"Thanks." Mal's tone was flat. He shut the bathroom door with a firm snap.

Reluctant to turn on the light, Grace rolled out of bed, gathered her robe, then hurried to the guest bathroom to clean up and dress. She'd told him it had been wonderful. They'd been wonderful together. Again. Her body still hummed from his touch. She bit her lip as an echo of the way he'd made her feel rolled over her. She took a breath and pulled her robe back on. Grace hesitated before pulling open the door. After making sure the hallway was empty, she hurried to her guest room to get properly dressed. She chose unattractive pale gray sweatpants, an oversized powder blue T-shirt and dark green slipper socks.

Get yourself together, Grace. Malachi Touré was a distraction. A wonderful, exciting, challenging, intelligent, caring, sexy distraction—but still a distraction. She needed to keep her mind on her research project and her quest to save lives.

Minutes later, Grace joined Mal in the kitchen. She forced herself through the wall of awkwardness to stand beside him at the stove. He was preparing to make one of his omelets, which she remembered were almost as delicious as he was. The raw eggs sizzled as he poured his mixture into the frying pan. He covered the pan to help the omelet cook.

"What can I do to help?"

He turned to her with empty eyes that ripped another hole in her heart. His voice was devoid of inflection. "Could you set the table?"

"Of course." She drew silverware and napkins from the drawers before crossing to the table to position the place mats. After four days in his home, she was able to navigate the kitchen. "There's something I've been wondering. You told me your parents started Touré Security Group out of your home."

"That's right." Mal tucked two slices of whole-grain bread into the toaster.

The scent of eggs, butter, cheese, onions and garlic escaped from the pan and expanded across the room.

"Were they inspired to start the company because of their military service?"

"Yes. They'd learned a lot about identifying weaknesses in security and systems coverage, and resolving those issues."

Grace filled two glasses with crushed ice and iced tea, then placed them on the table. "You and your brothers were really young when you started helping with the company."

"At first, we helped with the administrative stuff: sorting mail, answering the phone, updating the filing." A ghost of a smile touched his lips. "Jerry would repeatedly ask for copies of the state's child labor laws."

Surprised laughter burst from Grace. "I haven't known Jerry long, but I could easily imagine him doing that."

Mal laughed with affection. The awkwardness between them eased. Grace knew it wasn't completely gone, but at least it was more manageable.

The bread popped up in the toaster as Mal checked the omelets. She brought him the plates. It was a pure pleasure watching his tall, long-legged, broad-shouldered form move around the kitchen. She thought she heard music with every move he made.

"My parents made us equal partners in the business." Mal stepped aside and followed Grace to the kitchen table. "I'm wondering if it was a last punishment from them. Getting Zeke and Jerry to agree on anything requires diplomatic skills far beyond my training."

Grace took her seat on the far side of the table. "I thought I sensed some tension between them."

"Jerry thinks he has to prove himself to Zeke." Mal sat across the table from Grace. "All. The. Time. I think it's some version of the Youngest Brother / Eldest Brother Syndrome. I thought he would've grown out of it by now. It gets on my nerves."

"Maybe you need to talk with him again." Grace ate

a forkful of the omelet. It was fluffy and flavorful. She hadn't realized how hungry she was until that first bite.

"I've talked with him and with Zeke a bunch of times. Their arguing never stops. If anything, it's gotten worse. It always gets worse. The last time this happened, I left the company and moved to Chicago." His eyes said the rest: *And met you.*

Grace looked away. "The hostility between your brothers is the reason you moved to Chicago. You never mentioned that."

Mal flexed his broad shoulders beneath his black T-shirt before swallowing another bite of omelet. "I didn't think their dysfunction would impress you. Besides, their bickering didn't have anything to do with my parents or me."

"Have things between your brothers improved since you've been back?"

"Nope. They're still in top form. If juvenile squabbling was an Olympic event, they'd take the gold."

Despite his mocking tone, Grace could tell his siblings' rivalry was a heavy burden for Mal. And why wouldn't it be? With his parents' deaths, Zeke and Jerry were the only family Mal had left. Grace knew how that felt. With her father's desertion, and her mother's and Pam's deaths, her grandmother was all she had. Grace couldn't imagine what Mal was going through, refereeing battles between his only living relatives. She and her sister had always been close. Mal's grief made Grace want to knock Zeke's and Jerry's heads together. As pleasing as that thought might be, she set it aside and concentrated on a more constructive way to help Mal.

He continued. "And now I'm concerned that Jerry wants to leave the company."

Grace's heart leaped into her throat at the thought of the Touré Security Group going out of business. Ever. "Because of Zeke?"

Mal shrugged again. "I don't know. He won't talk about it. Meanwhile, Zeke wants to change the direction of the business and focus on bigger companies and richer contracts."

"Sounds like your company's in for a lot of changes." Grace noticed the tension lines bracketing his mouth and eyes. "What do *you* want?"

Mal held her eyes for a long, silent moment before dropping his attention to his almost-empty plate. "My parents founded this company to serve smaller businesses—the mom-and-pop stores that couldn't afford the high-tech solutions but still needed security systems. I want to stay true to that."

Grace nodded. "Could Touré Security serve both the smaller companies as well as the larger ones? Instead of having a flat rate for each service, perhaps you could offer tiered rates per service, depending on the size of the company?"

Mal gave her a slow smile that made her toes curl in her slipper socks. "That would make sense. Larger companies would require more resources for our services anyway. I'll discuss that with Zeke and Jer. Thanks for the suggestion."

"You're welcome." Grace felt the pulse in her throat flutter. "I hope everything works out. Your company's very special, Mal. It's the legacy your parents built and nurtured for you and your brothers. The three of you grew up in it. It would be heartbreaking if you had to let it go, for any reason. You owe it to your parents to do everything in your power to keep your family's company thriving. Fight for it."

Mal's throat worked as he held her eyes. "That's exactly how I feel. Thank you for understanding."

"You're welcome." Her voice was husky with emotion.

After all he and his brothers had done for her and her grandmother, it felt good to help Mal find a solution to a problem he was struggling with. If only she could do the same with her own. What could she do to find a successful balance between her promise to her sister to develop a cost-effective diabetes treatment and sharing her life with the person who'd proven he would never let her down?

"How was your run?" Grace searched her grandmother's features through the video on her cell phone early Saturday morning. She was looking for signs of fear or discomfort. Instead, Melba's dark brown eyes gleamed with satisfaction. Her warm brown cheeks were flushed with vitality. Grace could almost convince herself the account of someone impersonating her in an attempt to kidnap her grandmother had been a nightmare. Almost, except for the fact someone had tried to kidnap her, too.

"It was great." A triumphant grin flashed across Melba's round face. "One of Jerry's bodyguards joined me. We just ran around the grounds because it's safer than the open streets. But at least we were outside in this beautiful weather."

"I'm jealous." Grace sighed. "I haven't been able to run outside since the day of the break-in." Four days of running on the treadmill in Mal's basement. It was getting old.

She'd meant to talk with Mal about that during breakfast this morning, but things were still a little strained between them after last night. So she'd helped him clean up after their breakfast, wished him a good day and then called her grandmother to make sure she was well after yesterday's scare.

Melba chuckled. "They tried to keep me indoors today, too, but I made a fuss. The bodyguard's a young woman about your age. She understood, and when we got outside, I made her push me. She was surprised I was able to keep up as well as I did. Had to stop and walk a few times to catch my breath, but it felt great."

"You have everyone fooled, Gran." Grace smiled. "Did you tell her you get me to push you when we jog together?"

Melba snorted. "Of course not. With all these people underfoot, I have to have some secrets."

At eighty-five, her grandmother was still an avid jogger. She claimed to have kept to the same routine since before Grace's mother was born. She did strength training and ran a respectable number of miles six days a week. On the seventh day, she did yoga to stretch her muscles and rest her legs.

The weight on her shoulders grew heavier. "I'm so sorry to have turned your life upside down. And I can't even tell you how much longer this will continue."

But it had already been nine days since the hack, five days since they'd started their investigation. They were rapidly closing in on the two-week timeframe her chief science officer had given her to catch the hacker/murderer.

"No one can." Melba scowled. "And none of this is your fault."

Grace looked away from her cell phone. That's what Mal had said, too, but neither he nor her grandmother could absolve her of blame for this situation. "How can you say that? This entire situation is a direct result of a mistake I made. If I'd been better at my job—more focused—none of this would've happened."

"Does it ever occur to you that you're *too* focused on your job?" Melba arched a newly shaped eyebrow, courtesy of her recent trip to the salon.

"Gran—"

Melba cut her off. "You work twenty hours a day, seven days a week. If I didn't check on you, you wouldn't eat. If I didn't bully you, you wouldn't sleep. You're not a machine, Grace Anne."

Whoa. The Middle-Name Treatment. "I made a promise to Pam. It's too late for me to help her, but I have to keep my promise."

Melba gestured toward the screen. "Do you think this is what Pam would want for you? *No one* expects you to be a machine. *No one* expects you to give up your life to find a cure for diabetes."

"I know that."

"You don't act like you do." Melba shook her head. "I want you to be happy, Gracie. Pam would want you to be happy. What will it take for you to realize Pam never blamed you?"

"I know Pam didn't blame me." Grace clenched and unclenched her hand out of sight of her grandmother. "*I* blame me. I should've tried harder, worked faster."

Melba expelled another sigh. The look in her eyes

was familiar. It said she was at her wit's end. "How are things with Mal?"

Grace's cheeks burned as she thought about last night. "Everything's fine. Why?"

Melba searched Grace's face. Suspicion had entered her eyes. "Well, he's looking after my granddaughter. Why wouldn't I want to know how things are going?"

She tried for a casual tone. "We're working well together. At first, he thought I was a damsel in distress. He wanted me to hide instead of letting me help with the investigation. But it didn't take him long to start treating me like an equal partner."

"I'm sure your ability to defend yourself from that kidnapper yesterday helped change his impression of you." Melba's voice was grim. They both were struggling to get past the fear of their attempted abductions.

Grace had had a restless night, plagued by questions and frightened by visions of the danger her grandmother was in. What would have happened if Jerry hadn't been watching over Melba?

"Thank you for listening to me when I asked you to take self-defense classes." Melba gave her a more natural smile. "Have you and Mal had a chance to discuss your past relationship?"

Grace's cheeks burned again. Was her grandmother doing that on purpose? Did she somehow know something had happened between her and Mal? "We've been very busy with the case, on top of our regular jobs. There hasn't been time for anything else." *Mostly.*

"You need to make time, Grace." Melba's sigh held a trace of impatience. "You were so happy with him in Chicago. After years of studying and research, you were finally allowing fun into your life."

Memories of those seven wonderful months brought an ache of longing that started in Grace's chest and grew into her stomach. "But that fun distracted me from my promise to Pam."

Melba closed her eyes briefly. "We've already agreed Pam would want you to be happy." She hesitated. "Grace, it's just you and me now. Your mother died. Pam died. God knows what happened to your father. He hasn't been a part of your life in decades. When I die—"

Panic filled Grace's veins with ice. "Gran, I don't want to think about that."

Melba scowled. "Do you think I do? Ignoring it won't change the facts. I'm worried about you, Grace."

"Me?" She stiffened with surprise. "Why?"

"You don't have any close friends. You don't even have a pet. Who's going to look after you when I'm gone? Who's going to make sure you eat and sleep? Who are you going to turn to when you need someone to talk to? Find the balance in your life. Make time for love."

Grace lowered her eyes, trying to hide her emotions from her grandmother. "This probably isn't the best time for this conversation."

Melba rolled her eyes. "It's not as though this is the first time we're having it. Gracie, all I'm saying is it's been four years. It's past time to forgive yourself. You didn't let anyone down. Pam loved you. Bringing balance to your life and being happy is the best way to honor her memory."

Her sister had been her protector, her loudest cheerleader, her champion. Her grandmother was right: Pam would want her to be happy. She would have forgiven Grace. But how did Grace start to forgive herself?

She swallowed, easing her dry throat. "You're right, Gran. But I'm beginning to think happiness with Mal has passed me by."

"We appreciate you both coming in this morning." Eriq led Mal and Grace into a small, brightly lit conference room toward the front of the police station Monday. Taylor strode beside him.

Mal detected the scent of apples from the plug-in air freshener in the back of the room. He followed Grace across the threshold. He held out her chair as she took a seat on the opposite side of the rectangular blond-wood table from the detectives. He sat beside her.

His actions were in keeping with the good manners his parents had taught him. They also allowed him to assess Grace's reaction. She seemed calm. But there were telltale signs he knew her well enough to look for. The angle of her chin, the narrowing of her eyes, her stillness. The more uncertain Grace felt, the more assertive she became. It was as though she was overcompensating.

"You sounded urgent on the phone." Mal hoped the reminder would hurry Eriq to the point. What did the detectives want?

His attention shifted to Taylor. Her yellow blouse was a sharp contrast to her dark green jacket. Why had the homicide detectives investigating Dr. B's and Verna's murders contacted them? Mal wasn't under any illusions. This might be a more comfortable room, but he and Grace were definitely being interrogated.

Eriq adjusted the navy bolo he'd worn with his dark jacket and conservative white shirt. He fixed his attention on Grace. "Why would someone want to kidnap you?"

Grace didn't flinch. It was as though she'd prepared for his question. "As I explained Friday, I don't know. Mal and I suspect it has something to do with the research someone tried to steal from my computer."

Taylor sat diagonally across the table from Grace. "Had you ever seen the kidnapper before, maybe around your neighborhood?"

"Are you asking whether I'd noticed him following me? No, I hadn't." Grace seemed to shiver. Mal wanted to hold her, but they'd agreed to keep things between them professional.

Eriq leaned back on his seat. The look he gave them made Mal feel like something the cat wouldn't drag in. "What aren't the two of you telling us?"

Mal spread his arms. "You know as much as we do. Someone pretending to be Dr. Bennett MacIntyre tried to hack Grace's computer for research information on a drug she's developing to help treat diabetes. When she contacted Dr. MacIntyre, she learned he'd been killed before he supposedly sent that email. Grace followed the hack into Buckeye Dynamic's intranet. That's when someone killed my client, Verna Bleecher, and broke into Grace's home. Then Friday, someone tried to kidnap Grace and her grandmother, who lives in Florida."

Taylor frowned at Grace. "Your grandmother, too?"

Grace rubbed her upper arms as though the action would magically remove her from this nightmare. "We only learned about that Friday night."

"This must be some kind of formula." Was Eriq trying to draw details of Grace's research from her?

She didn't take his bait. "Why do you think we're withholding information?"

Eriq exchanged a look with Taylor before responding. "Because the man we arrested for attempting to abduct you made bail Saturday night."

Shock surged through Mal. The threat to Grace—and potentially her grandmother—was walking around free? "Why weren't we told?"

"Who posted bail?" Grace asked at the same time.

Taylor addressed Mal. "In their defense, the arresting officers didn't find out about the perp's release until this morning. They were going to notify you, but he was killed last night."

"What?" Mal and Grace spoke in stereo.

The kidnapper's murder after being freed on bail couldn't have been a coincidence. Mal's skin turned cold. He looked at Grace. The color had drained from her face. What did this new development mean for her safety?

Eriq's voice penetrated the buzzing in Mal's ears. "One of his known associates was also found dead last night. We're wondering if this second victim drove the getaway van."

"I didn't see the driver." Grace's voice was weak.

"Neither did I." Mal went through his mental checklist, which included updating Zeke and Jerry, and doing a background check on the kidnapper turned victim.

"It's possible the company's security cameras recorded him." Grace also sounded distracted.

Mal was certain she was thinking about her grandmother. Fortunately, Jerry had already increased Melba's security. He turned to the detectives. "We told the arresting officers about the security cameras. There could be images of the van, maybe even its license plate."

Eriq looked at Taylor. "We'll follow up with them."

Mal shared a look between the partners. "Where did this happen?"

How close had the attacks been to places connected to Grace, either her job, her town house or—worst-case scenario—Mal's home? Were the murders solely to mask the identity of the mastermind behind the attempted abduction, or were they meant to scare Grace into doing something that would jeopardize her safety?

Eriq nodded as though he knew the questions racing across Mal's mind. "The murders happened in separate places. The killer may have wanted to hide the connection between the victims." He paused, looking from Mal to Grace. "Perps think police are stupid. We're not. The kidnapper was found in an alley on the East Side near his apartment. The suspected driver's body was left in a garage near a white van."

Taylor turned her attention from Eriq to Mal and Grace. "Based on what we saw at the crime scenes, the attacks weren't expected. Both vics were shot twice at close range. The kidnapper took one in the leg and one in the head. The driver—*suspected* driver—was shot in the head and knee. There's gunshot residue and dimpling around the head wounds, as though the shooter pressed the gun against the vics' heads."

Beside Mal, Grace shivered in the warm room. She seemed paler than she'd been a moment before. Even the detectives looked concerned at her reaction.

Mal gave in to his greater need and took her hand. It was cold and clammy. "Are you all right? Do you need to step out?"

Grace shook her head, twining her fingers with his. "No, I'll be fine. I'm just not used to hearing about this in real life. It's hard to believe this involves me."

Mal looked again at the detectives across the table. "Based on your description of the crime scene and the wounds, it seems like the attack took the victims by surprise. It also suggests the killer isn't skilled with a gun."

Grace frowned. "What makes you say that?"

Mal saw the fear in her eyes and tightened his hold on her hand. "The first shots must've been the ones to the kidnapper's leg and the suspected driver's knee. Those wounds were meant to disable the victims. Then the shooter went in close for the bullet to the head that they hoped would kill their targets, permanently silencing them to ensure no one could identify them." He looked to Eriq, who was seated across from him. "Did you find anything helpful at the crime scene? Prints, DNA, something to point us in the direction of the killer?"

Eriq arched an eyebrow. "If we had, do you think we would have needed to call you two in?"

No, they wouldn't have. Mal's disappointment was crushing. He'd hoped they were close to catching the person—or people—threatening Grace and her grandmother. Who were they dealing with?

"Who posted bail?" Grace asked again. "Isn't it possible it was the killer?"

"That's our theory, too." Taylor gestured between Eriq and herself. "But the public defender doesn't know who posted bail. He got a call telling him to expect a courier with cash to cover the bail. We're following up with the courier and tracing the call."

"Keep us posted on what you know." Eriq got to his feet. Taylor stood with him. "We'll do the same."

Mal rose and inclined his head. "Thank you."

For the detectives to share information with outsiders meant they were struggling to solve the case. They weren't alone. The only clarity Mal had was his need to keep Grace and her grandmother safe. To do that, he had to identify the threat. But how?

Chapter 15

"The kidnapper must've known more than we thought he knew." Grace leaned in close to Mal as they used his cell phone to update his brothers and her grandmother via videoconference after their meeting with the homicide detectives late Monday morning.

"And maybe more than *he* thought he knew." Mal spoke from the driver's seat of his SUV.

After leaving the precinct, Mal and Grace had driven to Buckeye Dynamic Devices. It had been their destination this morning before getting Eriq's call requesting their presence at the precinct. Grace had included Dr. Roberta George on her original list of suspects. One of Dr. B's most promising former students, Dr. George was now a biological sciences researcher with the defense contractor. Roberta's division would benefit from Grace's research, and that benefit would most likely lead to a promotion for Roberta.

Roberta also had been a guest at Dr. B's table during the fundraiser. As such, she'd had access to the promotional thumb drive Grace received at the event.

Grace turned to look at Mal and found herself even closer to him than she'd thought. Her eyes dropped to his lips. They parted. A rush of heat shot through her at the invitation.

"What makes you think the kidnapper knew more than he thought he did?" Her grandmother's voice snatched Grace from the brink of doing something potentially unwise.

Startled, she leaned away from Mal and his talented lips.

He cleared his throat and looked away from Grace. "Because he's dead. He must've thought his silence would keep him alive, but the killer didn't want to take that risk. If the kidnapper didn't know anything incriminating, leaving him alive wouldn't have been a risk."

From his desk in his office, Zeke nodded his agreement. "The same goes for the victim the detectives think was the getaway driver."

Jerry spoke from his seat beside Melba. His tone was dry. "The killer must really want us to believe the second victim was the van driver. Why else would they go to the trouble of leaving his body beside a white van? It's like a billboard stating, 'These are the patsies you were looking for.'"

Grace caught Jerry's *Star Wars* reference. He'd paraphrased Obi-Wan Kenobi's line from *Star Wars: A New Hope*. Was *Star Wars* fandom something else the brothers shared? She took a moment to sink into the memory of watching a *Star Wars* marathon with Mal before returning her attention to the meeting.

Zeke was speaking. He pinched the bridge of his nose. "I agree with you, Jerry. Now the question is whether the killer will also come after the woman who'd tried to impersonate Grace?"

Mal grunted. "Especially since the guard on duty was able to provide a sketch good enough to give to the police and the media outlets."

Jerry spread his hands. "I've alerted the police. They're already getting tips from people who think they know the woman in the sketch. I've also updated our team here, so everyone's being extra vigilant."

Grace took her first easy breath of the day. She blinked her stinging eyes. "Thank you for taking such good care of my grandmother."

Melba sniffed. "Are you kidding? I'm the best client he's ever had."

Jerry glanced at Melba before giving Grace a cheeky grin. "Aunt Melba and I have become good friends. She talks about you a lot."

Oh, good Lord. "On that note, Mal and I need to speak with Dr. George. I'll check on you later, Gran."

They made plans to conference again in the evening unless another urgent situation arose. Grace hoped to avoid more of those. They were dealing with enough.

She climbed out of Mal's vehicle and joined him as they crossed Buckeye Dynamic Devices's parking lot.

"What's your plan for getting Dr. George to agree to speak with us?" He glanced at her as they strode to the entrance of the defense contractor's building.

Grace tossed him a teasing look. "I'm going to ask to see her."

Mal's thick eyebrows leaped up his forehead. "You think it'll be that easy?"

She smiled at his confusion. "We're CCSU alumnae. That connection matters." She sobered. "And we were both Dr. B's mentees."

Mal's hand on her shoulder brought them both to a halt. "She could also be his killer."

Grace closed her eyes and exhaled, gathering her resolve. "I'll cross that bridge if we get to it."

She'd never been to Buckeye Dynamic Devices. The defense contractor had tried to recruit her before she'd graduated from Central Columbus Science University, but she'd been more interested in the opportunities a health care–focused lab in Chicago had offered her. Perhaps that had been fate since that's where she'd met Mal. She glanced at him before they stopped at the front desk. The setup was similar to the lobby at Grace's company, except Buckeye Dynamic Devices had more guards at their desk.

She approached the male guard seated at the center of the lobby's black-and-white-marbled counter. His close-cropped red hair framed his pale face. He was hooked up to a hands-free phone device. "We're here to see Dr. Roberta George, please."

The security guard was impeccable in his pressed uniform. Its pale gray material matched his expressionless eyes as he seemed to assess her threat level. "Is she expecting you?" His heavy drawl tagged him as being from Southern Ohio.

"No. I'm Dr. Grace Blackwell." She gestured toward Mal. "This is my colleague, Malachi Touré. We'd like to speak with Dr. George about Dr. Bennett MacIntyre."

The thirty-something guard turned his silent evaluation to Mal. He frowned. "Malachi Touré of the Touré Security Group?"

Mal inclined his head. "That's right."

The security guard's stilted expression eased a bit. His cool gray eyes warmed with what appeared to be respect. He tapped some buttons on the table in front of him, out of sight from the counter, then spoke into the mic attached to this headphone. "Dr. George, this is Adams at the lobby. Malachi Touré of the Touré Security Group and Dr. Grace Blackwell are here to see you." He paused to listen. "I'll put them in visitor room three."

Grace and Mal were treated to a series of security measures, including providing state-approved photo identification, signing into the visitor log for passes, and going through a metal detector similar to the system used at federal and state buildings. A guard on the other side of the screening device showed them to visitor room three. Grace noticed the curiosity on the guard's smooth brown face. She wasn't surprised to realize Touré Security Group had earned celebrity status in the corporate-security industry.

"This is nice." Grace's modest heels tapped against the marble flooring as she entered visitor room three.

The space was cozy and empty except for four armchairs around a rectangular metal-and-glass table and a small circular metal-and-glass table in the corner. The smaller table balanced a lamp, black cordless phone, a container of pens and notepads, and a box of tissues. The smoked glass window provided the occupants with privacy.

Mal's steps echoed hers as he followed her in. "Does your company have meeting spaces like these?"

She continued looking around. "Similar. But this

room smells like money. Our rooms smell more like peppermint candies."

"I'd prefer the candies." Another female voice joined their conversation.

Grace turned to see Dr. Roberta George striding toward her. Before she could speak, the other woman had engulfed her in a tight embrace. The petite bioscientist reached only to her shoulders.

Grace had forgotten Roberta was a hugger. She returned the embrace. "Hi, Bobby. Thank you for seeing us."

"Of course." Roberta stepped back. She tipped her thick, navy-framed glasses back into place with the side of her small right hand, then offered that hand to Mal. "Hello. You're a handsome one." She gave Grace an approving look before returning to Mal. "You must be Mr. Touré."

Mal's eyes flared in surprise as he took Roberta's hand. "Call me Mal, please."

Roberta flashed a grin. "I'm Bobby." She gestured to the seats around the table.

Grace sat across the from Roberta, beside Mal. "How are you?"

The bioscientist had gathered her wealth of wavy strawberry blond hair into a small tower that balanced precariously on the crown of her head. "I'm heartbroken. Dr. B was so wonderful. I'm shattered that I wasn't able to attend his wake."

Grace nodded. "I was surprised not to see you."

Roberta turned away, wiping a tear from her eye. "I'd gone out of town with my boyfriend. I didn't know Dr. B had died until we got back a week later."

Grace exchanged a look with Mal. She could tell he

was thinking the same thing she was. If Roberta had been out of town when Dr. B was killed, she couldn't be the murderer—unless she was working *with* the murderer.

She returned her attention to the scientist. "You and Dr. B still kept in touch?"

Roberta's brown eyes were shadowed with grief. "Yes. We spoke and exchanged emails from time to time."

Mal's voice was gentle. "Bobby, when was the last time you'd spoken with him?"

Roberta seemed puzzled by the question. She frowned as though searching for a memory. "I spoke with him at least once a week. That week, I think I spoke with him Monday. I told him Jamie and I were going on vacation." Her smile was tinged with sadness. "Dr. B had introduced us."

"That's nice. How long have you been dating?" Grace hadn't meant to ask, but she was surprised the bioscientist had time for a romantic relationship. She was certain Roberta's career was as demanding as her own.

"A year." Roberta's smile chased away the shadows of bereavement. "Our vacation was to celebrate our anniversary."

"Congratulations." Mal's tone was sincere. "It was a great idea to plan a trip to celebrate. May I ask where you went?" He gave Grace an intimate look that immediately made her suspicious—and warm.

Grace couldn't look away from him. Was he trying to tell her something in the middle of their interview with Roberta? Her cheeks heated with a blush.

Roberta's smile blossomed into an approving grin. "The Rose Heart Inn in Mount Gilead. They offer a bunch of guest packages, including a romance one."

Grace had seen pictures of the bed and breakfast in Northern Ohio. Its Victorian architecture and period antiques were distractingly romantic. The idea of spending a week with Mal at the inn was tempting, especially when he looked at her like that.

Mal held her eyes a moment longer before turning to Roberta. "Thank you for the recommendation."

Grace saw the other woman's dreamy look of approval. She stiffened. Was Mal's besotted expression an attempt to make Roberta believe they were more than colleagues? Her breath left her in a stifled sigh. Of course it was. She'd hurt him once before. Mal would never trust her with his heart again.

She shook off her disappointment and brought her focus back to the interview. "How was Dr. B the last time you spoke with him?"

"He was fine. He seemed happy." Roberta's confusion returned with a vengeance. "What's going on? Why are you asking these questions? Dr. B's death was an accident. You sound like a scene from one of those police shows where the detectives interrogate a suspect."

Grace put her hand over Roberta's clenched fist on the table between them. "There are circumstances surrounding Dr. B's death that have raised concerns for us and for the police. We're working with them to investigate those inconsistencies."

"What are you talking about?" Roberta's voice lifted, as though she could drown out Grace's words. She turned to Mal. "Dr. B tripped and fell down a flight of stairs in McWorter Hall."

Mal shook his head. "Bobby, I'm afraid there's evidence to show that Dr. B was pushed."

"What?" Roberta's wide eyes sought Grace's, silently asking for confirmation. Grace nodded. "Oh, no. Dr. B."

Grace stood, taking the box of tissues from the corner table and bringing it to Roberta. She knelt beside the other woman and wrapped her arm around her shoulders in comfort as she struggled with her own tears. She was grateful for Mal's patience as they gave Roberta time to collect herself.

After a few minutes, Roberta drew a shuddering breath and straightened. "Thank you."

Grace returned to her seat, leaving the tissues with the other woman. "No need to thank me. I understand."

Roberta pulled out a notepad and one of the pens from the corner table. Her voice was thick with unshed tears. "I'm not in any way connected with Dr. B's death, and I can prove it." She scribbled something on the sheet of paper. "These are my boyfriend's home and work numbers. His name is Jamie Johns. He's an accountant with PricewaterhouseCoopers. He'll confirm my alibi."

Grace took the numbers Roberta offered. "Thank you. You said Dr. B had introduced you. Did he set the two of you up on a blind date?"

Roberta's smile was shaky. "Dr. B was always telling me how important it was to have balance in your life. Your personal life is a refuge from the stress and strains of your professional life, he'd say. And your professional accomplishments mean more when you have someone to share them with. He's—he *was*—right."

"He said the same to me." In fact, he'd said those words on multiple occasions. Watching Roberta now, seeing how happy she was every time she mentioned Jamie's name, Grace was beginning to think Dr. B was right.

"And now you have Mal." Roberta wiped her eyes again. "Without Dr. B, I wouldn't be where I am today. I have a great job I love, with lots of opportunities for advancement. If he was murdered, please, please find his killer. He was a great man, a kind man. He didn't deserve to die that way. Promise me."

Grace exchanged a look with Mal and saw the determination for justice she felt glinting in his dark eyes. She turned back to Roberta. "We promise."

"Zeke, Bobby said her boyfriend, Jamie Johns, can alibi her. He's an accountant with Pricewaterhouse-Coopers. Can you check on that and the dates they were on vacation?" Mal repeated Jamie's phone numbers and the information for the Rose Heart Inn.

He and Grace were using his cell phone to videoconference with Zeke and Jerry from the Buckeye Dynamic Devices parking lot immediately after their meeting with Roberta on Monday. They'd given his brothers a summary of their interview with Roberta.

Zeke made a note on his cell phone. "Of course. I'll get the dates from the inn and also update Eriq and Taylor."

"Thanks." From the driver's seat of his car, Mal turned his attention to Jerry. Melba sat beside his younger brother. "Any news from the local precinct?"

Jerry looked disgusted. "We aren't getting as much cooperation here as we get in Columbus—"

Zeke interrupted. "The Florida precincts don't know us as well."

Jerry rolled his eyes. "I know that, Number One."

Melba gave him a shaming scowl. "Now, Jerry. My

godson would know better than to be snooty to someone who's trying to be helpful."

"You're right. I'm sorry." Jerry sighed.

Stunned, Mal remained silent. He was certain Zeke
was also in shock. The youngest Touré had apologized?
Were they approaching the end-time, or was Melba having a strong, positive influence on him? If Melba could
get Jerry to be reasonable, maybe they should issue her
a 1099 tax form for independent contractors.

Jerry continued. "As I was saying, we weren't getting
anywhere with the local precinct until Lisa Mylar pulled
a couple of strings and got her contacts involved." He
referenced the residence's director. "The police believe
they've identified the suspect. They're on their way to
question her now." He checked his watch as though he'd
synced his time with theirs.

Mal was impressed. "We're fortunate the director
has such good contacts."

Melba grunted. "Are you kidding? This residence
has a better than ninety percent voting turnout. One
call to the mayor's office, and a positive response has
more influence than a campaign commercial."

Mal exchanged an amused look with Grace. "I'll
keep that in mind for the future. Grace and I are going
back to the university. Let's check in at the end of the
day."

"I'll call you tonight, Gran." Grace smiled when
Melba blew a kiss at the screen.

Mal ended the videoconference, then put his phone
back on the side cup holder. "Are you buckled in?" He
glanced over to check for himself that her seat belt
was fastened. Her amused expression gave him pause.
"What?"

"Jerry's right. You really would go the whole day without eating, wouldn't you?" Grace sounded more curious than annoyed. Jerry would've been annoyed.

It took a moment for Mal to switch subjects. He'd been focused on their next step to salvage their struggling investigation. "You're hungry?"

Laughter danced in her eyes. "Yes, I am. Thank you for asking. It's been five hours since our last meal."

"Come to think of it, I could eat." Mal tossed her a smile. "Let's go home."

He started to put his car in gear when his cell phone buzzed. He recognized the distinct sound; it was the alert he'd programmed into his cell for his home-security system. He threw his car back into Park. Myriad images paraded through his mind. Dr. B's murder. Grace's computer-security breach. Verna Bleecher's murder. Grace's attempted kidnapping. Melba's attempted kidnapping. His alarm system being activated three days after the foiled abduction attempts wasn't a coincidence.

"What's happening?" The tension was thick in Grace's voice.

"Someone's trying to break into my house." Mal unlocked his cell phone, berating himself for not moving faster.

A different bell rang on his cell. This one indicated an incoming call. It was his home-security company. Mal put them on speaker. "Malachi Touré."

"Mr. Touré, this is Go Bucks Home Security," a calm male voice responded. "An alarm has been triggered, sir."

"That's correct." Mal gave them his security word and his credentials as proof of his identity. "Please contact the police. I'm on my way home."

"I'm contacting them now, sir." Mal heard keys tapping on the other end of the line. "Do you want me to stay on the call?"

"No, thanks. I'll take it from here." Mal disconnected the call and pointed his vehicle in the direction of his Upper Arlington home.

"Mal, this break-in has to be related to the case." Grace was subdued. "How did they know I was staying with you?"

"We've been interviewing suspects together. I'm surprised it took them this long to figure it out." Mal's voice was grim. "We must have spoken with the killer. Now we need to go back and figure out who it was."

It felt like it took forever to get to his home, but the clock on his vehicle's dashboard reflected only a twenty-minute passage of time. Mal pulled up at the curb and climbed out of the car. He met Grace at the hood of the vehicle. Together, they walked to the front door, where two uniformed officers waited for them.

"Mr. Touré? I'm Officer Chanel." The older officer stepped forward and gestured toward the young woman to his left. "This is my partner, Officer Rice. We circled your neighborhood in our cruiser twice. No sign of the perp. Sorry. It's a good thing you have that alarm. We'll add an extra patrol in the area. Hopefully, our increased presence will prevent any further attempts."

To say Mal was disappointed would be an understatement. He'd had visions of the police capturing the would-be burglar and his connecting the burglar to the murders, attempted abductions and the hack. Case closed. Now his only hope was that at least one of his security cameras installed in the front or back of his home had recorded an image of the criminal, and he and his brothers—and law enforcement—could use it to locate the killer.

He and Grace thanked the police officers for their time and trouble before he led Grace upstairs to his home office. He wheeled the spare matching black cloth desk chair beside his and held it out for Grace. "I'm going to launch the security-video program so we can review the footage."

Grace folded her hands in her lap. Tension radiated from her. "You must be right. We've already spoken with the killer. Why else would someone try to break into your home now? There's no such thing as coincidences."

Mal sat in front of his computer. "Let's see." He double tapped the mouse pad to launch the security-camera program.

The video started automatically on his laptop screen. He fast forwarded to 12:03 p.m. when a slender figure entered the camera's range. The suspect was dressed in black pants and a black hoodie. The hoodie covered their head.

Grace groaned. "Oh, come on. Is that hoodie going to block their face the entire time?"

Mal narrowed his eyes. "The suspect's about five ten, maybe one hundred twenty or thirty pounds." He sped up the video.

"There!" Grace shouted the word at the same time Mal did.

He paused the video. In the frame, the would-be burglar glanced up at the security camera as though startled. The hoodie fell away from her head.

Grace gasped. "Oh my gosh!"

Mal's lips parted. "Martina Mann."

Chapter 16

"Thank you for coming, Detectives." Zeke's voice preceded him into the Touré Security Group conference room late Monday afternoon.

Mal looked up as his older brother led Eriq and Taylor to the table. He and Grace had already updated Zeke and Jerry, showing them the video that incriminated Martina Trenton Mann in the plot to steal Grace's formulation, murder Dr. Bennett MacIntyre and Verna Bleecher, and abduct Grace and Melba. Now they needed to lay out the case for the investigating homicide detectives.

He rose to greet the law enforcement officers he'd seen just three hours earlier. It felt like a week. Grace stood beside him.

Eriq took his hand. He wore a burgundy bolo tie with an ice-gray shirt, navy pants and a slate gray jacket. "We heard someone tried to break into your place."

Mal inclined his head toward the laptop in front of

him as he shook Taylor's hand. "My security camera caught a clear image of the burglar."

Taylor frowned as she released his hand. She split a look between Mal and Grace as she adjusted the jacket of her navy pantsuit. "And you think this attempted burglary is connected to your case."

"It is." Grace's voice was inflexible.

Zeke strode to the head of the table to take his seat. "Watch the recording first, then we'll explain everything to you."

Eriq frowned. "Then you *have* been withholding information." His tone was heavy with disapproval.

Grace settled onto her chair to Mal's right. "We haven't kept any evidence or updates from you."

"As my brother said, let's watch the video, then we'll answer your questions." Mal took his seat before adjusting the laptop so everyone at the table could see its screen. He tapped the keys to start the recording.

Everyone was quiet as Martina Mann's figure, masked in black slacks and an oversize black hoodie, came onscreen. She kept looking around, as though checking to see that no one was watching or following her. She crept up to the door, then tipped back her head and spotted the camera.

Eriq shook his head. "The rookies always look right into the camera."

Taylor gestured toward the screen. "And she still tried to break in even though she knew she was being recorded." Her voice was strained with disbelief.

The discordant buzzing of Mal's security system came through the audio. Onscreen, Martina froze for a split second before finally turning to run away. Mal stopped the video.

Eriq met his eyes. "Who is she?"

He wasn't surprised the veteran detective expected they'd know the identity of their would-be burglar. "Martina Trenton Mann. She's a member of CCSU's board of trustees as well as Buckeye Dynamic's board of directors."

"And the mother of one of Dr. MacIntyre's graduate student–research assistants," Grace added.

Taylor looked at Grace. Her eyes glinted with approval. "She checks all the boxes, connecting her to the players after your formula. Dr. MacIntyre, CCSU and Buckeye Dynamic."

Grace spoke faster. "She also sat with me at Dr. B's table during the fundraising dinner. That would have given her access to my thumb drive, which she planted at Verna Bleecher's home."

Eriq pointed toward Mal's laptop. "If you're right and she's the one who's after your formula, she's also responsible for four murders—Dr. MacIntyre's, Verna Bleecher's, the kidnapper's and the driver's—as well as two attempted kidnappings. The problem is, your prints are the only ones on the drive."

Grace's bright eyes widened in incredulity. "That could be explained. She probably used a napkin to pick it up."

"That's true." Taylor sounded almost apologetic. "But the bottom line is, her prints aren't on that drive. We don't have anything that says she's more likely to have taken it than anyone else at that table."

"Who else was at the table?" Eriq asked.

Grace looked down, as though bringing the scene to her mind. "In addition to me, Dr. B and Martina, there also was Martina's son, Trent, Jill Streep, Dr. B's other graduate student–research assistant and Dr. Roberta George, one of Dr. B's former students."

Taylor sat back on her seat. "Who's to say it wasn't one of them?"

Grace waved a hand toward the video paused on the screen of Mal's laptop. "Martina's the only one on the tape. She probably has more money than Mal and I combined, so why would she break into his home? Obviously, because she's after my formulation." She turned to Mal beside her. "No offense."

He shrugged. "None taken."

Zeke folded his hands on the table in front of him. "She's also seen Mal and Grace together, investigating the case. That's probably how she realized Grace was staying with Mal."

Eriq grunted. "I'm hearing 'probably' a lot, which isn't good for the case. We don't have enough to arrest her for these murders or the computer hack."

"We were afraid you'd say that." Zeke gestured toward the computer. "But you do have enough to bring her in for questioning for the attempted break-in of my brother's home." There was tension in his voice, as though the idea of someone threatening his family's safety triggered his temper.

Mal felt the same way. In this case, Grace's safety had once again been compromised.

Taylor interrupted his thoughts. "We could ask her about the break-in, but if we do that, she might destroy any evidence tying her to the murders. We need something more than her being at the event to tie her to the rest."

Grace's rounded eyebrows knitted. "What do you need to get a warrant to search her home?"

Eriq shrugged. "More than we have now. What we have amounts to speculation. It won't convince a judge to issue a search warrant." He leaned toward Grace. "Look, in our guts, we know you're right. The pieces fit. We just need tangible evidence to make it stick and convince a prosecutor."

Zeke crossed his arms. "Like her prints on the thumb drive, or testimony from the kidnapper or driver. Things she's already gotten rid of."

Mal had never been in a situation like this before. Touré Security Group provided protection services. They specialized in preventing crimes. But he and his brothers were quick studies and they were learning to adapt. "If you bring Martina Mann in for questioning, we'll put her under surveillance. Your interview may rattle her enough to do something that'll give us the link we're looking for."

Eriq and Taylor exchanged a look of silent communication before Eriq responded. "We'll ask her to come in now."

"Thanks." Mal took the thumb drive with the video from his security camera from his laptop and gave it to Taylor, who sat across the table from him. He stood, signaling the end of the meeting. "Zeke and I'll be ready to follow her after your meeting."

Grace rose, challenging him with a look. "So will I."

Mal met her eyes. "Why am I not surprised?"

"If your Mal is anything like Jerry, I can understand how you would've fallen in love with him." Melba's statement made Grace's head spin.

She'd called her grandmother from the privacy of Jerry's office late Monday afternoon. They were wait-

ing at Touré Security Group for the detectives to call
once Martina was on her way to the precinct for their
interview. It was a waste of time and gas to drive back
to Mal's home, only to return to the office for Zeke before starting surveillance on Martina.

Mal had set her up in Jerry's office. He'd cleared
towers of papers from the cherrywood desk to give
her space for her tablet. He'd also carried away several
empty and half-empty coffee mugs. Mal hadn't been
exaggerating when he'd called Jerry a slob. In contrast,
Zeke's and Mal's offices were almost obsessively well-
organized. Was Jerry's sloppiness an act of defiance or
a cry for help?

"Where's Jerry now?" If they were going to talk
about him, Grace hoped Jerry wasn't in the room. Melba
wasn't opposed to talking about people, even if they
could hear her.

"He went to the precinct. He thinks he'll get more
information about their search for the woman who tried
to abduct me if he's staring them in the face." There was
a hint of humor in Melba's voice. "But don't worry. He's
left me in Janice's capable hands. I'm making us some
tea. Now, tell me, is your Mal like Jerry?"

"He's not 'my Mal,' Gran." Grace rolled her eyes.
"And I don't know the Touré brothers well enough to
give you a good answer. They seem alike, but they're
also different." Grace's eyes drifted over the collection
of family pictures in Jerry's office.

There was a silver-framed photo on his desk beside
the port for his laptop. It appeared to have been taken
at the Columbus Park of Roses. The older couple in the
middle must have been their parents, Franklin Touré
and Vanessa Sherraten-Touré. Grace had read some ar-

ticles about them she'd found online. She wished she'd known them. The brothers looked so much like their father, but Jerry had his mother's eyes.

There were more photos on the shelf above Jerry's desk and a few on his bookcase: graduations, holiday celebrations, everyday scenes. There was a picture of the brothers flexing their muscles for the camera while they stood around their mother. It looked like the four of them had just completed the Columbus 10K fun run.

"What do you mean?" Melba prompted.

"They're all charming, but Jerry has the most obvious charm. They're all involved in the business, but Zeke seems to be the most hands-on. They aren't very talkative, but Mal says the least. He lets his actions speak for him."

"I do like a man of action." Melba sounded amused. "But Jerry's definitely a charmer. I've never had so much attention from the staff. The only reason they're being so solicitous is because they want to spend time with my fake-godson-slash-real-bodyguard. Even Gilda has a crush on him. Her eyes get big and bright when he's around." Melba chuckled. "The way she acts around him, you'd think she was in her thirties instead of her eighties like me."

Grace's lips curved into a smile. "I'm glad Jerry's been able to entertain you and to help distract you from the case."

Melba hummed her agreement. In the background, Grace heard the muffled words of a news update. Her grandmother must be watching a national media program. "From what you said about the attempted break-in at Mal's house, it sounds like the case is on the verge of being solved. Thank goodness. As much as I'm enjoying Jerry's company, it will be good to go back to normalcy and safety."

Indeed. "I doubt Martina will confess. If we don't have anything directly tying her to the murders and the hacking, she'll get away with these crimes." Grace's temper stirred. "But knowing she's under suspicion will hopefully be enough to stop her. And it may hurt her reputation. That's something, at least."

"It wouldn't be justice the way we'd want it, but if it keeps you safe, it's good enough for me." Melba's tone was a verbal shrug. A teakettle whistled in the background. "On another topic, have you given any more thought to what's going to happen with you and Mal once this terrible situation is resolved?"

Grace shifted on her seat with discomfort—and fear. "I didn't call to discuss my love life—"

"Or lack thereof." Melba's voice was as dry as dust.

Grace ignored her. "I'm calling to find out how you're doing."

"I'm fine. Now, what're you going to do about Mal?"

"I don't know, Gran." Grace inhaled, releasing her impatience and frustration on a breath. Jerry's office smelled like the mugs of stale coffee he'd abandoned around the room. "The truth is, I hurt him when I walked away. I basically disappeared. I don't know whether he'd be willing to give me another chance."

"Do you want one?" The gentle tapping of metal against china sounded in the background as Melba prepared tea for herself and Janice.

Grace thought about Roberta George and her boyfriend, Jamie. About Dr. B, his three children and his second wife—now widow—Tami. "Yes, I do."

Dr. B had warned Grace like he'd warned Roberta

that she needed a personal life. Unlike Roberta, Grace hadn't listened. She'd buried herself in her work without giving herself a chance to remember what she'd given up. It had taken Mal coming back into her life, reminding her that he was what she'd been missing, to make her realize the truth of Dr. B's warning and her grandmother's advice. Now she wanted to find that work-life balance—with Mal's help.

"If you want a second chance with Mal, you'll have to find the courage to ask for it." Melba's words broke into her thoughts.

They chatted for a while longer—long enough for Grace to be convinced her grandmother felt safe and was in good spirits despite the circumstances—before they ended their call and Grace went back to work.

Her grandmother was right: she had to be brave enough to ask for what she really wanted. But suppose the answer was no?

Mal rolled a pen between the fingers of both hands. "Touré Security doesn't have to limit its services to the small companies we were founded for or big corporations, as you've proposed for our expansion. We can do both."

Zeke had followed him into his office late Monday afternoon once the detectives had left. He now sat in the visitor's chair directly across from Mal. "How do we make that work with our pricing? If we charge what the bigger corporations can afford, we price out the smaller companies. If we adjust our pricing for the smaller companies, we undercut ourselves."

"Tiered pricing." Mal's conversation with Grace played back in his mind. "Instead of a flat rate based on the service, we offer tiered rates per service based on the size of the company: small, medium or large. We can base their size on the number of people they employ. But we'll figure that out later, if we agree to go this route."

Zeke tipped back his head and studied the ceiling as he contemplated Mal's proposal. He gave a slow nod. "We would post our definition of small, medium and large companies on our website and in our collateral to keep our price structure transparent. That would work." He smiled at Mal. "Good thinking."

"I can't take the credit." Mal shook his head. It was a relief to have Zeke accept the compromise between their different visions of their family company's future. "Grace suggested it. She said we owe it to our parents to fight for the legacy they built for us. She's right."

Zeke set his right ankle on his left knee above this dark gray pants. "Smart lady. Do you think Jer will go for it?"

Mal sat back on his executive chair. It was a win to have Zeke on his side; Jerry was another matter. His younger brother was the wild card. "Let's discuss it as a group once this case is over."

Zeke sighed. "Yeah, Jerry's fuse has been even shorter than usual. I don't know what I've done to tick him off this time. I asked him, but he's not talking."

Mal glanced at his brother. "You're right. Something's bothering Jerry, and we need to deal with it. But I don't think it has anything to do with you." He checked his watch again. "The detectives should be back at the precinct by now."

"It'll take them a few minutes to park, then get to their desks." Zeke hesitated. "I know you've been busy with this investigation and your cybersecurity clients, but have you thought about what's next for you and Grace?"

Mal stiffened. He'd barely thought about anything else when he should've been thinking about everything else. As Zeke said, in addition to solving their client's murder, he had several cyber clients to serve, but all he'd been able to think about was Grace, morning, noon and night. Keeping her safe. Making her happy. Holding her in his arms.

"We don't have time for that." Mal pushed away from his desk with more force than he'd intended. He stood to pace to the floor-to-ceiling window at the back of his office. "There's a killer after a biological weapon, and we're the first and last line of defense between her and the scientist who's risking her life to protect that formula."

"Your words say you don't have time." Zeke's pensive tone carried to him from across the room. "But the passion in your voice says you don't want to let go of this woman."

"What does that matter?" He spat the question over his shoulder. "She made up her mind four years ago. When it was me or her research, she chose her research. The end."

"But she has feelings for you. It's clear whenever she looks at you."

Really?

Mal turned to stare wide-eyed at his brother. His breath caught in his throat.

Stop it!

He turned back to the window, shoving his fists deep into his pockets. His movements felt stiff with bitter disappointment. "She considers me a distraction. Her research is important. It could improve the lives of billions of people all over the world. What do I have to offer her?"

"Love."

Mal squeezed his eyes shut. Zeke was killing him. "I don't want to be responsible for her not achieving her goals—"

"Cut the crap, Mal." Zeke's angry response sounded closer. "The past week has proven you're both better together. You've come out of the shadows. You're more decisive, more engaged. You're the leader you used to be before Jerry and my constant arguments drove you away from the company. With Grace, I have the old Mal back. I'm sure Grace is better with you, too."

Mal turned to find his older brother an arm's length from him. He cocked his head. "What makes you think that?"

Zeke stepped forward and put his hand on Mal's shoulder. "Because, Mal, you have that rare ability to make everyone around you better versions of themselves— even Jerry."

That brought a reluctant smile to Mal's lips. Rubbing his forehead, he stepped around Zeke. "Even if that was true, you keep forgetting one important thing: Grace is focused on her career. She doesn't have time for anything else, especially not a relationship. At least not with me."

"That's ridiculous." Zeke turned to keep him in sight. "Mom and Dad made it work with three children."

"We're not Mom and Dad." Mal tossed the truth over his shoulder.

"That doesn't change the fact that they made a relationship work even as they built this company from scratch and raised three kids." Zeke followed him back to his desk. "You are your parents' son. You can do it, too."

Mal settled back on his chair. He spread his arms. "Pointing out the obvious: none of us are in a relationship. When was the last time you even went on a date?"

Zeke stood behind the closest visitor's chair. "We're talking about you. You deserve to be happy, Mal. Why are you giving up on that? You're in love with Grace. She still has feelings for you. If you want a relationship with her, you're going to have to convince her to make room for you."

"I—" Mal's cell phone rang, cutting him off. "It's Eriq. I'll put him on speaker." He accepted the call, then tapped the phone's speaker icon. "Eriq, I'm here with Zeke. Has Martina arrived?"

"That's why Taylor and I are calling you." The detective's voice was grim. Traffic noises, footsteps and conversations sounded in the background. "Martina Mann isn't coming in. She's dead."

Chapter 17

Mal stood with Grace and Zeke outside of the Mann residence in Bexley late Monday afternoon. He had flashbacks to the scene at Verna Bleecher's house after she was found dead. Patrol cars were double-parked at the curb. Their flashing lights warned neighbors against approaching the activity. Uniformed officers examined the Victorian-style home's perimeter, including its winding driveway, large front and side yards, and the wraparound porch.

His eyes slid from the entrance to the porch. His heart clenched when he discovered one major difference between this scene and Verna Bleecher's home—a grieving relative. Trent sat in a wooden folding chair on the porch with Eriq and Taylor. Martina Mann's son was sobbing his heart out. Both detectives regarded him with empathy as well as confusion. Mal took a breath to ease the tightness in his chest. His mother's death two years earlier and his father's passing three months before that were fresh enough for him to remember his grief and loss. Fortunately, he'd had his brothers to help him through the pain. Grace and Melba had been there for each other after her sister, Pam's, death. Who did Trent have?

Mal stepped up to the yellow crime scene tape. "Excuse us, Officer."

A slight young woman with a wealth of red hair tugging free from the hairclip at the nape of her neck turned to him. Her brown eyes were tired and impatient in her white face. Her badge displayed her surname as Nelley. "Can I help you?"

Mal inclined his head toward the porch. "Detectives Duster and Stenhardt asked us to join them here."

Interest nudged out the fatigue in her expression. Her eyes swept across him, Grace and Zeke. "And you are?"

"Malachi Touré." He gestured in turn to Grace beside him and Zeke on her other side. "Dr. Grace Blackwell and Hezekiah Touré."

She gave him and Zeke narrow-eyed stares. Her demeanor warmed slightly. "Touré Security Group? Wait here."

Grace nodded toward the porch. "I wonder if there's anyone we can call for Trent? He shouldn't be alone now."

Zeke shook his head. "You're right. Poor guy."

The afternoon was warm. The air was still and carried the faint scent of fuel, grass, spring blossoms and gossip.

"…found her when he came home from classes."

"…shot. It was probably a home invasion. Are *we* safe?"

"Does anyone know if anything was taken?"

As he half listened to snatches of the neighbors' conversations, Mal watched Officer Nelley maneuver through the handful of officers and crime scene techs between her and the detectives. She jogged up the four steps to the porch and spoke with Taylor and Eriq. The young officer gestured toward Mal, Grace and Zeke, who waited in the street behind the tape. Eriq nodded and the officer returned to escort them beyond the crime scene tape.

The detectives led Mal, Grace and Zeke to the other side of the entrance, several feet from Trent.

Eriq looked at each of them. "Martina Mann was the killer."

Mal's eyes widened with surprise. His eyebrows stretched upward. "How can you be so sure?"

Taylor handed Mal a clear evidence bag. Inside was a single sheet of plain white printer paper. "She confessed."

Mal held the bag so Grace beside him and Zeke on her other side could read the message along with him.

I killed Dr. MacIntyre and Verna Bleecher to prevent them from connecting me to the hack of Dr. Blackwell's system. I killed the men I'd hired to kidnap Dr. Blackwell for the same reason. But now I regret the embarrassment my actions will cause my family. Killing myself seems the best solution.

Mal shook his head. He looked at Grace. "Does this seem right to you?"

She looked as skeptical as Mal felt. "I didn't know Martina well, but this letter seems very stiff. It doesn't sound like her. And who's the letter to? "

"That's because my mother didn't write it." Trent's voice was still thick with tears. "For the millionth time, my mother didn't commit suicide. Someone murdered her. You should be looking for her killer."

Mal looked at the young man. His brown eyes were red and puffy. His white features were blotchy.

Grace went to Trent and put her hand on his shoulder. "I'm so sorry for your loss, Trent. Is there anyone we can call for you?"

Trent's voice was muffled by sorrow and his hands covered his face. "My aunt's on her way from Cleveland."

Mal's muscles relaxed at the news that Trent had family who'd soon be with him. He turned to the detectives, lowering his voice. "What's your theory about what happened?" He didn't want Trent to go over the traumatic report again.

Taylor glanced at Trent before returning her attention to Mal. "We need to check the gun for prints, but based on the position of the weapon and the body, it looks as though Ms. Mann shot herself. There was no sign of a break-in."

"You're wrong," Trent shouted. His tone was hard with fury. "My mother wouldn't have committed suicide. She wouldn't have wanted me to find her like that. She loved me. She wouldn't have left me."

Taylor spread her arms. "You identified the weapon as your mother's gun."

"So what?" Trent clenched his teeth. "That doesn't mean she used it on herself. You need to find her killer. Now!"

Mal turned to Eriq. The older detective shook his head as though he was at his wit's end.

Mal approached the grief-stricken son. "Trent, which door did you use to enter your home?"

Trent scrubbed his face with both hands. He shrugged

his narrow shoulders. "The back door. I always use the back door."

When he was growing up, he'd always used the back door, too. Why was that? "Did you need your key to unlock it, or was it already open?"

Frowning, Trent looked up at him. Uncertainty shadowed his features. "I think the door was locked. I used my key."

"Was it just the lower lock, or was the dead bolt secured as well?" Mal asked.

"I don't remember. I think so, but I'm not sure." Trent's scowl darkened. "What does it matter?"

Zeke slipped his hands into his front pants pockets. His tone was gentle. "If the door was locked, chances are no one broke in." His implication that Trent could be wrong about someone killing his mother hovered between them.

Grace caught Mal's attention, leading him away from the group. "Trent's right. Martina Mann may have been involved in the hack and the murders, but she didn't kill herself. She loved her son too much to have him find her like that. And she would've addressed her suicide note to him."

"So the question is, who was Martina's partner?" Mal looked at Trent over his shoulder. "Once we answer that, we'll find the killer."

Grace sat cross-legged on the center of the bed in the guest room early Monday evening. She looked up at the knock on the open door, taking a moment to drag her thoughts from the notepad on her right thigh.

From the doorway, Mal held two mugs of coffee. He was casually dressed in a copper cotton jersey and lightweight, knee-length navy shorts. "I thought you could use a break."

"And the caffeine." Grace untangled her legs under her cloud gray shorts and pressed off the bed to stand. She struggled to find a smile as she took one of the mugs from Mal. "Thank you."

"How's the revised suspect list coming?" Mal asked.

Grace turned back to the bed. She felt the warmth of Mal's presence behind her. "I'm spinning my wheels. I've tried prioritizing the list by people who're connected to both the university and Buckeye Dynamic."

"That makes sense." Mal sat on the edge of her bed with her. "You, Zeke and I—and Trent—agree Martina's suicide scene seemed staged. Martina was connected to both the university and Buckeye Dynamic. It would fit that her partner—and her killer—would have connections to both places as well."

"Except I keep coming back to the same suspects we've had since the beginning."

Grace pulled her notepad onto her lap. She massaged her neck as she studied the list. "With Martina dead, we're left with Roberta and Trent. We know Trent didn't kill his mother, and Roberta has a solid alibi for the night of Dr. B's murder: She was forty-five miles away in Mount Gilead."

"You're right. We're missing someone." Mal stared at the colorful area rug beneath their feet as he drank his coffee.

Grace's heart tripped as Mal's soap-and-pine scent drifted closer to her. The room seemed smaller with him in it. He was larger than life to her. A series of images cycled through her mind: Mal reviewing the original suspect list with her; laughing with her grandmother;

cooking with her like old times; sprinting to her rescue outside of MARS.

They were so close to solving these crimes. Grace could feel it. And this is what she wanted—what she needed. She didn't want lives to be in danger. Her grandmother's, Mal's and his brothers', the lives of the people in her community and across the world, even her own were in jeopardy. But she didn't want to lose Mal, either. She didn't want to lose who she was when she was with him.

Grace refocused on their case. "We've been missing someone since the beginning, but I can't identify them."

"Maybe you need to step back for a few minutes." Mal took her half-full coffee mug and crossed the room. He set both mugs on the dressing table, then turned to face her.

Grace's lips parted in surprise. She looked from the mugs to Mal as he leaned against the table beside them. A startled laugh escaped her lips. "What're you doing?"

"I'm distracting you." Mal tossed her a cheeky grin. "Zeke liked the idea of a tiered pricing system so Touré Security can continue to cater to small companies while expanding our customer base to include medium-sized and larger corporations."

Grace's spirits lifted with the first happy news she'd received in too many days to count. "Mal, that's wonderful. I'm glad."

Mal grinned, giving her another glimpse of the man she'd fallen in love with in Chicago. "So am I. And I'm grateful to you." He returned to the bed. "Thank you for helping us find a way to make our two visions for the company's future work."

"You're giving me too much credit." Grace shook her

head. "You would've come to the same conclusion eventually. Sometimes it takes someone from the outside looking in to help you see the solution a little faster."

"Now we just have to bring Jer on board." His dry tone and the frown lines between his eyebrows indicated to Grace that Mal wasn't optimistic about their chances for success with the youngest Touré.

"What would he object to?"

Mal shrugged restless shoulders beneath his jersey. "I don't know. Jerry can be a wild card. He may not object to anything. But then he might object to everything. He's been even more unpredictable lately."

"I'm hoping for your success. Touré Security Group is well regarded in the community." Grace thought of the reactions of the security guard at Buckeye Dynamic Devices, and comments from the officers and detectives at the Columbus Police Department. She put her hand on Mal's where it rested on his inner left thigh. His skin was smooth and warm beneath her palm. "I want to thank you as well, especially for the way you and your brothers jumped into action to protect my grandmother. She's all I have, and you kept her safe for me."

"It was our pleasure." His voice was husky, causing her heart to skip again.

Grace cleared her throat. "Your company should consider offering investigative services as well as protection. You're really good with your research, background checks and connections with law enforcement."

Mal laughed. "I don't know about that." His ebony eyes warmed as they searched her face.

Grace's chuckle wavered, exposing her nervousness. "At least think about it." She drew back her hand.

Mal caught it. "We couldn't have done it without you."

The look in his eyes made her heart jump into her throat. "Mal." She whispered his name, shifting toward him without conscious thought.

Grace covered his mouth, moving even closer to him. Her arms slid around his tight waist and up his broad back. Her fingertips pressed into the hard muscles of his shoulders. She inhaled, then moaned as his scent filled her head. A restless hunger built inside her. Leaning into Mal, she closed every inch of space between them. His arms wrapped around her, pulling her tighter. She sighed her approval. Mal lay back against the mattress, bringing her with him.

She lay on top of his hard, lean muscles as she drank from his lips. He tasted of strength, warmth and caffeine. Desire was burning inside her.

Grace broke their kiss, pressing her lips to the side of his neck. "Oh my God, Mal."

"Do you want to stop?" The dread in his voice kept her from weeping.

"No. Do you?" She had to be sure.

He cupped her face between his palms. "No."

Mal pressed his mouth to hers and stroked his tongue across the seam between her lips. Grace didn't need any other urging to open for him. Mal's tongue stroked hers. He swept inside, caressing her, toying with her, stoking the fires that fed her passion. Grace felt the pull in her breasts. A pulse beat slow and heavy between her thighs.

Their arms and legs stretched and tangled as they helped each other undress. Mal took a condom from his wallet and set it beside them. Grace's eyes moved over his long, fit body as he lay across the bed.

"I could look at you for days." She traced his broad

pectorals with her fingertips. She stroked her hand over the ridges of his torso.

Mal cupped her breast. "You make me ache."

The look in his eyes made her feel beautiful, magical, powerful. Feverish. Grace pushed herself up to straddle him. Mal caught her breast in his mouth. Grace gasped as he suckled her, stroking and kissing her taut nipple with his lips. Her body moistened. She closed her eyes. Pressing her right palm to the back of his head, she brought him closer to her.

Her muscles shaking, Grace released Mal. Straddling his legs, she kissed and licked her way down his body to his hips. His groans and deep breaths broke the stillness of the room. His muscles tightened and flexed between her knees. Grace kissed his right hip bone and nipped his left with her teeth.

"You're killing me." Mal's words were tight.

"I'm loving you." Grace kissed his tip. She stroked her tongue up his length.

"Grace." Mal panted her name. "I need you now." His voice was hoarse.

Grace leaned away from him. Her body was heated. Her skin was damp with perspiration. Her hands shook as she tore the condom from its packet. She rolled it over him, and his hips rose from the mattress.

I love you. Her heart wanted to set the words free. Instead, she pressed her lips together to keep them trapped inside.

She leaned forward, guiding him to her as she whispered in his ear, "I want you."

Mal met her eyes. His features were tight. His face was flushed. "I want you, too."

Grace's heart thumped against her chest. His words

seemed to have more meaning than just this moment in time. Was she wrong?

Mal closed his eyes and pressed his head back as he surged up into her. Grace gasped. Her body bowed back. She moved her hips, setting the rhythm for their passion. Waves of pleasure slid over and through her with each thrust of Mal's hips. She tightened around him, drawing out their movements.

"That's it." Mal voiced his encouragement. "Come for me."

"I will," she whispered back.

Catching her hips, Mal rolled over. Grace gasped as he pulled himself free. He pressed his lips to hers in a demanding kiss, then rasped in her ear, "I want you to come for me now."

Sliding to the side of the bed, Mal drew her to him. He cupped her hips, moved between her thighs and kissed her there. Grace pressed the back of her head into the mattress and cried out her desire. Mal stoked her passion with deep kisses and long, slow licks. Her body shuttered. Her muscles stretched and tightened. Her core clenched. Need—hot, full and deep—raced to the edge and leaped free. She convulsed as wave after wave of pleasure broke within her.

Mal pulled himself up over her. The hairs of his chest and torso teased her sensitive skin. Her chest heaved as she worked to catch her breath. Her heart raced. The pulse between her thighs galloped. Mal surged into her, and she gasped. He worked his hips, and Grace felt another climax building. Her body responded to his thrusts, rising to meet him, not wanting to let go. She wrapped her legs around his hips to keep him close, tight. She didn't want to let him go. Not now. Not ever.

But how would she put that into words? How could she ever make amends for leaving him once before?

Mal's movements quickened. He held her to him with one arm. His free hand slid between them and found her. Grace shattered again. Her body trembled in his arms. He held her tightly, but Grace still felt herself slipping into oblivion.

"I don't regret last night." The words burst free from Mal early Tuesday morning.

Grace shook her head. "Neither do I."

Mal managed to hide his surprise. Relief threatened to overwhelm him. He reminded himself to breathe.

He and Grace sat across from each other at the kitchen table, eating breakfast. She'd been unusually preoccupied, as though lost in thought since they'd woken beside each other that morning. They should have been famished; they'd missed dinner last night. Not that he minded, but her deafening silence during the meal almost ruined his appetite until she assured him that her distraction had nothing to do with one of the best nights of his life.

"You've been so quiet." He finished his coffee. "What's on your mind?"

Grace hesitated. "I still haven't updated our suspect list."

What had he thought had been on her mind? Lives depended on their identifying the person who was trying to steal Grace's formula. Of course the suspect list had been on her mind. It also should've been on his, but his thoughts lingered on last night.

He glanced at his watch. "I have a client meeting—"

Grace spoke at the same time. "Actually, I wasn't—"

Mal stopped and gestured to her. "I'm sorry. What were you going to say?"

Grace hesitated again. "Can we talk?"

Mal searched her big, bright eyes. There was sadness and dread in their depth. Oh no. Those were *not* good signs. She didn't regret last night, but what made him think that meant she was willing to give a relationship with him another chance?

Stupid! Stupid! Stupid!

He checked his watch again. He stood and carried his cereal bowl, juice glass, coffee mug and silverware to the dishwasher. "I have that client meeting I mentioned. I need to leave now, but could we talk over lunch?" *Once I've had time to prepare myself for another heartbreak?*

"Thank you." Grace followed him with her dishes. "In the meantime, I'm going to call my chief science officer and to update him on our investigation. It's been almost two weeks."

"All right." Mal shrugged off the sense of defeat. They still had two days to crack this case. He forced a smile. "Are you sure you can trust him?"

"Funny." Grace helped Mal load their dishes. "I did check, though. He doesn't have ties to CCSU or Buckeye Dynamic."

"That sounds like the Grace I know and… Know." *Stupid!* Mal straightened from the machine. "So you're going to call your chief science officer from here, right? Be careful. Remember not to tell anyone where you are or with whom. Until the case is solved, the killer's still out there."

"I'm not likely to forget." Her voice was dry. She stepped back, putting more space between them.

He felt a cold breeze separate them. "I'm sorry, Grace. I just want to make sure you remain vigilant until we're certain the killer has been stopped."

"I promise to be careful." Grace held his eyes. "But you have to be careful, too. It's obvious the killer knows you're helping me. I don't want anything to happen to you, either."

"I promise."

Grace's look of concern didn't ease. "You'd better get going. You don't want to be late for your meeting."

"My what?" He shook his head to clear his thoughts. "Oh, right. Thank you."

"I'll see you this afternoon for lunch."

He let his eyes linger on her face. "Yes, you will."

Mal didn't give himself time to think. He didn't want to consider the repercussions. Instead, he reached out on impulse, bringing her close for one last kiss. Whatever happened this afternoon, he wanted a final kiss before goodbye.

He dropped his arms and stepped back.

Grace opened her eyes. They were soft and unfocused. "What was that?"

"That was no regrets." *At least, not until this afternoon.*

Chapter 18

Mal's doorbell rang shortly after he left Tuesday morning. Grace absently acknowledged the chime as she focused on her formula. Mal had helped her set up her work at the smaller desk in his home office. She didn't see any reason to stop what she was doing to react to the interruption. It wasn't her doorbell; it was Mal's, and he was meeting with a client. He wouldn't return until lunchtime. Grace kept her head down and focused on her task.

The doorbell sounded again, longer this time.

Grace scowled, muttering under her breath. "All right. You're persistent."

Irritated by the interruption, Grace marched to the iPad Mal kept on top of one of his metal filing cabinets. Was this a package delivery that required a signature? If so, the courier was out of luck. She wasn't going to sign for anything. They could play with the doorbell until Mal came home for lunch, which wouldn't be for another three hours at best.

Grace used the login information Mal had given her to access the device. During the tour of his home, he'd told her the iPad was connected to the alarm system and explained how it worked. Grace launched the security program. The computer screen displayed real-time video feeds from six strategic camera positions: west rear, side and front; and east rear, side and front.

Grace muttered to herself as she cycled through the footage. "Nothing to see. Nothing to see. Nothing to—" She froze, frowning at the screen. "Hold on."

The two rear cameras provided images of the back of the house. Evergreen and burning bushes followed the maple-wood fencing that enclosed the backyard. Cameras to the left and right of the home captured rosebushes and junipers. But the two front cameras sent back images of their uninvited guest.

The person had turned their back to the camera mounted to the overhang on the west side of the porch. They wore a long, belted black trench coat and clutched a large black briefcase. Judging by their figure, Grace guessed the visitor was a woman. She'd lifted the coat's collar to obscure her identity. A woman's wide-brimmed black hat covered her hair and blocked the rear camera from a clear view of her profile.

However, the camera mounted on the east side of the porch provided a better prospective. Large black sunglasses masked most of her face, but Grace had known their unexpected guest for almost three years. She'd recognize her anywhere: Dr. B's administrative assistant, Doris Flank.

Grace's muscles froze with shock. Her mind went

blank. She stared at the screen in disbelief. "How did you know I was here, Doris?"

The question was rhetorical. Grace suddenly realized that Doris knew everything because she'd been behind this plot the entire time. Partnering with Martina Mann provided her with a connection to Buckeye Dynamic Devices. While Martina had taken point, Doris had remained in the shadows. She'd tied up loose ends like Dr. B, Verna Bleecher, the attempted kidnapper and the getaway driver. She'd also set up Martina to take the fall in the event their scheme unraveled and Touré Security Group identified the hacker—which they had. Last night, Doris had sacrificed Martina, her queen, in this criminal game of chess. But now, apparently, she was getting serious. She'd come straight for Grace. Game over.

Grace was through playing as well. She looked around Mal's meticulous office. She put the remote alarm trigger in the front right pocket of her powder blue pants and her cell phone in her left.

The doorbell chimed for a third time.

"Coming, Doris." Grace wasn't going to hide.

Yes, she was scared. She'd be a fool not to be afraid. But as frightening as this situation was, it also was the best opportunity Grace had to bring the killer to justice for Dr. B's and Verna's families. She also wanted Doris behind bars so she, her grandmother and the Tourés would feel safe enough to reclaim their lives.

She pulled the thumb drive from her laptop and hurried to the guest bathroom. She shifted the screen from the fluorescent lighting above the sink, tucked her drive on the structure's lip and then replaced the screen. In case anything happened to her, she had to hide the formula to the best of her ability.

Grace took a deep breath in an effort to slow her pulse before jogging down the steps to the front door. She pulled her cell phone from her left pocket. She activated the voice-recording app, then tucked it away again. She checked her right pocket to make sure the alarm was still there. On the video, Doris didn't appear to be armed, but Grace couldn't tell with that trench coat and briefcase. She wanted to wait for the right time to call in backup, whenever that may be.

Showtime!

She took another deep breath and opened the door. Grace feigned surprise. "Doris?" She gave the older woman a quick once-over. Was there a weapon in that briefcase? "What're you doing here?"

"Grace!" Doris removed her sunglasses and gave her a relieved smile. "I was beginning to think no one was home."

"But you kept ringing the bell." Grace gripped the doorknob, trying to get her right hand to stop shaking. Was she actually face-to-face with Dr. B's murderer? She felt sick.

Doris lifted the briefcase. "I came across some documents among Dr. MacIntyre's belongings. I was anxious to share them with you because I think they might shed light on who killed him."

She'd been anxious to share them with me? The doorknob was slick from Grace's sweating palm. "How did you know I'd be here, Doris?"

Grace's heart shattered. Until right now, she'd been holding out hope that Doris was innocent. She didn't want to believe Dr. B's trusted admin had betrayed and killed him. She'd thrown him down a flight of stairs like trash. And why? Because she'd wanted to profit from a mistake Grace had made in which Dr. B had had no involvement.

Doris frowned. "You told me when I let you into Dr. MacIntyre's office."

There!

Doris's lie was the signal Grace hadn't known she'd been waiting for. She slipped her sweaty right hand into her pants pocket and activated the remote alarm. "No, I didn't. No one was supposed to know where I was. But somehow Martina Mann had found out. Did she tell you?" *...before you killed her?*

Doris slammed her left shoulder into the door. The impact of the blow sent pain rocketing up Grace's right arm. Doris forced her way into Mal's home. She pulled a gun from her right coat pocket. "You're right, of course, Grace. Martina did tell me you were staying with Malachi Touré—right before I killed her."

Grace stood her ground.

Mal is on his way—if I could just hold on.

"Ankle Antiques approved our cybersecurity proposal this morning." Mal sat on one of Zeke's guest chairs Tuesday morning. Jerry's image appeared on the laptop on the center of the eldest Touré's desk.

The brothers were continuing to conduct their company meetings virtually until they were 100 percent confident the killer had been caught and Melba was safe. To date, that hadn't happened.

Zeke turned to Mal. He sat behind his desk in a crisp snow-white shirt and garnet tie. His navy suit jacket hung on the coatrack in a corner of his office. "And you met with the clients in person at their office?"

Mal regarded his older brother with amusement. "That's right."

Zeke's eyebrows shot up his forehead. "I'm impressed."

"Give it a rest, Number One." Jerry's sarcasm threatened to derail the sibling banter.

He was meeting with them from his motel room, having entrusted two of their security consultants in addition to the residence's guards with Melba's safety. Today was Jerry's eighth day in that room. It looked like it should be condemned. There was a pile of clothing on the bed, other piles on the floor and empty food containers on every visible surface. It was as though the room didn't have trash cans. Mal knew better than to acknowledge the disaster. He needed to get through this meeting so he could get back to work and to Grace.

Aside from a flash of irritation quickly masked, Zeke ignored Jerry's comment. "As usual, Mal, you have a lot on your plate. Do you have any concerns with any of your other projects?"

Mal sat with his right ankle on his left knee above his gunmetal gray slacks. He scanned the printout of his project list again, which rested on his right thigh. "No. I should have the Zoose Financial security eval done around eleven, right before I leave to meet Grace for lunch."

"Like a date?" Jerry's voice was tinny as it came through the laptop audio. His midnight eyes glowed with interest.

Mal prayed he wasn't blushing. He and Grace had crossed the line on more than one occasion. The situation was complicated because of their previous history. His brothers didn't need to know any of that, though, especially since he was pretty sure their lunch conversation would consist of her telling him goodbye.

"I want to check on her." Mal was relieved his voice sounded steady and relaxed. "The house has a state-of-the-art alarm system, but I'd feel better if I saw her. Martina Mann's dead, but none of us believe she was acting alone. There's a second person involved in these crimes that we haven't identified yet."

Jerry ran his hand over his hair. "Do we have any clues that could give us a starting point for looking for the second suspect?"

Mal rubbed his forehead. His eyes settled on the meeting agenda and his project list, both printed on plain white paper. But in his mind, he pictured Central Columbus Science University's Division of Math and Science's faculty office the day Grace and Doris had shown it to him.

"Grace was confident Dr. B hadn't discussed her formula with anyone other than her." Mal rose to pace his brother's office.

"I remember." Zeke's voice carried from his desk. "She'd been adamant about that point because he'd given her his word."

Mal stared blindly through Zeke's floor-to-ceiling window. "She'd discussed it with him in person at his home office and in his office at CCSU, and she'd called him on his office phone."

"That's once in his house and twice in his office." Jerry blew a breath. "We believe the people involved are linked to CCSU and Buckeye Dynamic. It makes sense the leak would've happened in or around his office."

A leak in or around his office.

Mal turned back to the room, imagining again the layout of Dr. B's office. One door. His desk was on the other side of the room. A window, but his office was on the third floor. Unless the killer had a jetpack, there was no way anyone could've eavesdropped from outside his window. A leak, as though there was another phone. Could someone have put another phone or phone line in Dr. B's office?

A second phone line.

"That's it." Mal held out his arms.

Zeke frowned. "What's it?"

Jerry spoke at the same time. "Come back to Zeke's desk. I can't see you."

"Sorry." Mal returned to his seat and jabbed an index finger toward Zeke's desk phone. "The leak didn't come from someone standing outside of Dr. B's office. It came from someone listening in on his phone line. Doris Flank, Dr. B's admin, has a phone with extension buttons she could use to transfer calls."

"That's old-school." Jerry's comment was dry.

Mal shrugged. "The school's administrative building's like a time machine. These buttons light up whenever the extension's active. Doris could listen in on Dr. B's calls without anyone knowing."

"Oh, man." Jerry covered his eyes with his left hand, shaking his head in disbelief. "I can't imagine having someone invade my privacy like that."

Zeke turned his attention from Jerry's image on his laptop to Mal sitting in front of him. "She works for CCSU and she's connected to Buckeye Dynamics through Martina Mann, whose son was Dr. B's research assistant."

Mal nodded. "We need to speak with Doris right a—"

An alert came over Mal's cell phone. His blood ran cold. It was the signal for his home alarm. Grace was there alone. He ignored his brother's questions about the alert and, with shaking hands, launched his house-security-system app. The image on his screen caused him to spring out of his chair.

"Someone forced their way into my house. Call the police." He shouted the command as he raced for the door to Zeke's office.

"I'm coming with you." Zeke called from behind him. "Jer, call the police."

Grace is alone. Grace is in danger. I have to get to Grace—before it's too late.

Hurry, Mal. Please hurry.

Grace resisted the urge to check her watch. All she knew was that it was Tuesday morning. She didn't know where Mal was or how long it would take him to get home. She just knew he was on his way. In the meantime, she had to figure out how to distract Doris, who stood less than two arm lengths away from her. The other woman had already killed five people.

She returned Doris's stare, trying to avoid looking down the barrel of her gun. "How did you learn about my formula? I know Dr. B didn't tell you."

"I'm not here to chat." A sneer twisted Doris's thin, pale lips. She'd dropped the briefcase and taken off the sunglasses, but she still wore her wide-brimmed hat and trench coat. "Give me the formula. Now."

Grace's mouth went dry. Sweat rolled down her spine. As long as she'd known Doris, the other woman had al-

ways seemed cool, almost cold. It was terrifying to see
her like this. Angry, out of control, homicidal.

What have I gotten myself into?

Grace pulled the tattered remains of her courage together. "Let's not kid ourselves, Doris. Once you have
my formula, you're going to kill me. I deserve answers."

Doris giggled. Her gray eyes glittered with excitement. The gun shook in her hand. Grace caught her
breath. Her heart stopped, then raced to make up for
lost time.

Oh, dear Lord. The woman is insane.

Mal, I hope you get here soon.

"You 'deserve'? You *deserve*?" Once again, Doris
giggled and the gun jerked in her hand. Once again,
Grace thought she was going to die. "You graduate
students think you're so special because you have an
advanced degree. You think that makes you better than
other people. You think you're entitled."

Grace's lips curved in disgust. "Is that how you jus-
tify yourself? You tell yourself you don't have an advanced degree, so that entitles you to kill people?"

Don't anger the woman with the gun.

Doris glowered at her. Grace could feel the admin's
hatred like a wall between them. "I'll allow you three
questions."

"Five."

Doris's eyes widened with disbelief. "I said three."

"Five." She was trying to buy herself as much time
as possible, but she didn't want to provoke Doris into
shooting her to shut her up.

Doris narrowed her small gray eyes. "Ask what you
want. You'll only get three answers."

Fair enough. "I've already asked this question. How did you learn about my formula?"

"I suppose I can answer that." She waved the gun. "I listened to Bennett's phone conversations through the extension on my desk." She shrugged. "I've always done that. The university's facilities department has tried to give me a new phone for years, but I wouldn't let them."

Grace arched an eyebrow. "So it was your idea, not Martina's, to hack my system."

"Of course it was." Doris used her left hand to steady her right. Was her arm getting tired? "Martina was useless. I had to take care of everything. She thought sitting on a university's board of trustees and a research facility's board of directors made her smart." She snorted. "It didn't."

"That wasn't my second question. This one is: Why did you do it?"

"For the money, of course." Doris lowered the gun. Her arm *was* getting tired.

"Do you have any regrets over killing those people? Martina, Verna Bleecher, the people you sent to kidnap me?" The third question was the most important. "Do you regret killing Dr. B?"

"No, I don't. They were in my way." Doris's voice was flat, her response final. She pointed the gun at Grace again. Her eyes glittered with anger. "Now, give me the formula."

Everything happened at once. The front door burst open behind Doris. It was as though someone had kicked it in. The crash seemed to echo across the house. Mal led Zeke and several uniformed police officers into the house. "Enough, Doris. Put the gun down."

Doris grabbed Grace. Using her as a human shield,

she spun to face Mal, Zeke and the officers. She pressed the barrel of the gun against Grace's temple. "You drop yours!"

Grace saw the look of terror on Mal's face. Doris dragged her backward, away from Mal and the officers, toward the back door. The older woman was making her a hostage.

Oh, no, no, no!

Techniques from Grace's self-defense classes played across her mind like life-saving flash cards. She stomped on Doris's foot with all the pain and anger she felt toward the woman for taking Dr. B away from her. She drove her elbow into Doris's ribs with vicious intent for threatening her grandmother's life. Twisting her torso backward, she grabbed hold of Doris and flipped the older woman over her shoulder, landing her on her back.

With the threat neutralized, the officers hurried forward to take Doris into custody.

Mal ran to Grace in three long strides. He wrapped his arms around her, holding her so tight. His muscles were shaking almost as much as hers were.

Grace leaned back to look up at him. Her smile was unsteady. "I knew you'd come."

Mal wiped her cheek. She hadn't realized she'd been crying. "You didn't need me."

Foolish man. Grace pressed her face into the center of his chest and let the tears of fear and relief fall.

Chapter 19

"It's a good thing Grace had the foresight to record her encounter with Doris." Zeke paced Mal's kitchen late Tuesday afternoon.

Seated at the table, Mal scrubbed his face with the damp palms of his still-shaking hands. When would his nerves settle down? It had been six hours since he'd charged through his front door, desperate to rescue Grace. That image would reappear in his nightmares for weeks to come. His older brother was working off his nervous energy by wearing a path across his laminate flooring. Mal would do the same, but his knees weren't yet steady enough.

He and Zeke were updating Jerry on the case using the videoconference feature on Mal's cell phone. Meanwhile, upstairs, Grace was speaking with her grandmother. Mal understood their need for privacy. There were probably sentiments and emotions they needed to express but not in a group setting.

Jerry spoke from his motel room. His tone was disbelieving. "The police found Doris holding a gun on Grace, but she still tried to deny being the serial killer?"

"That's right." Mal cleared his throat. "She claimed she thought Grace was involved in Dr. B's murder, and she'd brought the gun as protection while she confronted her. But Grace had recorded her confessing to not only killing Martina, Verna and the kidnappers but Dr. B as well."

The recording also had captured the sounds of Grace fighting off Doris and flipping the other woman over her shoulder. If she hadn't been able to free herself, Doris would've taken her as a hostage, and God only knows what would've happened after that. Mal swallowed to ease his dry throat.

"Doris has retained a lawyer." Zeke finally joined Mal at the table. "But Eriq and Taylor believe they have more than enough to hold her in custody because of the recording as well as several eyewitnesses to her threatening Grace, including officers on the scene."

Jerry ran a hand over his hair. "Wow. She killed her boss and four other people just to get her hands on a potential biological weapon. That's next level. I hope Grace is able to correct her formula and destroy every trace of this mistake."

"She will." Mal was confident. "She's brilliant. And no one wants to repeat this experience."

"No kidding." Jerry shook his head.

"When should I pick you up from the airport?" Zeke directed his question to his youngest sibling. "Mal and

I have some thoughts on next steps for the company, and I'm anxious to get your input."

It was like a curtain closed over Jerry's face. His expression went blank. His features tensed. His midnight eyes grew watchful. "What thoughts?"

Mal frowned in concern. He exchanged a look with Zeke. They needed to tread carefully with Jerry, or he'd close himself off. "Tiered pricing. That would give us a way to expand our services to bigger corporations and keep working with smaller companies."

Jerry's sigh lifted his broad shoulders beneath the black button-down shirt he wore with a silver tie. "Look. That sounds great. I think you should go for it if that's the direction you want to take the company. I'm sure it'll be great. But I'm leaving—"

"What?" Zeke rose halfway out of his chair. "Why?"

Jerry's features eased. "I'm going to become a fitness and self-defense trainer. A colleague asked me to teach some classes at a gym she owns."

Zeke gave Mal a look. What the hell?

Mal shrugged his confusion.

Zeke turned back to Jerry's image on Mal's cell phone. "Why, Jer? Why do you want to leave our family's company?"

Jerry spread his arms. "It's time, Z. I want to do something on my own. You and I, all we ever do is fight. It's not good for us. It's not good for Mal. It's not good for the company. Maybe my leaving will actually bring us closer together."

Mal looked at Zeke. They were thinking the same thing: *Bullshit*.

Mal frowned at the cell phone. He lowered his voice.

"Does this have to do with your last personal-protection detail, the one with that boy band singer?"

"No, it doesn't." Jerry denied it, but the tightness around his mouth and eyes called him a liar. "I know I messed up, but my leaving the company has nothing to do with that case."

"When are you coming home?" Zeke's tone was abrupt.

Mal caught the hard look in his brother's eyes. It was the same expression their father used to get. The elder Touré may have changed the subject, but he was not done with this discussion.

"I can't believe you let a serial killer into the house with you." This was the third time Melba had made that statement. It sounded just as bad as it had the first two times. Grace's grandmother blew her nose, then tossed the tissue into a garbage can off camera.

Grace half sat, half reclined on the bed in Mal's guest room. She was using her laptop to videoconference with her grandmother in private. The Touré brothers had invited Melba and her to join their debriefing, but she'd declined their offer. Now that the week-long nightmare was over, she wanted to make sure she and her grandmother could express all their feelings and emotions freely with one another. This was something they had never experienced before. She prayed they never would again. She wanted to make sure they said everything they needed to say before they put this past week behind them and moved forward.

Grace pulled the box of tissues beside her closer. "I know you're angry, Gran—"

Melba interrupted. "I'm not angry. I was terrified for you."

"I understand that." Grace breathed to ease the tightness in her chest. She was still shaky and uncertain. She'd had a gun pressed to her temple. How long would it take before the terror from that encounter dissipated? "But with everything that was at stake, I felt it was worth the risk."

"The risk was too high."

Grace shook her head adamantly. "The stakes were even higher. Your life, Mal's life, Zeke and Jerry. Jerry put his life on the line for you." She flung her arm toward the window her grandmother couldn't see. She clenched a tissue in her fist. "If I didn't take that chance this morning, Doris might still be a threat to us."

Melba drew another tissue to wipe her eyes. "You're in science, not law enforcement."

Grace's tone was dry. "Believe me, I know that."

She let several beats of silence pass as she combed through images of the past week. Speaking with Dr. B's children during his wake. Interviewing Verna Bleecher's widower. Comforting Martina Trenton Mann's son. Finally, all those families would have justice. And if the prosecutor was allowed to use the recording of Doris's confession, they wouldn't have to suffer through a trial. That would also keep Grace's formula out of the news.

Melba wiped her nose before discarding another tissue. "Are you going to break the news to Martina Mann's son and Dr. B's and Verna Bleecher's families?"

Grace had thought about calling Elsie, Toran and Alana MacIntyre. She'd promised to keep them apprised of the case. But in the end, she'd decided against it.

She shook her head. "No, I gave everyone's contact

information to the investigating detectives. I think the victims' loved ones should hear the official announcement from the police. I'd be willing to meet with them if they want to talk with me afterward, though."

Melba nodded her understanding. "It must've devastated you to learn someone close to you and Dr. B had killed him."

"*Devastated* is one word for it." Grace massaged the side of her neck. "I wasn't close to Doris. She seemed cold and off-putting. That's why I was surprised Dr. B liked her. He was so warm, outgoing and approachable. But he'd sing Doris's praises. He'd said she was well organized and efficient, calm in the face of every deadline. Her eavesdropping on his conversations sheds a new light on his claims that she always anticipated his needs."

Melba closed her eyes, shaking her head. "Why had she misled him for so long?"

"I don't know." The way the serial killer had preyed on her friend infuriated Grace. "When she forced her way into Mal's house, it was as though her mask dropped. She sounded and acted unbalanced."

Grace recalled the way Doris's gray eyes had glittered. Her voice had been almost strident. She hadn't recognized the woman she'd thought she'd known for almost three years. That had added to her terror. She shivered at the memory.

"I'm so sorry he'd put his trust in the wrong person." Melba's words pulled her back to the present. "It wasn't his fault."

"No, it wasn't." Grace curled her hands against her laptop table. "That's the reason I have trust issues."

Melba frowned. "Gracie, you know I love you, but

you've allowed your wariness against trusting other people to go too far."

Grace stared wide-eyed at her grandmother. "How can you think that, after what we've just been through? You agreed Dr. B trusted the wrong person. That person killed him and four other people, then tried to kill me. I have good reason to be wary."

"We should all be a little cautious. But it's been four years. Can we talk about the real reason you left Mal?" Melba's dark brown eyes filled with kindness and understanding.

"It was because of my promise to Pam." Her lips were numb with shock.

"No, it wasn't, Gracie." Melba's words were gentle but firm. "It was because you fell in love with him. The same way your mother fell in love with your father. The same way Pam fell in love with the man who turned out to be a jerk."

"Gran, I—"

Melba ignored her interruption. "But Mal isn't like them. He's someone you can count on. Mal is someone you could trust. Your words, 'What we've just been through.' Mal was right there with you from the beginning. When he realized you were in danger, he opened his home to you—even after *you* were the one who broke *his* trust. He took excellent care of you. Because of that, he's someone *I* can trust."

Grace swallowed the burning lump in her throat. "Yes, Gran, but I'm—"

"When that stranger tried to snatch you, Mal ran to you. When Doris pulled a gun on you, he ran to you and brought the police. Now, I've told you this before, Gracie—I'm not going to live forever. Before I die, I want to see my granddaughter married to someone I know I can trust."

Grace pulled another tissue from the box, using it to dry her cheeks. "Gran, I'm afraid."

Melba's brow furrowed in confusion. "Afraid of what? Telling Mal how you feel about him?"

"Yes!"

Melba straightened on her overstuffed, flower-patterned armchair and squared her shoulders. "Grace Anne, you confronted a serial killer with a gun because you said the stakes were too high and it was worth the risk. Well, the stakes are high now—your heart and your future. I know you can find the courage to tell Malachi Touré you're in love with him."

Grace took a shuddering breath. "Suppose he won't give me a second chance?"

"Then tell him again that you love him. If he still won't hear you, show him how much he means to you. And keep showing him even after he hears you."

Grace wanted to take her grandmother's advice, but fear kept her body rooted in place. "You make it sound so easy."

Melba smiled. "I know it's hard. But isn't he worth it?"

Grace's tension eased. "Yes, he is."

She wrapped up her videoconference with her grandmother, then checked her appearance in the mirror before leaving the room. In the hallway, Grace paused, wiping her sweaty palms on her powder blue pants. What should she say to convince the lover she'd walked out on to give her one last chance with his heart?

Grace started down the stairs, hoping by the time she reached the bottom, something would occur to her.

* * *

"I've booked an early flight for the morning." Jerry gave Mal and Zeke his itinerary details. "I'm staying one more night to take Melba and Gilda to dinner. We're going to celebrate closing this case."

Mal smiled for the first time that day. "That's a great idea, Jerry. Thank you."

Jerry flashed his movie-star grin. "No need to thank me. Melba and Gilda are great company. And if Grace is anything like her grandmother, you'd better hold on to her with both arms."

Some of the tension seemed to ease from Zeke. "You have to tell Grace how you feel, Mal. People can't read your mind. You have to speak up. Just tell her."

"Easy for you to say." Mal pushed himself away from the table to pace the room. "When was the last time you put yourself out there?"

Jerry huffed his displeasure. "I hate when you guys walk away from the table. You move out of the camera and I can't see you. It's like talking to an empty room."

Zeke grunted. "When has that ever stopped you?"

Mal ignored their exchange. "Grace doesn't need me."

"You're wrong, Mal. I do need you." Grace's voice carried into the room from behind him.

Mal spun to face her. He felt like a deer in headlights. For one painful moment, his heart stopped, then restarted at a gallop.

"That's our cue to leave, Jer." Zeke's words sounded like they were coming through a tunnel.

"Do we have to?" Jerry protested.

"Goodbye, Jerry." Zeke paused, presumably to log out of the videoconference app. "I'll use my key to let myself out." He winked at Grace before striding out of the kitchen.

Mal watched his brother leave before moving across the room to prop his hip against the table. "How much of that did you hear?"

Grace hesitated. "I'm grateful to Jerry for taking Gran and Gilda to dinner tonight."

Oh, crap! She'd heard everything. Was he blushing? Mal rubbed his forehead. "I'm sorry, Grace. My brothers got carried away."

"Carried away about what?" She sounded confused. "What made them say those things about us if—"

Mal interrupted before she said anything that would cause him further embarrassment. "I know your research is important to you, Grace."

"It is, but—"

"And I don't want to be responsible for getting in the way of that."

"You wouldn't—"

"A lot of people would benefit from your work. You're saving lives."

Grace raised her voice. "I'm still in love with you, Mal." She stepped forward. Her movements seemed stiff and uncertain. "I *never* stopped loving you."

The blood rushed out of Mal's head. He gripped the edge of the table with both fists. "You're being cruel, Grace. I'm in love with you. You're telling me you love me, too, but the fact that you refuse to be with me because of your work makes it hurt more."

"I'm not telling you that anymore." She took another step forward, stopping close enough for him to sense her warmth. "I want to spend the rest of my life with you, Mal. I never should've left you. I was a coward and I was wrong, but if you'd be willing to give me another chance—"

Mal surged away from the table and gathered Grace in his arms. He covered her mouth with his, sipping the words of love from her lips. His heart punched his chest. His pulse pounded in his ears. He couldn't think. He could barely breathe. The day had started with heartache and terror but was turning into the best day of his life.

He raised his head. "I am so in love with you."

Grace's smile was uncertain. "You'll give me another chance?"

"Absolutely." Mal grinned. "All I've ever wanted was forever with you."

Grace threw her arms around his shoulders and gave him a hard kiss. "I've wanted forever with you since your mail kept showing up in my mailbox."

Mal's smile faded. "About that. I have a confession. *I* put my mail in your mailbox myself."

"I know. I've always known." Grace rested her forehead against his. Her voice was hushed. "You won me over with utility bills and frozen cookie dough."

Mal laughed. "I'm so glad you hacked into my computer." He lifted her into his arms and pressed his lips to hers.

* * * * *

COMING NEXT MONTH FROM

⊕ HARLEQUIN
ROMANTIC SUSPENSE

#2251 COLTON'S MONTANA HIDEAWAY
The Coltons of New York • by Justine Davis

FBI tech expert Ashlynn Colton's investigation into one serial killer has made her the target of another one. Only the suspect's brother—handsome Montana cowboy Kyle Slater—will help. But as the duo grows closer, their deadly investigation isn't the only thing heating up...

#2252 LAST CHANCE INVESTIGATION
Sierra's Web • by Tara Taylor Quinn

Decorated detective Levi Greggs just closed a high-profile murder case and took a bullet in the process. But when his ex-fiancée, psychiatrist Kelly Chase, returns to town with another mystery, saying no isn't an option. Searching the wilderness for a missing child reignites long-buried desire...and more danger than they bargained for.

#2253 HER SECRET PROTECTOR
SOS Agency • by Bonnie Vanak

Marine biologist Peyton Bradley will do anything to regain her memory and finish her important work. Even trust former navy SEAL Gray Wallace, her ex-bodyguard. Gray vows to protect Peyton, even as he falls for the vulnerable beauty. But will the final showdown be with Peyton's stalker, her family, her missing memory or Gray's shadowy past?

#2254 BODYGUARD MOST WANTED
Price Security • by Katherine Garbera

When his look-alike bodyguard is murdered, CEO Nicholas DeVere knows he'll be next. Enter security expert Luna Urban. She's not Nick's doppelgänger, but she's determined to solve the crime and keep the sexy billionaire safe. If only they can keep their arrangement all business...

YOU CAN FIND MORE INFORMATION ON UPCOMING HARLEQUIN TITLES, FREE EXCERPTS AND MORE AT HARLEQUIN.COM.

HRSCNM0923

Get 3 FREE REWARDS!

We'll send you 2 FREE Books plus a FREE Mystery Gift.

FREE Value Over $20

Both the **Harlequin Intrigue®** and **Harlequin® Romantic Suspense** series feature compelling novels filled with heart-racing action-packed romance that will keep you on the edge of your seat.

HARLEQUIN
PLUS

Try the best multimedia subscription service for romance readers like you!

Read, Watch and Play.

Experience the easiest way to get the romance content you crave.

Start your **FREE TRIAL** at
www.harlequinplus.com/freetrial.